Plugged

Also by Eoin Colfer

Artemis Fowl
Artemis Fowl and the Arctic Incident
Artemis Fowl and the Eternity Code
Artemis Fowl and the Opal Deception
Artemis Fowl and the Lost Colony
Artemis Fowl and the Time Paradox
Artemis Fowl and the Atlantis Complex

Benny and Omar
Benny and Babe

The Legend of Spud Murphy
The Legend of Captain Crow's Teeth
The Legend of the Worst Boy in the World

Airman
Half Moon Investigations
The Supernaturalist
The Wish List

And Another Thing . . .

Eoin Colfer
Plugged

headline

First published in Great Britain in 2011
by HEADLINE PUBLISHING GROUP

1

Cataloguing in Publication Data is
available from the British Library

ISBN 978 0 7553 7998 9 (Hardback)
ISBN 978 0 7553 7999 6 (Trade paperback)

Typeset in Electra by Ellipsis Books Limited, Glasgow
Printed and bound in Great Britain by CPI Mackays, Chatham ME5 8TD

Headline's policy is to use papers that are natural, renewable and
recyclable products and made from wood grown in sustainable
forests. The logging and manufacturing processes are expected
to conform to the environmental regulations of the country of origin.

HEADLINE PUBLISHING GROUP
An Hachette UK Company
338 Euston Road
London NW1 3BH

www.headline.co.uk
www.hachette.co.uk

For Ken Bruen who made me do it.

With thanks to Declan Denny for his invaluable attention to my details.

CHAPTER 1

The great Stephen King once wrote *don't sweat the small stuff*, which I mulled over for long enough to realise that I don't entirely agree with it. I get what he means: we all have enough major sorrow in our lives without freaking out over the day-to-day hangnails and such, but sometimes sweating the small stuff helps you make it through the big stuff. Take me, for example; I have had enough earth-shattering events happen to me, beside me and underneath me to have most people dribbling in a psych ward, but what I do is try not to think about it. Let it fester inside, that's my philosophy. It's gotta be healthy, right? Focus on the everyday non-lethal bullshit to take your mind off the landmark psychological blows that are standing in line to grind you down. My philosophy has gotten me this far, but my soldier sense tells me that things are about to come to a head.

There isn't much call for deep thinking in my current job in Cloisters, New Jersey. We don't do a lot of chatting about philosophical issues or natural phenomena in the casino. I tried to talk about National Geographic one night, and Jason gave me a look like I was insulting him, so I moved on to a safer subject: which of the girls have implants. This is one of our regular topics, so it's familiar territory. He calmed down after a couple of swallows from his protein shake. Me talking about issues scared Jase more than a drunk with a pistol. Jason is the best doorman I have ever worked with, a rare combination of big and fast and with a lot more smarts than he lets on. Sometimes he'll forget himself and reference a Fellini movie, then try to cover his tracks by giving the next guy through the door a hard time. Guy's got secrets; we all do. He doesn't feel like burdening me and I am absolutely fine with that attitude. We both pretend we're dumb and we both suspect we aren't as dumb as we pretend. It's exhausting.

Most nights we have time for chit-chat out front. Everything's quiet until ten thirty or so. Generally just a few small-time players, under-the-radar guys. The party crowd doesn't show up until the regular bars close. The bossman, Victor, who I will describe in detail later because this guy deserves a movie of his own he is such a dick and to talk about him now would ruin the flow; anyways Vic still wants a couple of bodies out front. Sometimes it takes two to shut down a fight if there are accusations flying around on the back table. It can get pretty heated in there, especially with the little guys. I blame Joe Pesci.

So I generally do the night shift, not that there's a day shift per se. Twice or three times a month I pull doubles. I don't really mind. How am I going to pass the time at home? Do push-ups and listen to Mrs Delano bitch?

Tonight I get in at eight on the dot. It's midweek so I'm

looking forward to a quiet evening chewing power bars with Jason and talking surgery. Just simple distraction, which is the closest to happiness I'm expecting to get in this lifetime.

Jason and I are watching this Russian throw around kettlebells on YouTube when I get a call from Marco on my headset. I have to ask the little barman to repeat himself a couple of times before I get the message and hustle back to the casino floor. Apparently my favourite girl, Connie, leaned in to slide cocktails on to a table, and this guy goes and licks her ass. Moron. I mean, it's on the wall on a brass plaque. Not ass-licking specifically. *Do Not Touch The Hostesses*, it says. Universal club rule. Some of the hostesses will do a little touching in the booth, but the customer never gets to touch back.

When I arrive, Marco is trying to hold this guy away from Connie, which is probably more for the guy's safety than he realises. I once saw Connie deck a college footballer with her serving tray. Guy's face was in the metal, like a cartoon.

'Okay, folks,' I say, doing my booming doorman voice. 'Let's get this handled professionally.'

This announcement is met with a couple of boos from the regulars, who were praying for a little drama. I grip Marco's head like a basketball and steer him behind the bar, then loom over the offender.

The licker has his hands on his hips like he's Peter Pan, and Connie's fingers have left red stripes on his cheek.

'Why don't we take this into the back room,' I say, giving him five seconds of eye contact. 'Before things get out of hand.'

'This bitch hit me,' he says, pointing in case there's some doubt about which bitch he's talking about.

His finger is coated with the remains of a basket of buffalo wings, and sauce on fingers is something that has always irritated me more than it reasonably should.

'We got a time-out room just back here,' I say, not looking at the brown gunk under his nails. What is wrong with people? You eat, you keep your mouth closed, you wipe your fingers. How hard is that? 'Why don't we discuss your issues back there?'

Connie is quiet, trying to hold her anger in, chewing on some nicotine gum like it's one of the guy's balls. Connie has a temper, but she won't slap without good reason. She's got two kids in a crèche over on Cypress, so she needs the paycheque.

'Okay, Dan,' she says. 'But can we move it along? I got people dying to tip me. This is an open-and-shut case.'

The pointer laughs, like it's funny she should use that terminology.

I shepherd them into the time-out room, which is barely more than a broom closet; in fact there are a couple of mops growing like dreadlocked palms out of a cardboard box island in the corner.

'You okay?' I ask Connie, glad to see she's not smoking. Six months and counting.

She nods, sitting on a ratty sofa. 'Dude licked my ass. Licked it. You got any wipes, Daniel?'

I hand her a slim pack. You always carry a pack of antiseptic wipes working a bottom-rung New Jersey casino like Slotz. There's all sorts of stuff you can catch just hanging around.

I look away while Connie is wiping the barbecue sauce off her behind. You can't help noticing cleavage in this place, but

4

I figure you can avoid the lower regions. I try to keep my eyes above the waist; leaves everybody with something. So while she's cleaning up, I turn to the guy. The licker.

'What were you thinking, sir? There's no touching. Can't you read?'

The guy is going to rub me the wrong way. I can tell just by his hair, a red frizz sitting on his head like a nest fell off a roof.

'I saw the plaque, *Daniel*,' he says, pointing towards the casino floor. This guy is a pointing *machine*. 'It says do not *touch*.'

'And what did you do? You touched.'

'No,' says the guy, switching his pointing finger over to me, so close I can smell the sauce, which is putting me off barbecue for a month at least. Except ribs. 'I didn't *touch*. You *touch* with your hands. I *tasted*.'

He stops talking then, like I need a second for this brilliant argument to sink in.

'You think I never heard that stupid shit before? You seriously think you're the first guy to try that on?'

'I think I'm the first *attorney* to try it on.' His face lights up with smugness. I hate that look, maybe because I get it a lot.

'You're an attorney?'

More pointing. I'm tempted to snap this arsehole's finger right off. 'You're goddamn right I'm an attorney. You try anything with me and I'll shut this shithole down. You'll be working for me.'

'I'll be working for you, sir?'

Sometimes I repeat stuff. People think it's because I'm stupid, but really it's because I can't believe what I'm hearing.

The guy goes for option A.

'What are you? A parrot? A fucking retarded *Oirish* parrot? *Kee*-rist almighty.'

This is probably the way it goes in the office for this guy. He doles out garbage and people take it. I'm guessing he's the boss, or close to it. Only the boss or the mail guy can not give a shit how they look to this extent and get away with it. Suit and spectacles that could have been stolen from Michael Caine circa 1972, and of course the Styrofoam ring of ginger hair.

'No, sir. I'm not a parrot,' I say, nice and calm, like I learned in doorman school. 'I'm the head of security and you touched the hostess, whatever way you want to dress it up.'

The guy laughs, like he's got an audience. 'Dressing things up is what I do, Mister Daniel Head of Security. That's my motherfucking business.'

He says *motherfucking* all wrong, like he learned it from the TV. It doesn't sound right coming out of his attorney's face.

'It's your motherfucking business?' I say, saying the word like it should be said. I learned it from a Romanian mercenary working for the Christian militia in Tibnin. Anghel and his boys would tool past our camp most days in their beat-up VW, stopping to strike deals for long-life milk or pasta we'd traded from the French garçons. I liked Anghel okay; he never shot at me specifically, his whole head was a beard and I appreciated the way he said motherfucking.

Only one carton, Paddy? I give you perfect good mozzerfokken hairdryer.

Made it sound real; the double z. So sometimes if I want to

make an impression I say it the Romanian way. Often it's enough to confuse a guy, put him off his stride.

But not this guy. The ginger monkey is seriously unimpressed by my double z and proceeds to make his second mistake of the evening that I know about. He steps up to me, cock of the walk, like I don't have eight inches and fifty pounds on him.

'What is this parrot shit?' he says, and believe it or believe it not, he taps me on the forehead. 'You got a goddamn plate in your head? *Kee*-rist almighty.'

I am surprised by this tap on the head but also happy, because the guy has touched me now.

'You shouldn't have touched me, sir,' I say sadly. 'That's assault. Now I got to defend myself.'

This takes the wind out of his sails. Being an attorney this jackass knows the letter of the law regarding assault. He is aware that now I got the right to put a little hurt on him and claim I felt threatened. I practise my *threatened* face so he can visualise how it will look in court.

His pointing finger curls up like a dried turd, and he takes a couple of steps back.

'Now listen. You lay one hand on me . . .'

He can't finish the threat, because I got a free shot and he knows it. At this point I would dearly love to take that shot and put this attorney out of everyone's misery. But Connie's got her kids in the crèche and the last thing she needs is a court appearance hanging over her head. Plus the courtroom is this guy's arena. Before the judge he's a gladiator. I can just see him, jumping around like a little ginger monkey, pointing like there's no tomorrow. And in all honesty, my *threatened* face ain't all that hot.

So I say, 'How much money you got in your wallet?'

The guy tries a little bluster, but I'm giving him an out and he knows it. 'I don't know. Couple hundred maybe.'

Bullshit he doesn't know. Attorneys and accountants always know. Generally they stash little wads of notes all over, in case they get stuck with a pushy dancer or hooker later in the evening. This guy probably knows how much cash his sick momma has rolled into her tooth jar.

'Gimme three,' I say. 'Gimme three hundred for the hostess and I won't have to act in self-defence.'

The attorney physically flinches. 'Three hundred! For a lick. *Kee*-rist almighty.'

He'll go for it. I know he will. The alternative is explaining to his high-roller clients how he got his face rearranged in a dump like Slotz, where we got mould on the carpet corners and toilets with chains.

The guy is fumbling with his wallet, like the bills are putting up a struggle, so I grab it, making sure to squash his soft attorney's fingers a little.

'Here, let me count that, sir. You're shaking.'

He's not shaking, but I want to plant the idea that he should be. This is not a tip I picked up in doorman school. The army shrink gave me a few conflict tips before my second tour.

It's true I snag the wallet to hurry this whole thing along, but I also want to help myself to one of this guy's business cards. It's good to have details about troublesome customers. Let them know there's no place to hide. Once I have his card,

I can find his wife, and I'd like to see him try the taste defence at home. His monkey head would be on a plate and no jury would convict.

I count out six fifties and toss him his wallet.

'Okay, Mister Jaryd Faber,' I say, consulting the card. 'You are hereby barred from Slotz.'

Faber mutters something about not giving a shit, and I can't really blame him.

'We thank you for your business and urge you to seek counselling for your various issues.' Standard *get out and don't come back* spiel.

'You're making a big mistake, *Daniel*,' says Faber, something I hear so often they should carve it on my tombstone. 'I got serious friends in this town.'

'We all got serious friends,' I say, and surprise myself by coming up with a mildly witty rejoinder. 'I got an army buddy hasn't smiled since Desert Storm.'

Nobody so much as acknowledges the effort and Faber mutters something else, possibly a *fuck you*. Still a little fire left in this attorney. I decide to extinguish it.

'Take your ass home,' I growl. 'Before I hit you so hard you'll be pressing charges from the afterlife.'

That's not a bad line either, but it's a little Hollywood. I've used it a dozen times and it's all Connie can do not to groan when I trot it out again.

I crack my knuckles to make my point and Faber wisely decides to leave. He's a bad loser, though, and tosses another two hundred at Connie from the doorway.

'Here,' he sneers. 'Buy yourself a boob job.'

I fake a lunge and the attorney is gone, door swinging behind him. I feel like hurting this guy, I really do, but I know from experience that it won't make me feel much better. So I swallow the instinct like it's a ball of medicine and put on my funeral face for Connie.

'You okay?'

Connie is on her knees, fishing for one of the fifties that has floated under the couch on the breeze of a flapping door.

'Screw him, Dan. This is two nights with a sitter.'

I lever the couch with my boot so she can snag the note and avoid all the other crud under there.

'Is that Al Capone's missing rubber?' I say, trying for some humour.

Connie sobs. Maybe it's the bad joke; more likely it's the last straw that this jerk Faber probably was, so I put my arm around her, raising her up. Connie is the kind of girl a man feels like protecting. She's beautiful like she belongs in a fifties movie; Rita Hayworth hair that ripples when she walks like lava flowing down a mountain, and wide green eyes that still have some warmth in them in spite of a shitty job and shittier ex.

'Come on, darlin', he's gone for good. You'll never see him again.'

'No one says *darlin'* any more, Dan. Only in the movies.'

I squeeze her shoulder. 'I'm Irish, *darlin'*, we're different.'

Connie adjusts the polka-dot bikini that passes for a uniform in this place.

'Yeah? *Good* different, I hope. That creep was *bad* different. What would you call a worm like that in Ireland?'

PLUGGED

I think about this. 'In Ireland he would be referred to as a galloping gobshite. Or a worm.'

Connie smiles a watery smile, but at least it's something. Better than the despair in her eyes when I came in here.

'Galloping gobshite. I like that. I gotta visit Ireland; I say it every year. Little Alfredo would love it, and Eva too. Green fields and friendly people.'

'Not so much of either any more,' I confide. 'Not since the country got moneyed.'

'You could bring us, Dan. Show us around. Give us the authentic tour.'

My stomach flips. 'Any time, Connie. You know how I feel.'

Connie reaches up and tugs at the band of the black watch cap I wear every waking hour.

'So how's it looking, baby?'

I am sensitive on this subject generally, but Connie and me go back nearly two years, which is a lifetime in this business. We got history, as they say. One weekend a few months back, she got a sitter and we had ourselves a fling. It could have gone further but she didn't want a new dad for her kids. *I just want to feel young for a couple nights, Dan. Okay?*

Twenty-eight and she wants to feel young again.

Every guy's dream, right? Couple of no-strings nights with a cocktail hostess. I didn't push it; now I'm thinking I should have.

'It's looking fine,' I tell her. 'I got my check-up with Zeb tomorrow.'

'Can I see?' she asks, long nails already peeling off the watch cap.

11

My hands jerk up to stop her, but I force them back down. About time I got an opinion.

She folds the cap into her long fingers, then pushes me back under a recessed spotlight.

'Zeb did this?'

'Yeah. He had a few nurses too, preparing the follicles. Students I think.'

'This is not a bad job,' says Connie, squinting. 'I've seen plenty of hair plugs before, but this is good. Nice spread and no scars. What is it, rat hair?'

I am genuinely horrified. 'Rat? Christ, Connie. It's my own hair. Transplants from the back. They'll fall out in a couple of weeks, then the new hair grows in.'

Connie shrugs. 'I hear they're using rat now. Dog too. Tough as wire, apparently.'

I reclaim the cap, spreading it over my crown like a salve. 'No canine or rodent. Irish human only.'

'Yeah, well it looks okay. Another session and you won't know the difference.'

I sigh like it's cost me a lot of dollars, which it has. 'That's the idea.'

I roll the hat back down and take Connie's elbow, steering her back to the floor.

A Formica bar, low lighting that's more cheap than fashionable. A roulette wheel that bucks with every spin, two worn baize card tables and half a dozen slots. *Slotz.*

'Here,' she says. 'Take fifty. You squeezed it out of him.'

I fold the note back into her hand. 'It was a pleasure, darlin'. The day he licks my arse is the day I take fifty.'

Connie laughs full and throaty and something stirs in my stomach. 'Oh, baby. The day he licks your *arse* is the day I buy tickets to witness the consequences.'

She's back on an even keel, but it's temporary; this place really takes it out of decent people. A toll on the soul.

'You okay to go back on the floor?'

'Sure, *darlin'*. You know Victor will dock me for the whole night if I quit now.'

I lean down to whisper in her ear, smelling her perfume, noticing not for the first time how long her neck is. Feeling her peppermint breath brushing my cheek. Remembering.

'Between the two of us, Victor is also a galloping gobshite.'

Connie laughs again, something I would pay money to hear, then she grabs a tray from the bar and she's back on the floor, hips swaying like a movie star from back when movie stars had hips worth swaying.

She throws a couple of tantalising sentences over her shoulder.

'Maybe we got another weekend coming up, baby. Maybe a whole week.'

Connie darlin', I think, then raise my gaze.

Stick to the code. Eyes up.

Eyes up, for now. But me and Connie have unfinished business.

One more look at the hips, my dark side whispers. *Then back to work.*

As is often the case, my dark side wins.

I give myself a moment to get my head back in the game. That's the most common rookie mistake in the security business: complacency. Thinking I'm big and scary and what fool

13

is gonna take a swing at me, even to impress his girl. The key word in that sentence is *fool*. They come in all shapes and sizes and most of them are juiced, coked or both and would take a shot at the devil himself if they thought it would buy them a little respect from their crew or a special treat from a hostess.

So I shut the drawer on Faber and Connie and give the crowd a once-over. Couple of college boys eyeing the hostesses, a few divorcees, and old Jasper Biggs playing the big shot. Tossing in one-dollar bills like they're hundreds. No danger signs. Still, I decide to send Jason back here to throw around the steroid stare. Can't hurt. Sometimes trouble begets trouble.

Unfortunately, I am not wrong. Before the ghost image of Connie's hips can fade, a dozen yeehaws barrel through the double doors. One of them either has a very dainty dick, or a flick knife in his jeans pocket.

Jason, I think. *These guys should never have made it in the room.*

As Bob Geldof once sang, *Tonight, of all nights, there's gonna be a fight*. Unfortunately, Bob's not wrong either.

CHAPTER 2

After my first stint with the Irish army's peacekeeping corps in the Lebanon, I was flown home to a zero's welcome and found the green green grass not so lush any more. Apparently the general public were of the opinion that peacekeepers don't fight wars; we just stand between the two armies who *are* fighting the wars and say stuff like: *Ah, lads, that's a bit much* or *Show me the passage in your holy book that says 'minefields are okay sometimes'*. And then the armies say: *You know what, you Irish guys have hit the nail on the head, no offence Christians, plus you have such a good record in your own country that we should all be thoroughly ashamed of ourselves for all this border conflict stuff and just accept our differences.*

I decided that the best way to fill the crater that had been blasted in my soul by none of this happening, plus all the exploding and stuff that did happen, would be to volunteer for a second tour, and my application apparently rang a few warning bells, because the sergeant major ordered me to sashay on over to Dr Moriarty's office at my convenience. Minus the words *sashay* and *convenience*, plus the words *hustle* and *right fucking now, retard.*

I know that traditionally I should have been outraged, smashed my fist into my palm and blurted *this is outrageous, Sarge* or *I still got the stuff*, but honestly, the notion of being probed kind of interested me.

So I showed up prompt at o-seven-hundred the next morning only to find out that consultant shrinks do not *do* enlisted hours and spent the next two hours in Dr Moriarty's waiting room reading a magazine that I swear to God was called *Head Cases*.

Dr Moriarty? I know, almost a professor. Hilarious, right?

By the time Dr Simon Moriarty finally showed up, I was starting to get a handle on the psychology of the whole psychiatry thing: if bad things happen to you when you're young, then you're liable to blame someone for it when you grow up, possibly someone with a similar hairstyle to whoever did the bad things in the first place.

I explained my conclusions to Dr Moriarty, when he finally rolled in looking like the guitarist from Bon Jovi and smelling like the drummer from the Happy Mondays. Not a dickie bow or elbow patch in sight.

'Nice theory,' said Moriarty, collapsing on to the couch. 'I told Marion we shouldn't leave psych mags strewn around the waiting room.' He lit a thin cigar and blew the smoke in a dense funnel towards the ceiling, while I tried to remember if I'd ever heard the word *strewn* spoken aloud before. 'The charming Colonel Brady suggested that I leave *Woman's Own* out there so we can weed out the gays. Man's a genius.'

'Good kisser, too,' I said, straight-faced.

Simon Moriarty grinned through a mouthful of smoke.

'There might be some hope for you, soldier.'

I thought it best to burst that bubble. 'I want to volunteer for a second tour in the Lebanon.'

Moriarty expertly flicked his cigar through a half-open window. 'Then again, maybe not.'

So we talked for an hour. A bit like your normal pub chat, when you've been out for a few days with your best mate and your eyeballs are filmed with vodka.

I sat behind the desk while Moriarty lay on the couch and frisbeed questions at me. Eventually he came around to:

'Why'd you join the army, Daniel?'

I remembered something from the magazine. 'Why do *you* think I joined the army?'

Moriarty did the kind of long hard fake laugh that would make a Bond villain proud. 'Wow, that is hi-larious,' he said with a confidence that made me feel I'd been saying hilarious wrong all these years. 'I feel quite the fool now, wasting all that time in university when all I had to do was read a magazine. Have a nice time in the Lebanon.'

I sighed. 'Okay, Doc. I joined up because . . .'

Moriarty actually sat up. 'Because?'

'Because the uniforms set off my eyes. Come on, Doc. Work for the money.'

Simon Moriarty blinked away the previous night's party. 'They flew you home early, McEvoy. Remind me why they did that?'

I shrugged. 'I called in some gunship fire on my own position.' The shrug was to make this seem like no big deal, but it was a big deal and my legs were shaking as I said it and my mind flicked back to the tracers criss-crossing the night sky like something out of *Blade Runner* or maybe *Star Wars*. Whichever one was in space.

'That does sound like the action of a moron.'

He was baiting me, but that was okay, because we were both smiling a little now. 'What was left of Amal decided to overrun the entire compound,' I explained. 'Old-school style. An honest-to-God battle; couple of them had swords. Everybody made it into the bunker except the watch. I had a radio so I called in a gunship.'

'Was that a good decision?'

'Not according to the manual. Lots of property damage but not as much as there might have been. Plus a general got to live.'

'So they shipped you out?'

'Cos I was shell-shocked.'

'And were you?'

'Absolutely. No bowel movements for three days.'

Moriarty hit me again. 'So why did you join the army, Daniel?'

He was good. I wasn't expecting the change of tack. I mean, that gunship thing is an interesting story. 'Because I reckoned dying overseas was better than living at home.'

Moriarty punched the air. 'One nil,' he crowed.

Most nights after work at the casino I take a couple of Triazolam to nod myself off. I go for as long as I can trying to tune out Mrs Delano in the apartment above, but she grinds me down with her ranting, so I pop the pills just to shut her out for a few hours.

PLUGGED

Usually we have a little exchange through a hole around the ceiling light fitting.

I'll lead off with something like:

For Christ's sake shut up.

To which Mrs Delano will reply:

For Christ's sake shut up.

I could follow this with:

For one night? Could we have a little bloody peace for one night.

Which she might cleverly twist to:

One night I'll give you a little bloody piece.

You get the idea.

Tonight I'm thinking about Connie, so I add the Triazolam to a shot of Jameson and manage to grab a few hours of sweet dreams, but by eight my crazy neighbour's piercing tones have ruptured my rest, and I lie in bed listening as Delano lets fly with a few nuggets that wouldn't sound out of place in *The Exorcist*.

'If I ever find you, baby, I will poison your coffee.'

That gets me out of bed sharpish. I've lived in this building for five years and for the first couple Mrs Delano seemed like a normal, non-homicidal human. Then, in year three, she starts in with the *poisoning coffee* spiel. I'm starting to believe that nobody really knows anyone. I'm pretty sure no one knows me.

A hair-obsessed ex-army doorman. What are the odds of those Venn diagram bubbles intersecting?

Venn diagrams? I know. Another nugget from Simon Moriarty.

I jump in the shower thinking about Connie, so the shower is the right place to be. Everything about her stays with me.

19

All the usual suspects. The way she walks like there's a pendulum inside her. How her Brooklyn accent gets a little stronger when she's pissed. The sharp strokes of her nose and chin. Wide smile like a slice of heaven.

Oh baby, she'd said. *Oh baby*.

Inside a cloud of steam, my imagination adds levels. A husky catch at the end of the phrase.

Oh baaby.

How could I not have noticed this at the time? Connie was sending me a message.

I turn the shower knob way over in the blue.

Sunshine is slanting through my bathroom window, warming the chequered vinyl shower curtain. It's going to be hot today. Too hot for a woollen hat.

That's okay. I got lighter hats.

I quite like this time of year in New Jersey. The air on my skin feels like home. The old sod, the emerald isle. Ireland. Sometimes, on a clear day, the sky has the same electric-blue tinge.

Just go home then and stop bitching.

I'm even beginning to irritate my own subconscious. Is there anything more pathetic than a Mick on foreign soil, wailing 'Danny Boy'? Especially one who never liked the country when he was there.

It wasn't the country, I remind myself. *It was the people in the country and the things that happened there.*

My apartment is two floors up, three blocks north of Main Street and ten blocks south of the line of buildings with mildly risqué fronts that pass for a strip in this town. I stroll down the cracked concrete, trying to rein in the menace. I dated a gypsy once who told me I had an aura that looked like shark-infested water. Sometimes I piss people off just by walking by, so I hunch a little and keep my eyes on the ground, trying to radiate friendliness. Think hippies, think hippies.

Dr Kronski's surgery is in a part of town where there aren't any trees set into the sidewalk. The trashcans are generally teeming with beer bottles, and if you stand in one place long enough someone's going to offer you whatever you need.

All of which would suggest that Zeb Kronski isn't much of a surgeon, which would be totally not true. Zeb Kronski is a hell of a surgeon; he just doesn't have a licence to practise in the United States. And he can't apply because he had a boob job die on the table in Tel Aviv; not his fault, he assures me. Implant-related death.

The building is maybe twenty years old, but looks five times that. Part of a mini strip mall, mostly glass and partition walls. In winter, accountants and dental nurses freeze to death in these boxes.

Zeb's is wedged between Snow White's dry-cleaners and a Brite-Smile. Chemical sandwich. No wonder my doctor friend has his off days, with fumes like that eating his brain. I make sure my appointments are in the mornings, before depression takes hold.

The sign is flipped to *Closed* when I arrive. Surprising. Usually Kronski's homeopathic centre is doing a brisk business in powdered crocodile penis capsules by this time. Zeb tells me that the homeopathic bit started out as a front, but now he's having to file returns.

People are fucked up, Dan, he confided one night at Slotz, down to a film of whiskey in the bottom of his glass. *Everyone's looking for the magic pill. And they don't give a shit whose horn gets ground to make it.*

Wooden blinds stretch across the shop front; reminds me of a schooner deck I worked on in Cobh harbour. *Kronski's Kures* reads the decal. This mall is big on misspellings. Two doors down is Close Cutz, and around the back there's a roomful of Krazy Kidz slugging down Ritalin.

I feel a little irritated. Zeb better not be face down in an empty jacuzzi, sleeping off a bender.

Again.

Last time it cost me two hundred bucks to pay off the madam. I've been working up to this session, mentally, running through the scenarios, playing devil's advocate with myself.

What if the follicles didn't take? What if I end up scarred? What if I'm a vain asshole who'll still be ugly after the next operation?

And now that I have myself totally psyched, as my adopted countrymen would say, Zeb Kronski is running late. And when Zeb is running late, he is generally running tanked.

I thumb the flap in my wallet for the spare key; at least I can get the percolator bubbling while I'm waiting. Then I notice the door is open a crack.

A little odd. But no more than a little. Zeb doesn't remember to zip his own fly when he's drinking. One time in a bar, honest to Christ this happened, one time Zeb was five steps out of the john before he remembered to tuck his dick away.

I nudge the door open with my toe and duck inside. The

light is sepia, and heavy with swirling dust spores. Something has been moving in here.

Little moments like this, I can't helping thinking of patrols in Tibnin. I try to avoid the whole flashback thing when I've got stuff to do, but some moments are more evocative than others. Some moments are fat with menace. For some reason, this is one of those moments.

Suddenly Corporal Tommy Fletcher is in my head for the second time in so many days. Huge Kerry bastard, arms like Popeye, always complaining. Even on an early-bird mine sweep, Fletcher was mouthing off. *This weather is murder on my complexion, Sarge*, he was saying. *My freckles are fucking multiplying.*

Then a Katyusha rocket took out the US M35 truck behind us and flipped it on to Fletcher's leg, severing it at the knee. I walked away lugging Tommy on my shoulder, with a coating of B+ and a case of tinnitus.

And . . . we're back in the present. I try not to get bogged down in those days, but when the memories hit me, it's like being there, except you know what's coming next. You surface in the present and for a moment you are that scared boy again. Once I wet my pants. I wouldn't mind, but I held it in during the real incident.

I love watching the TV flashback guys. Tom Magnum, Mitch Buchannon, Sonny Crockett, all the greats. They have a ten-second jitter scene about 'Nam, then wake up bare-chested with a pained frown and maybe a light sweat on their smooth foreheads.

Fletcher, I think. *Jesus Christ*.

Inside Zeb's unit, the dust is settling.

This place is a real dump. Pills heaped in untidy pyramids on the shelves, a filing cabinet, its drawer hanging open like a drunk's mouth. Papers everywhere, a few sheets still fluttering to earth.

There's somebody here, I realise, and miss a step, catching my toe on the carpet.

'You okay there, bud?' says a voice. There are crossed legs and loafers sticking out of the shadows in the waiting area. Penny loafers, with actual pennies. Who is this guy? One of the Brat Pack? But the pennies strike a chord with me; I half remember something.

I cough to give myself a second, then answer, 'Fine. Goddamn rug. Doctor is trying to kill me.'

A low growling laugh, followed by a statement I get a lot. 'You talk weird.'

'I get that a lot,' I say.

'What is it? Dublin?'

That's pretty good. Most people get Irish, but never Dublin. 'I'm impressed. You got relations?'

The legs uncross and stretch. 'Nah. I work with a guy, he watches this Irish TV show on the net.'

The pennies drop. I know who this is, and all it takes is a flick of the light switch to confirm it.

Macey Barrett. One of Michael Madden's soldiers.

Okay. This could be trouble.

We don't really have much organised crime in Cloisters. Too small. But there's one guy trying to upgrade from hood to boss. He spent a summer with his cousin in the Bronx and picked up some ideas on how to run an organisation.

Irish Mike Madden. Prostitution, protection and a burgeoning crystal meth business, to pull in the weekend tweakers. And here, sitting in my friend Zeb's waiting room, is one of Madden's boys. In the dark.

What the hell is going on?

I tell myself to be calm. After all, hoodlums get bloated stomachs too. Maybe this guy's here for some aloe.

Barrett looks like an accountant. Expensive haircut, expensive smile, nice golden tan. But he isn't an accountant. Jason pointed him out to me one night in the club.

You see this guy, with the permatan and the penny loafers. Macey Barrett. Irish Mike brought him back from New York. They call this guy the Crab, on account of this little sideways shuffle he does before he sticks you.

Sticking people is apparently Barrett's favourite pastime. I knew guys like that in the army; they liked to get their hands red. Liked the feel of the blade sliding in.

'You waiting on the doc?' Barrett asks me, like he's just passing time.

I help myself to a cone of water from the cooler. 'Yeah, sure. I have an appointment.'

'You don't say? You're not in the book.'

He's reading the book now. Doesn't even bother hiding the fact.

'I'm not an in-the-book sort of a guy.'

Barrett rolls himself out of the chair, coming to his feet casually.

'So, you and the doc, pretty tight? Talks to you and shit? Confides in you?'

I shrug, conveying: *you know, whatever*. It's not much of an answer, and Barrett is not happy with it.

'I'm just saying, you don't have an appointment and you got a key in your hand. You give a key to someone, he's your friend. You meet for a beer after work, shoot the breeze. Talk about who's getting what done in the back room.'

'Zeb doesn't talk about patients. He's like a confessor with that stuff.'

Barrett doesn't listen past the first word. 'Zeb? Zeb, you say? Shit, you two *are* tight.'

Then he changes tack altogether, goes all buddy-buddy. 'So, pal. How do I know you? I know you from somewhere, right?'

'Small town.'

Barrett laughs, like this is some kind of joke. 'Yeah, sure. Small town. Nail on the head, buddy. But I know you. Come on, man. Don't tell me you don't know me.'

Barrett makes *knowing him* sound like a wonderful gift.

Screw it.

'Yeah, Macey. I know you. I see you on the strip. Madden's boy.'

And the friendliness shoots up a notch. 'That's right. I work for Mike. It's that shithole club, isn't it. Slotz, right? Daniel McEvoy, that's you, tell me I'm wrong. I seen you work, but never heard you talk.'

And he does a little sideways shuffle, dropping his right hand low.

This is not a great development. The sideways shuffle.

'You're a big guy, McEvoy,' says Barrett, shaking something

down his sleeve. David Copperfield he ain't. 'I bet you knock shitkickers around pretty good.'

I'm having a hard time believing this is actually happening. Barrett is really going to make a move on me just for being here. Wrong place wrong time for one of us. His hand comes up quick and in his fist there is what looks like a shaft of light.

It looks like a shaft of light, but unless he's Gandalf it probably isn't.

Good point, and it's more than enough for my fighter's instinct to stand up and dance a jig.

I step to one side, dig my heel into the carpet for stability. Adrenalin shoots through my system like nitrous oxide, slowing the whole thing down. The shaft of light flashes past my eye and I put the key through the side of Barrett's neck, watch him bleed out, then sit down and think about what I've done.

CHAPTER 3

When I finally parted ways with the army after my second tour, I quickly realised that there was nothing for me in Dublin. Every minute I spent in the dirty old town sent me further into the whirlwind of my own mind. I couldn't find a good memory in there that didn't end in tragedy. And I have a tendency to live in my head. Shit happens, right? So deal with it.

I did. Took advantage of being born in New York City and boarded a transatlantic jet to JFK. Wore the uniform that wasn't mine any more to check in and even got myself an upgrade. Oldest trick in the manual, after loading a shotgun with tea bags to scare the crap out of looters. Dumped the beret and jacket in the lounge bathroom. Walked out a civilian with a first-class ticket.

My mother may have been from America, but with her family apartment way up high and hanging over Central Park, she wasn't what you might call a typical New Yorker, and after touchdown it took me a while to credit the local accent. One day it's *bejaysus* and *begorrah* and the next it's *fugeddabout it*.

They're putting this on, I thought. *Yadda yadda yadda. Badda bing. Bullshit, no one talks like this.*

But they did, and worse. I took a couple of beatings in the early days just because I didn't understand what the hell people were saying to me. *Wadda fucku starin' at? You fuckin' retahded? Lookit dis fuckin' guy.*

It got so that I didn't wait around for the chit-chat. Some guy started strutting my way along a bar, and I let him have it with whatever I could reach. An ashtray, barstool. Whatever. Pre-empting fights comes naturally to me. I always know which guys are gonna go off. Something Simon Moriarty taught me once we got to know each other a little.

Seeing as you're determined to go back, Dan, I may as well pass on a few useful nuggets.

Such as?

Such as when it's time to stop peacekeeping and start shooting.

It's in the eyes and the shoulders, Simon had explained. They get to a point and then think *screw it*. At that moment consequences mean nothing, so you need to take your hands out of your pockets and start swinging. I swing good, too. Twelve years in the army taught me that much at least. But I still get pains in my back whenever I take a swing, especially in deep dark winter, even though the doctors swore they got every sliver of Hezbollah mortar shrapnel. *Phantom pains*, they said. Doesn't seem phantom when the frost is creeping up my window like a silver cobweb and my lower back feels like some demented leprechaun is driving rivets into it.

I stuck New York for four full years, working meatpacking during the day and clubs at night. But my fresh start was starting to seem like a dead end; love never walked around the corner, plus my hair was falling out. A decade in the grave and still my father was sending gifts my way. Four years of New York living and I was up to here with wiseguys and weisenheimers. My knuckles were like acorns from punching people. That's right, *people*. The women and children are dangerous in the Big Apple. I see a needle coming at me and I don't care if the person holding it has got braids and milk teeth. One humid autumn evening I gazed down on the baby-faced Asian hooker I had just decked, and decided to get out of the city. I took her knife, though. Nice butterfly with something Chinese on the handle. I've had it ever since.

So I packed my army duffel and took a train to the satellite town of Cloisters, Essex County. Only reason I got off there was because of a billboard they had in the station. *Cloisters. For People Who Are Tired Of The City*. I sure did like the sound of that.

It turns out that *here* isn't much better than *there* was. For a start, Cloisters has gambling only a bus ride across the Hudson. Which means on the weekends all the city arseholes come to throw away their hard-earned, watch one hundred per cent nude ladies and crash in hotels that are a lot cheaper than Atlantic City. Plus we've got our indigenous arseholes too. Six years have gone by and sometimes I think I should have stayed in New York. More than sometimes.

I'm moving on as soon as the hair grows in. Once I have hair I'll be happy. That's what I tell myself. I may have left it too late.

* * *

I make myself watch Macey Barrett die, because that way it means something. I don't want to kill a man then shut my eyes while he dies. You make these things hard, or else they get easy. I've killed men before, but only three, and never like this. Never so close that I can see eyelashes flickering or hear the rattle in their chest like there's a handful of beads in there. In the army you could always tell yourself: *This is war. You get a pass for war.* But here and now, in a pill shop in Jersey, it feels like this sort of thing shouldn't be happening. Violent death is supposed to be consigned to my past. Dr Moriarty would call it an anachronism.

Barrett goes slow, jerking like there's a current passing through him. Blood everywhere.

What do you expect? You put a spike in his jugular.

For some reason, my subconscious sounds like Zeb.

In the final spasm, Barrett loses his grip on the stiletto in his fist. It twirls straight up like a cheerleader's baton, burying itself in a suspended-ceiling tile.

I relax a little. That's justifiable homicide in my book, but perhaps not in every book. Michael Madden, for example; his book might read a little different. Irish Mike will cut me down for killing his man. Simple as that. I need to confuse this issue as much as possible.

First step, lock the goddamn door, stupid.

The key is still where I put it. I'm not a squeamish individual, but pulling that key out makes me cringe a lot more than sticking it in did. It comes loose with a familiar sucking noise, as though it's found a nice warm home and doesn't want to leave.

Familiar sucking noise? No one should be familiar with that particular sound, but I am. It reminds me of the time I decided to have a go at pulling a triangle of shrapnel out of my own side; it was just before I passed out.

I fumble the key into the lock and twist it, about fifteen seconds before one of Zeb's customers tries the handle.

'Kronski, you asshole,' she calls out, in a voice ravaged by thousands of cigarettes. 'Your tablets gave me the shits. Twenty-six fifty for the shits? Open the door, dammit. I can see you moving.'

The woman's silhouette trembles with fury, or possibly flatulence, and I'm starting to wonder if maybe I shouldn't be letting Zeb poke holes in my scalp when he can't even hand out the right tablets.

I play statues until the lady moves on, looking for a bathroom maybe, then turn my attention to Macey Barrett, lying blue faced and weirdly cross-eyed on the carpet. Looks like a vampire bit him. Poor bastard.

No. Not poor bastard. Murdering bastard.

Just like me.

No. Self-defence. Even God is okay with that.

Definitely Zeb's voice. My subconscious has figured out something that I don't want to face.

I have plenty of training in the art of killing but zero in the art of clean-up, and any jackass with a TV remote knows how important it is to get rid of trace evidence.

This is a problem. There are litres of blood soaking into the carpet, not to mention a two-hundred-pound family man lying deceased *on* the bloodstained carpet.

PLUGGED

Move the evidence. All of it. No body, no crime.

It's a big ask, but once I get my head around the job, it's calming to have something to do. Army mentality: idle hands are the devil's tools. Busy hands too in this case.

Zeb has a tiny supply closet in the rear. I liberate some scrubs, gloves and a mask. There's a power bone-saw, but I'm not ready to face that yet. A key in the neck is one thing, dismemberment is another.

I pat Barrett down for his keys, phone, watch and wallet. All the things a thief would lift. The search is rewarded with top-dollar goods. Lexus keys, Prada phone, Omega watch and a stack of fifties thicker than a quarter-pounder.

The carpet comes away easily, just a few glue strings to stretch and ping.

Typical Zeb. Cheap everything.

I yank up the entire waiting room section, rolling Barrett in three layers. Tape around the carpet, trash bags over the tape, more tape. No blood on the tiles underneath, that I can see, but I give them a swab of bleach just in case. They got all sorts of UV lights now; even the criminals have them. There isn't much you can't purchase on eBay.

Now I have myself a Cleopatra carpet package that needs moving. It's heavy, but I've humped a couple of bodies in my day, just not directly after killing them. I sling the burden over one shoulder, then take three quick steps out the back door to a white Lexus SUV, this year's model, blacked-out windows, door even opens itself. Talk about convenient.

The enclosed car park seems deserted, but even if a curtain-twitcher spies me, all anyone can ever testify to is that a masked man rolled a rug into a car. Of course Michael Madden won't care about due process or reasonable doubt.

I'm adjusting the driver's seat for my legs when a text buzzes through on Barrett's cell.

'I'll check that, shall I?' I say to the corpse in the back. He doesn't object, so I open the text.

It's from Mike Madden. Irish M reads the caller ID. Barrett has his phone set to display a photo of his boss. This massive guy at an Irish wedding, looks like, stripped to the waist, two of his boys in sweaty headlocks. Mad eyes, flat tweed cap with a shamrock pin on the peak.

I shudder. This person is bad news. I know the type. Irish borderline alcoholic. Death before disrespect. I would be better off swinging by his house and putting an end to this right now. But I won't, because this is not a war zone, there might be another way, and maybe Zeb is still alive.

I read the message.

Did you get it?

I sigh and pocket the phone.

Did you get it?

Shit. Zeb is most likely dead.

So who is this Zebulon Kronski guy? And how did I bump into him? That's nearly better than the gunship story. Surprise, surprise, the answer to those questions lies back in the Lebanon, so I'll keep it brief because this story is about now rather than then, although *then* seems to be pretty much a part of now most of the time. Someday I'll tell the full *then* story when I can even think of a Russian bear without throwing up.

PLUGGED

In a nutshell, the UN peacekeepers patrolled the border between Israel and the Lebanon, trying to keep the Israeli troops and the Shi'a Hezbollah and Amal from blowing themselves, each other and us to kingdom come. Those groups had been fighting for so long that they couldn't even agree which kingdom they would get blown to. Our main objective was to keep civilians safe, but our main function seemed to be as human shields for the Shi'a to hide behind while they fired rockets up at Israeli encampments. Most of the time we wore camouflage, went on patrol and were baked by the sun until our skin cracked, but sometimes things got a little primal, which tends to happen when bunches of hot, grumpy men have loaded weapons and different ideas about God.

One weekend I'm on a supply run in UN headquarters with Tommy Fletcher and he insists on a little detour to Mingi Street, an organic souk that grows like a reef around HQ and where anything is available for the right price. At this point in our military careers I am the corporal and he is the sergeant so I have no choice but to follow his unexplained lead.

Tommy is being a little mysterious about what he's looking for, so I am less reluctant to tag along than I pretend; curiosity has always been the cat that skinned me. Whenever I ask what we're after, he just taps his nose and says *that's actually funnier than you'd think*.

So we wade our way through the kids nipping at us like cleaner fish, we ignore the electronics merchants, the T-shirt vendors, the gold guys and hashish boys. I keep my finger on the trigger of my Steyer and thumb on the safety. It's not that I didn't like the concentrated life of these oven-like alleys,

35

but just because you like a place doesn't mean it's gonna like you.

Tommy walks ahead of me, the thousand resentful stares bouncing off him like pebbles off a rhino's back. With long strides he negotiates the souk, brushing through the hanging sheets of fine silks and elbowing past forests of rolled rugs. About ten minutes after I have totally lost any sense of place, he pounds his fist on a poster of Michael Jackson, which apparently has a door behind it. Michael's eyes slide back to reveal another set behind and I cannot resist saying, 'Oh for God's sake, Sarge! You're going to buy something from these people?'

But Fletcher is undeterred and passed a few dollars through the slot, which is enough to get us inside. The poster goes up like a roller blind and there's a steel door behind, which is hilarious because the wall is made of plasterboard.

I'm laughing openly now. 'You know what, Tommy? We should beat it. Yeah, this is bad. You know it.' I draw the line at *shamon*, too obvious.

I follow Tommy into the low-ceilinged corridor and continue walking forwards, even when I see what looks like a waiting room full of locals reading US *Weekly* and *Cosmopolitan*. A large *No Smoking* sign dominates the wall, and amazingly for the Middle East, no one is ignoring it. A pretty nurse talks rapidly on the phone as we enter and ignores us until Tommy taps on her desk with the barrel of his weapon.

'I need to see the doc,' he says pleasantly.

The nurse looks American with all the benefits. Big Julia Roberts teeth and boobs that could have some lucky guy's eye out.

PLUGGED

'Does sir have an appointment?' she says, and I would guess California by the way she wobbles her head on *appointment*.

Tommy nods equably. 'Yep, sir does. Fully loaded with another few clips in his bag.'

The nurse waves a pink nail towards the waiting room. 'We're all armed here, sir. I got a Colt pointed at your privates right now. So take a seat, cos if this thing goes off, even the doc can't do much about it.'

It's strange, all this melodrama in one afternoon. But it doesn't seem real or wrong in the heat. My brain sizzles inside the gourd of its skull and the walls sizzle and crack.

Bloody flies are huge.

Two women in floral head wraps argue over a Madonna article.

'Sorry, miss,' says Tommy. 'We're on a schedule.'

Things happen quickly then, and when I try to piece it together, images jump and flicker like an old VHS that's been taped over one too many times.

The nurse comes out of her seat and she does indeed have a large handgun in her tiny fingers. Suddenly the gun is in my hands. I must have twisted it away from her. Don't recall really. Training took over. Tommy's gone down the corridor and I remember thinking: *Okay, enough is enough. I don't know what this is, but I need to extricate myself. Hell, I could bash my way out into the street through one of these walls.*

But I don't go anywhere except after my sergeant.

The corridor is lined with posters, faded in the sun. I remember seeing *ET* and one of the Connery Bonds, then we're at a door. Someone has written DOCTOR in thick marker.

'Oh Jaysus,' says Tommy. 'Isn't that handy now?'

And in he goes, with me at his elbow and the nurse close behind cursing us both for sons of bitches. Inside the door we see a rudimentary surgery with plastic on the floor and a man in a white coat sticking a large needle of reddish gunk into another man's dick.

I'm suddenly no longer curious, and Tommy throws up on the covered floor, sending rivulets running along the polythene.

'Bloody bastards,' says the doctor guy. 'This is a sterile environment.'

And that was how I met Zebulon Kronski.

More later.

Once upon a time, I could have driven the Lexus to Newark airport and abandoned it in the long-term. Now with Homeland Security they'd be shoving mirrors under it in a New York minute, so I pick the local bus station instead and park the SUV by the dumpsters. I should get ten days' grace before the blues are called. With any luck some kid will jack the vehicle, dump the body and screw up the chain of events for anyone trying to follow it.

I walk half a dozen blocks from the station, then pay for a cab with one of Barrett's fifties. Guilt free.

Screw him, he tried to stick me.

I can't say this aloud, even mutter it, because I have never killed anyone outside a combat zone and I am shaken to my core.

You don't think that was a combat zone? What would you call it then?

PLUGGED

In the taxi, I give myself brain ache trying to wrap my head around the morning's events. Zeb has a good phrase for this kind of situation. A poor hand of poker or bad luck with a woman could set him off.

A total donkey's cock, this is, Dan. Donkey's fucking cock.

I don't know what that phrase means exactly, but somehow it catches the mood.

My friend has something that Irish Mike Madden wants. Something so important that Macey Barrett was cleared to stick any witnesses without even calling it in. If Zeb were alive, there'd be no need to toss his place; he'd give the *something* up. No doubt about it, zero pain tolerance. I once took him to emergency for a heart attack that turned out to be a trapped nerve. A trapped bloody nerve. Shit, I got a dozen of those a week in the army.

So this means that Zeb is probably gone. And if he's not, what am I supposed to do about it?

Nothing. Head down and pray the storm passes over. Grieve quietly and wish it away. All that movie soldier crap about never leaving a man behind is just that. Movie soldier crap. A man goes down behind enemy lines and he's gone. First rule of combat.

CHAPTER 4

I spend an hour and a half over a ten-minute lunch in Chequer's Diner by the park. I expect the turkey club to taste like ash, but it doesn't. Sweetest sandwich I've ever had in this place, and I've had plenty.

I'm alive, I realise. *And food tastes good.*

I remember now. You make it home from reconnaissance, and gritty water from the neck of an oil can tastes like nectar. This trauma is bringing the memories back. I'm starting to think like a soldier again; maybe that's no bad thing.

Once I get over the magical goodness of food, I start brooding on Zeb. He's a friend, I suppose. The only one I have. A man passes forty and he's supposed to have a handful of guys in his inner circle. Maybe in Ireland there's a couple of army buddies who would step up for me, but here, no one. Even Zeb wouldn't have tolerated any actual discomfort on my behalf. One night I made him get out of bed to pick me up, and I had to listen to it for a month.

Probably dead. More than likely. No sense hoping.

The park is still green. That's unusual for this time of year;

even the leaves are hanging in there. Through the railing I see a dad and his boy tossing a baseball like something from a happy-family TV show.

It's too late now for me. No baseball-tossing, or kids with my eyes. All I have to look forward to is staying alive until tonight so I can listen to my crazy neighbour mouthing off upstairs.

It's true what they say about Irish people: we have a great love for the maudlin. For every silver lining there's a cloud. Maybe that's why I get on with Zeb so well. It has to be said that the two of us love a good moan, though Zebulon's beyond moaning now.

Don't count on it, you Mick asshole.

Except in my head, apparently.

I spend the afternoon watching my own apartment from across the street. There are three delis and an Italian restaurant within ten yards of my front door, so I load up on comfort carbs and coffee. With that concoction inside me, my brain is telling me to get up and go while my stomach is begging for a nap.

I am knocking back my fourth espresso when a couple of suits mount the steps to my building, but they're peddling the afterlife rather than an end to this one. Definitely not pros of any sort. They walk up side by side and don't even check the door before knocking. Anyone so inclined could shoot both these guys through the mail slot.

I keep up my vigil for a couple more hours, but nobody suspicious or even suspiciously ordinary shows up. But that doesn't mean I'm clear. Macey Barrett won't even be stiff in his rug yet.

*   *   *

Eventually the caffeine in my bloodstream beats down the dough balls in my gut so I make the short walk to the club and arrive at eight, mildly surprised to find myself alive and unmolested. Not so much as a crooked look from a passer-by. Well, no more than the usual. Because of the way I look, people project stuff on to me as I walk past. All of a sudden I'm their mean old daddy, or their arsehole boyfriend, or their handsy boss.

Maybe if you smiled once in a while, Simon Moriarty had suggested during one of our sessions.

So I tried that, until my fixed grin reminded a new girl at the club of some serial killer on the FBI's most-wanted list and she phoned it in. That was an interesting afternoon in the tombs. Especially with me being handy with a knife and all. Luckily for me, the actual killer was caught the same day when he passed out under a park bench having hit a vein trying to tattoo a psalm on to his dick. It pains me mightily to say it, but the guy did look a little like me.

The upshot of all this is that I don't smile now unless someone I like says something to me that they think is funny. One of the people I like is too young to get my humour and the other is missing presumed dead.

It doesn't really surprise me that no one is on my tail.

Still too early, I tell myself. *Macey Barrett hasn't been gone more than half a day.*

Which hasn't stopped Irish Mike sending a dozen texts wondering where his employee has gotten to. They start civil enough.

Hey, M. What's the story?

Deteriorate a little.

M. You trying to be funny? M.

And by the end are openly hostile.

You report in, Barrett, or I'll cut your forking head off.

Forking? Predictive text.

I don't read any more after that.

I get to the club early, but hang back for almost an hour, see if anyone is making enquiries. Nothing suspicious. The only dangerous-looking Irish guy around here is me, so I push through the black leather doors. Jason is at the coat check shooting the breeze with Brandi, one of the older hostesses. I say older, but Brandi is barely thirty, which is just out of her teens as far as I'm concerned. Brandi has been angry at the world for about a year, since she had to hang up her stripper's G-string and downgrade to a hostess job at Slotz. Forced retirement at thirty.

Jason is leaning on the counter with that fond faraway look in his eyes that tells me tonight's subject is childhood memories.

'I remember getting pissed on by my old man,' he says dreamily.

Brandi shoots me a look like maybe she should hide in the coats.

'Yeah, Jason,' she says, rolling her eyes at me. 'That sounds swell.'

Jason catches the tone. He's big, but not stupid. 'No. Nothing like that. It was a game we had, you know, two of us at the bowl, pissing as hard as we could. A race. Dad always let me win, even if he was blue in the face holding on. Sometimes there'd be spray, you know.'

43

'Those were the days,' I say sincerely, passing my coat to Brandi. Any good memory is a valid good memory.

Jason tears the foil from a protein bar, bicep bulging in his sleeve. 'You got anything, Dan? Any good memories of your pappy back home in Ireland?'

'Yeah. There was this one day when he beat me with his hand because he couldn't find the shovel. I'll never forget it, still brings a lump to my throat.' I try not to be bitter, but it's hard.

People are usually embarrassed when I start in on my father, but Brandi has heard a million sob stories in her years on the podium. 'Jesus, Dan, lighten the hell up. This place is gloomy enough with Connie scaring away all the big tippers.'

Some of the girls are not opposed to getting frisky in a booth if it means an extra few bucks. Most of the guys, too.

'Come on, Brandi. Guy licked her arse.'

'You can say ass, Dan. You're in America now.'

I sigh. 'Arse is the last piece of Irish I have.'

I decide then and there to give half of Macey Barrett's wad to Connie. Her kids could probably do with a weekend away; maybe they'd take me along. We could toss a baseball.

I'm clutching at straws now. Never look out the window in a diner.

'Where is Connie? She in yet?' I'm already seeing myself making the gesture.

'No sign,' says Jason, checking his teeth in a tiny mirror on the back of his phone. 'She better get here soon, Victor's due.'

Vic's favourite pastime is docking the staff. Any excuse he can find. A while back he put a timer on the staff washroom, which lasted about ten minutes before someone set fire to it and took out half the rear wall. Still, gives you an idea of the kind of person he is.

'Yeah, that Vic, what a prince,' says Brandi with a sneer.

Everybody's on the same page on the Victor subject.

Then the man himself stumbles in. Victor Jones, the world's oldest white rapper, fifty-five, resplendent in a Bulls sweatsuit and cap, wraparound shades and gold ropes up to his chin. More than a stereotype; a cartoon stereotype. Simon Moriarty could spend the rest of his life analysing this guy. I'm surprised Victor doesn't get beaten up on a daily basis.

Matter of fact, he looks like he got beaten up tonight. There's a drool pendulum swinging from his chin, and what looks like puke in little triangular pools between the laces of one ruby sneaker.

Ruby sneakers? I mean, come on, man. You're mid-fifties from Hunterdon Country. Have some self respect.

Brandi is all over the boss, plumping his shoulder with a boob. 'Hey, Vic, honey. What's up? What happened to your shoe?'

Hypocrisy is a survival skill in Slotz. Five minutes ago she was spitting on Vic's name.

Victor bends over, wipes his chin.

'In the . . . fucking . . . out in the . . . I don't fucking believe this . . .'

He pukes on the other sneaker.

'Hurghhh . . . fuck it . . . fuck.'

I am not too upset. To be honest, seeing Victor doubled over is kind of amusing, takes my mind off my own gangster trouble.

'Get it out, Mister Jones,' I say, winking at Jason. 'You'll feel better.' And then I add, 'Bejaysus.' To let Victor know I'm being Irish and charming.

'Yeah, get it out, boss,' adds Jason, smiling so wide I can see the little diamond in his fang. 'Musta been one of those kebabs.' He shoots a few seconds of video with his phone.

'Shut the hell up the both of you,' gasps Victor, spitting into the puddle between his feet. 'We got work to do.'

He's up straight now, wiping the tears from his scheming eyes.

'Okay, McEvoy, make sure there's nothing sub-v going on in the club. I mean nothing. You find someone holding, toss 'em. Any of the girls doing side business, tell 'em to zip it up. Jason, I want you to make absolutely sure there's no disk in the security camera's recorder. If there is, wipe it. Wipe them all. I want us squeaky clean before the cops get here.'

Brandi is snuggling his elbow again. 'What can I do, baby?'

Vic shrugs her off like a wet jacket. 'You, *baby*? You can clean up the puke.'

Kissing arse doesn't get you anywhere with this boss.

Then I register what Victor said.

Before the cops get here.

Why would the cops be coming here?

Connie generally parks her old Saturn out back and slips in through the delivery entrance. She's not ashamed of herself, just her job, and she doesn't want any of the cling-ons to doorstop her at the front sidewalk. The police eventually cordoned off a ten-metre square around the Saturn with yellow crime-scene

46

tape. But not before I ignored Victor's instructions and rushed outside.

Connie lay dead beside her car. One shot through the head it looked like, between her arched eyebrows. She'd struggled some; her blouse was ripped and her right shoe lay apart from the body.

I felt numb; it was too much. Sensory overload. My brain steamed as though it was packed in ice.

I'll feel this later, I thought.

I was right.

Generally I'm not much for scenery. I don't slow down to gaze at the stars, never rise early to watch the sun pulse over the skyline, but sometimes a picture gets etched on to your brain and you know it's there for good. Always the violence, shit and misery. I barely remember my own baby brother's face, but every night dear old Dad haunts my dreams. Three-quarter profile, hooded eyes, tacks of grey stubble, and me falling away from his fist, left eye filling up with blood.

I will remember this night too. Connie lying beside the Saturn, slightly on her side, as though turning in her sleep. One cheek scuffed like a boy's shoe, limbs brown, elbows sharply pointed. Car door open, cab light casting a yellow glow on her face. Cracked and buckled asphalt with cigarette butts in the grooves. Blue shift dress with some kind of sparkly material, sequins or metallic thread, I don't know. Hip curved. Hair frizzed on the wet road.

And a hole in the head.

I stumbled back inside, gasping for air.

Did I have something to do with this? Is it connected?

*   *   *

The cops assemble us in the bar and announce that we are shut down for the foreseeable. Vic goes ape.

'What the hell?' he rants, going nose to nose with a detective, who's got that look in her eyes that should tell Vic that there's a shit-limit and he's fast approaching it. 'Shooting didn't even happen on the premises. This is victimisation, fucking police brutality. Something.'

Vic never could see the line between saving face and talking stupid.

'There's a bakery on the other side of the lot. You pricks better shut that place down too or I'm suing somebody.'

'I'm a cop, sir,' says the detective, black, thirties, strong features like you'd get on a wood carving. 'We don't shut down bakeries.'

Vic almost has an aneurysm. 'Fucking funny, lady. If I wanted to take shit from a bitch, I coulda stayed at home.'

The cop has a comeback for that too. 'Yeah? Well maybe if you click the heels of those ruby slippers together, you could do us all a favour and magic yourself off to whatever dream world manufactures culture-raping assholes like yourself . . . sir.'

These are strong words, but Vic started in with the B word, so the cop is probably on safe ground complaints wise. I decide not to get on her bad side.

The blue puts up with five more minutes of Vic's obstruction, then gets tired of making the effort and sends him up to the plaza for a night in the cells.

Brandi objects loudly until the door closes behind her boss, then she sparks a cigarette and says, 'Thank heaven. That boy was about to feel the sting of my boot on his behind.'

I am surprised. *Behind* is a delicate word to be coming out of Brandi's mouth.

So for two hours we sit around in the bar, waiting for a crime lab crew that has to come all the way from Hamilton in their paper suits. Then another ninety minutes while they scrutinise the area for trace. Good luck to them. That back lot has seen more pot deals and blow jobs than the Amsterdam red-light district. I bet they get semen samples going back to the nineteen fifties.

I keep an eye on the scene through the high window. All I can see of Connie is her foot, but it's enough to make me want to cry for every sadness I've ever known. I don't break down, though. Tears from a big man are as good as an admission of guilt to a zealous cop.

A couple of the CSIs are not as professional as they might be, pulling down their masks to smoke cigarettes and bobbing along to whatever's on their headphones. Maybe that's how they deal, or maybe they genuinely do not give shit one.

And all the time, while the trail is growing cold, the staff is sitting jittery around the casino's poker table; that is until Brandi hits upon the notion of getting hammered on the boss's dime. Victor's locked up, Connie's shot dead. So, screw it, we all need a drink.

After a while the only ones sober are me and Jason, and he's been chewing steroids like they're Juicy Fruit.

'This is fucked up, man,' he says for the hundredth time.

Some of the hostesses echo the sentiment back to him, but the number dwindles each time he says it.

I know how Jason feels; there are no words for this kind of situation. Nothing covers it. The numbness is leaving me now, and I miss it. In its place there's a ball of nausea in my gut.

Have they told little Alfredo and Eva? Who's going to take them in?

I feel myself getting Irish maudlin again, asking the big questions. Where has my life gone? What have I got? I remember my brother Conor and the look he always had on his face. The look you see on dogs in the pound, the ones they find in burlap with chains coiled at the bottom.

Fresh wounds are like doors into the past. Who said that? Hope to Christ it wasn't Zeb. I don't want to be therapising myself with any of his skewed wisdom.

Thanks a bunch. I said plenty of wise shit. Who told you not to fuck with the Jews? Who told you that?

By the time we run out of silver tequila, the cops are ready for interviews. They set up in Vic's office and summon us one by one. I go second, after Brandi, who comes out snapping her fingers, like she's won some kind of victory.

There are two local detectives in the room, both African-American females, which is not as much of a long shot as it used to be. They've squeezed themselves behind Vic's desk and swept some of his porn memorabilia into a drawer. The junior detective is the lady who gave Vic grief over his trainers. I want to take a liking to this girl, but she's got her arms folded across her chest and is wearing a pretty clear *I don't make friends* face. I duck from habit under the steel construction beam that spans the ceiling, even though it's a couple of inches above head height, and sit opposite the detectives.

50

I point at a Pirelli calendar on the wall. 'You might want to take that down too.'

I am not being a smartarse here; it is important to me that this investigation goes well. The first forty-eight hours, as they say.

The younger detective rips the calendar out of the wall, taking a chunk of Sheetrock with it.

'Satisfied, Mister McEvoy?' she asks, giving me the bad-cop eyeball. We are off on the wrong foot; she has me down as non-cooperative.

'That was a genuine suggestion,' I protest, calmly and sincerely. 'Connie was my friend and I want her killer caught.'

The cops are not won over by my Irish brogue; if anything, a foreigner seems to make them more suspicious. They sit up, shuffle papers and stuff, bump shoulders in the tight space. They were going for authoritative, lining up behind the desk like that, but they look like two school kids squeezed behind a bench.

'Cornelia DeLyne was your *friend*, Mister McEvoy?' says the older of the two.

Cornelia? I don't know why Connie's full name surprises me, but it does.

'Mister McEvoy?'

I focus on the lead detective. She is maybe forty, striking, a slash of rouge on both cheeks, strands of silver in her cropped hair. She wears a grey suit and a colourful Jamaican parrot shirt that kind of jumps out at you.

'Yes, Detective . . . ?'

'I'm Detective Goran, this is Detective Deacon.'

Deacon, the smart mouth, is early thirties. Severe grey suit, wearing anger on her face like latex. I know the type; very serious about her work.

'Well, Detective Goran, Connie and I were good friends. More than that, briefly.'

I figure Brandi has already told her.

'So she broke up with you, and you were pissed off.'

I don't sigh dramatically; I was expecting this.

'We never broke up, as such. We had a weekend together, and I think there was another one coming up. If you want to talk pissed off, we had quite a ruckus in here last night. Bunch of college kids.'

'We know all about it,' says Deacon, cutting across me. 'Harmless hijinks, I'd say. We want to talk about you, Mister McEvoy. You're saying *you* were this beautiful young lady's booty call?'

I heard this phrase once maybe five years ago. Nobody uses it any more.

'Booty call, Detective?'

'Fuck buddy. How does that suit you?'

From *hijinks* to *fuck buddy* in a couple of heartbeats. We're down to this level already? I expected another minute of civility, but this is how it goes. It's not personal, except with Deacon I have the feeling that maybe it is.

'Okay, I get it, Detective. I know, she's . . . she was twenty-eight and I'm . . .'

'You're what? Seventy?'

I don't get riled. 'I'm forty-two. I counted my lucky stars, believe me.'

Deacon goes for it. 'You want to know what I think? I think you were fixated on Miss DeLyne. Obsessed. She kept turning you down. It's disgusting, right? You're an old man in a silly hat. So you freaked and shot her. Why don't you sign the paper and we can call it a day?'

I can't see myself, but I bet my jaw is jutting stubbornly. 'Not that easy, Deacon. You're going to have to work on this one.'

'Come on, Danny, give it up. I'm tired and the coffee stinks.'

'What? You think I'm going to break down and blubber out a confession?' I turn to Goran. 'She always this lazy?'

I shouldn't be smart-arsing, but Deacon needs to refine her style a little. This shooting has to be solved and the detective is throwing spears into the ocean hoping to hit something.

Goran shields her face with a file and I suspect she's smiling. 'You know the young 'uns, Mister McEvoy. Instant gratification.'

And suddenly Deacon is smiling too and I realise that this bull-in-a-china-shop attitude of hers is the oldest trick in the book.

'You do bad cop pretty good,' I tell her. 'But time's a-wastin' and I am not the guy.'

Deacon flips open a field laptop. 'Really? You have quite a file here, Mister Daniel McEvoy. And looky here, an interview with the FBI tagged on at the end.'

Groan. Word travels fast over the internet. Some tool in the army records department e-mailed my info to the FBI last year. Not so much as a court order and he shoots it across the pond.

'I know what the file says. If you look at the end of that page, you'll find it was a case of totally mistaken identity. I got an official apology, for Christ's sake.'

Deacon ignores this, reading with great melodrama like she doesn't already know what's on the screen.

'Company Sergeant Daniel McEvoy. Active service in the *Lebanon*.' She says Lebanon with jazz hands, like it's Disneyland. 'Extremely dangerous individual. Trained in close-quarter combat. Expert knife man.'

'I don't like bazookas,' I say, straight-faced. Luckily my file doesn't mention sniper and marksman skills. I learned those on my own.

'You've done some things, Daniel.'

'Not murder.'

'*Not murder*,' she jeers, doing my accent. 'Sez you. What are you, Daniel? Albanian?'

'I'm Irish, American too. My mother was from Manhattan. It's on the screen.'

She checks it. 'Your mom moved *to* Ireland from New York? Isn't that a little ass to mouth?'

Now she's talking about my mother, it's like we're in the schoolyard. But it's tactics, might even rile someone a little shorter in the tooth. I have to admit, this Deacon woman stirs shit good.

'I think you mean *ass backwards*.'

I'm watching Goran through all this. The senior officer taking everything in, letting Deacon have her head, for now. This is their routine. Mother and tearaway daughter, I can see how it could work on a guilty person. Not that I ain't a guilty person; I'm just not guilty of this.

What I want to do is cut through the bullshit, stop playing the game and really talk to these people.

'Look,' I say, palms up, which is body talk for *trust me*. 'I liked Connie, loved her a little maybe. Can we skip the regulation back-and-forth and see if I can't actually help out? Come on, I'm not right for this. Once upon a time I was a professional. Do you seriously think I would shoot Connie, then leave her not ten yards from where I'm sitting drinking coffee? How does that make sense?'

Goran nods slowly, accepting the truth of my argument.

Deacon believes it too, but she sticks to her role just in case I'm a better actor than she is. 'How do we know what kind of psycho you are, Daniel? Maybe you didn't get enough killing in the army. Maybe you *want* us to catch you.'

I'm staring at Goran now, head to one side. 'Okay. I see what you're doing. You've got nothing, so you're shaking the tree.'

Deacon closes the laptop. 'Shaking the tree? Is that some kind of racist comment, McEvoy?'

I do my best to ignore this accusation. 'Ask me something relevant,' I say to Detective Goran. 'The clock is ticking. Your actual murderer is probably halfway across the GW bridge by now.'

Goran is not ready to share just yet and covers the file with her forearm. 'This looks like a crime of opportunity, Mister McEvoy. Right place for him, wrong place for her. Some crackhead looking for bag money.'

It's a theory, but not a great one. In Ireland we would say she was patting my bottom and closing the door behind me.

'You're in Cloisters, Detective. We're not exactly overrun with crackheads. This is the roughest joint in town and I haven't even seen a needle in a couple of years. How many crackheads you know can make a shot right between the eyes?'

Goran's chin comes up. 'You saw the wound, Daniel. How'd that happen?'

That was a little slip. Maybe it's time to stop talking so fast.

'I made it my business to see before the tape went on. Wanted to be sure it was Connie.'

'Touch anything?'

'Not one damn thing.'

Goran gives me a long look, searching my eyes for the lie, which she doesn't find, or maybe she does find it and decides to give me a little rope to tie myself up with.

'Take a walk, but not too far. I'll be dialling your number.'

My shoulders sag. 'You don't want to ask me anything useful?'

'You want to tell me something useful?'

I leave without saying another word.

CHAPTER 5

I had a whole six months of sessions with Simon Moriarty before the medical discharge finally came through after my second tour. Twice a week I took a bus to his Dalkey practice and waved a cup of coffee under his nose until he rolled out of bed.

'Come on, Sergeant,' Moriarty said to me one day, with a grin that told me he knew a whole lot more about the world than I did. 'Make it difficult for me. This is too easy, textbook stuff.'

I was lying on an oxblood leather sofa, feeling about as comfortable as a cat in the doghouse. Usually Simon lay on the sofa, but this was our last session and he was taking me to task.

'I'm an open book, huh?'

'A pane of glass, Sergeant. Trans-parent.'

'Let me in on the secret, Doc. What's my problem?'

Simon lit a thin cigar. 'With Irish and Jews usually it's the mother; with you it's daddy dearest.'

I sat up, gave him a serious look. 'Are you trying to tell me that having an abusive father leads to problems in later life? You must be some kind of genius.'

'Hilarious, Sergeant. Hiding behind humour. Good tactic. How's that been working out for you?'

Simon could be a pain in the arse, but he generally hit the nail on the head.

I lay down. 'Not so good. Listen, Doc, everyone's got problems, issues, whatever. You just get on with it, try to stay as calm as possible.'

Moriarty flicked ash from the front of his Ramones T-shirt. 'That's what we're here to as-certain, Daniel. Can you stay calm? We can't go releasing a trained murder machine into the big city if he can't keep his talents to himself.'

'Don't worry about that. I've seen enough bloodshed.'

'You have plans?'

'I'm free on Tuesday and I know a nice bar.'

More ash-flicking. 'Life plans, smartarse. With your tendencies, you need to be careful what kind of situations you put yourself in.'

'Tendencies? You make me sound like a pervert.'

'Here's my theory, Daniel. You had a violent father who beat up on your mother, yourself and your baby brother, got the entire family, except you, killed drunk driving. So now you feel like you have to protect the defenceless. That's why you joined up. Not to kill, to pro-tect. The problem is that you also have difficulties with authority, father figures. So, you felt compelled to join the army, and you also felt com-pelled to clock your superiors. Do you see the conflict?'

I felt I had to defend myself. 'My superior officer left three of his own men pinned down between Israeli troops and the militia and he refused to order any covering fire. Some people need to be clocked.'

Simon pretended to write something. 'There are protocols for these things, Dan.'

'I know. Fired upon twice, blah-blah-blah.'

'So you broke protocol and *once again* drew fire on your own twenty by deciding to ignore the chain of command and providing some covering fire of your own.'

'Twenty? That's CB, not military.'

'I'm reaching out; cut me some slack. So you break protocol, this time getting half a mortar shell up yer hole.'

'It was a whole shell.'

Simon frowned. 'A shell made specifically for holes?'

'Whole with a silent w.'

'Oh, I see. But my point stands: you felt compelled to protect.'

'Com-pelled to pro-tect. Got it. Where were you when I was signing up?'

'Also you have the gambling addiction.'

This was a new one. 'Addiction? Come on. Who told you that? I like a hand of poker, it's true, but no more than the next man. It's hardly a problem.'

'Wishful thinking,' Simon admitted. 'I grow weary of this analysis, plus I like a game of poker myself.'

'I don't think you're a man to be bluffed.'

Simon closed his notebook with a snap. 'All in all, I think the medical discharge is the best thing for you.'

'Medical discharge? Sounds disgusting.'

'Find yourself a nice conflict-free position,' continued Moriarty, ignoring my attempt to hide behind humour. 'Somewhere you don't have to protect anyone.'

I can't help it. 'Don't you mean pro-tect?'

Simon ha-ha'ed drily. 'Very good. Wisecracks, the fast track to mental health. Seriously, Dan, find yourself a stress-free position. No cards, no boss and no one depending on you for their well-being.'

So now I'm a doorman at a casino. But it's not my fault; I'm com-pelled.

The town is busy tonight, but I don't feel connected. It's like I'm watching everything through a dirty window. The world I've been holding together with spit and dreams is finally coming apart. The cops toss us out on the street like we're trespassers and tell us to get lost. There won't be any rickety roulette or polka-dot bikinis tonight.

Connie is dead, Zeb is missing. I killed a person with a key, for Christ's sake.

I know that really the key part of it is not important, but there seems to be some kind of irony in it.

Instead of locking the door, I opened Barrett's doorway to the next life.

Forced. Laboured.

There is no key to life, just a key to death.

Better, but I won't be writing slim volumes of poetry any time soon.

I feel sick deep in my stomach and there's bile in my throat. Bile and tequila. I stop and spit in the drain, and as I hawk it up, bent over with my hand on a pole, I see a glint of street-light on a gum wrapper and remember something.

Macey Barrett's stiletto spinning like a cheerleader's baton, burying itself in the ceiling.

The stiletto. It's still there.

Shit.

Shit. Shite and bollocks.

What can I do about it? What *should* I do?

I straighten slowly, like a very old man, and actually admonish myself aloud.

'Okay, Daniel. Think about this calmly.'

In the third person now? Christ, things are bad.

Unfortunately my calm thinking space is out of service at the moment. I try to swat aside the waves of grief and tequila fumes, but my brain is fogged and buzzing.

It should be fine.

So the stiletto is up there; it shouldn't lead back to me unless there's a spy-cam in the handle.

The way my luck's been going . . .

I chuckle and spit one last time to restore my manhood after all those thoughts of irony.

Think this thing through.

Going back to the surgery would be a big mistake. Irish Mike could be keeping an eye on the place, and showing up would only put me on his radar.

What about Zeb?

I want to think something positive, I would kill for some kind of bright shining answer, but there's nothing coming out of my brain but fog and sadness.

Connie, darlin'.

Zeb is dead.

Call him and find out. It's a thought.

I block the ID on Barrett's Prada cell and punch in Zeb's number.

Couple of rings, then a man answers.

'Yeah?'

Not Zeb. I can tell from a single syllable. Zeb's got this asthma voice, all in the nose.

'Dr Kronski?' I ask, like it's a professional call.

'Who's speaking?' says the man.

'*You* are,' I say, and hang up. I should probably have invented some medical yarn and promised to call back later, but I can't be bothered.

They're answering his calls too. Whatever Macey Barrett was looking for, they haven't found it yet, otherwise Zeb's phone would be at the bottom of the reservoir, along with his body.

I shouldn't have called. I don't want any of this information; it's funnelling me towards a choice.

There's a dawn glow cupping the clouds by the time I get home. I feel like crap and probably look like week-old crap. The last thing I need is my upstairs neighbour Mrs Delano going off on an abuse bender, not to mention the fact that Mike Madden could have cottoned on to my being a fly in his ointment by now.

So with all this in mind, I use my army stealth training to creep into the apartment. There could be a cell of jittery terror-ists holed up on the second floor and they wouldn't hear

Company Sergeant Daniel McEvoy slipping down the hallway to his own door.

Which is open. The busted triple-bar lock lying shamefaced on the floor.

I forget all about operation under the radar when I see the whirlwind that has rolled through my apartment.

'Christ Almighty!' I shout, wading through the detritus that was my life. I used to do that metaphorically with Simon; now I'm doing it for real. It's just as painful and I don't feel better with every step.

The place has been wrecked. Destroyed. I've seen bomb sites with less shredding. They pulled down the wallpaper, disembowelled the sofa, dismantled the appliances. My fridge is lying on its side, leaking mayo; looks like a dying robot. The AC unit is in pieces on the table; reminds me of a mechanic's course I took once. Pictures on the floor. A Jack Yeats West of Ireland print I carried in a tube from Dublin, slashed for malice.

I walk around flapping my arms, kicking through the debris. Where do you start? How can you fix this?

Then Mrs Delano pipes up. She was waiting for me to come home, I'm sure of it. Probably been up all night injecting her eyeballs with caffeine. I know that sounds crazy, but when you live underneath crazy, some of it drips downwards.

'Kee-rist almighty,' she calls, voice wafting through the light fixture. 'Kee-rist fucking almighty.'

I am absolutely not in the mood for this lady right now. The best tack, I know, is not to rise to the bait, because if I react she wins, and we could be at this all morning and at the end of it my stuff is still trashed.

'You down there, Irish? Can't you keep your monkey friends under control?'

Monkey friends? Screw it. Zeb, Barrett and sweet Connie. I need to loosen the valve, let off some steam. So I throw my head back and roar like Tarzan.

'Shut the hell up, you crazy bat.'

She comes back with 'Hell is shut for crazy bats.'

'Shut up,' I shout, and I can feel my tendons stretch. 'Or I swear to Christ I will come up there and wring your neck.'

'No Christ in this neck of the woods.'

This kind of carry-on is infuriating, and now that Delano has me on her hook, she could keep it up for hours.

'Drop dead, you lunatic. Why don't you drop bloody dead?'

My face is red and tight. I'm not just shouting at Delano, I know, but I keep shouting anyway.

'That's right. Drop dead. The world would be a better place.'

'Dead is a better place? You think dead is a better place for lunatics, Irish?'

There's a new note in her voice. Wild, past caring. I'm a bit that way myself.

'You heard me.'

She doesn't respond, which is unusual. Ominous, even. Echoes of my own voice circle me like ghosts.

If this was a movie, something really bad would be just about to happen.

What is she going to do? What's the big tease? How can Delano haunt me for ever?

There's one sure way.

Something thumps on the ceiling overhead.

Four dead? Four in one day? Come on.

I race to the door, skirting my ruptured easy chair. The corner of my eye notices that they even took the weights off my barbells. Thorough.

Up the stairs three at a time, sick to my stomach, heart bouncing around like a lottery ball in the cage.

Please God, not too late. What the hell did she do?

Delano's door is pretty solid, with a couple of extra bolts, but I'm running on adrenalin and take them out with a bull charge. Momentum carries me inside, and I lurch across the threshold, heaving breaths, shoulder throbbing, afraid to look and see.

I do look, in case time is of the essence, and I see Delano sitting in a straight-backed chair, a cigarette between two slim fingers. There is a large book on the floor beside her. A bible, I think.

'Hello, hero,' she says, smoke leaking from between her bow lips. 'You owe me a door.'

I am such an idiot.

'Sucker,' Delano adds, which is a more accurate word.

My first thought is to launch into a rant, but by the time I draw breath I realise there's no point. It's funny; this whole thing is hilarious. Not ha-ha funny, so I don't laugh.

'You might cut me a break,' I say quietly, 'if you realised the kind of day I've had.'

'I've been up all night listening to your friends,' she snaps, without a shred of mercy.

This is the closest I've stood to Delano. She's my age, a few years younger. Blonde hair, straight and long. Maybe a figure, hard to tell in a towelled robe. And blue eyes rimmed with kohl, staring right into me like she's got mind powers. I notice for the first time that this lady has got cat's eyes, like Ava Gardner or Madonna. Beautiful but dangerous.

The apartment is freaky neat, but cold. There's a tube of wind coming in through a hole in the window.

She notices me looking. 'I was having a moment,' she explains. 'Goddamn satsuma. Can you believe that? Made a helluva hole.'

Something to do, thank Christ. Take my mind off those eyes.

Get those idle hands to work, soldier, and do not even contemplate strangling this woman.

You learn to use your hands in the army. Things break down in the field and they need to be fixed; no use waiting for a requisitions crate. Ireland is a long way from the Lebanon, and even if your package makes it through the grifters on both ends of the pipeline, you're still talking half a year. There was a guy in my squad fixed an old 77 radio with parts from a Rolf Harris stylophone he bought on Mingi Street. A real live MacGyver. I wasn't good with electronics, but I could manage basic household repairs.

So I size up the window with a squint, then go foraging underneath the sink for something I can use.

'Hey, Irish, what are you playing at?'

Maybe Delano thinks I'm looking for trash bags to wrap her body.

Good.

A pity she doesn't know about my pro-tective instinct. Perhaps I'll tell her later.

Nothing under the sink to plug a hole, so I rifle the storage.

This woman has more pills than a New York pusher and more drawers than an underwear store.

Boom-boom, chuckles Ghost Zeb. *You're a funny killer, Daniel McEvoy, yes you are.*

'Stay out of my drawers, Irish.'

I laugh. 'No need to worry on that account, Mrs Delano.'

'Screw you.'

'You screw?' I say, twisting her words. Childish I know but I need a laugh.

Most of the drawers are half empty, so I pour one into another and punch the board out of the first. The wood comes away clean, nails red with rust like they've been sealing a coffin.

Stay away from the imagery, Simon told me once.

Because it deepens my pain?

No. Because you are shite at it.

I'd like to read the manual that came from. Chapter Six: Shiteness At Imagery and its Effects on Latent Arseholery.

Delano doesn't ask what I'm playing at, but she's pulling hard on that cigarette now, tip pulsing red and white.

Showboating is what I'm doing. I could just tape over the hole, there's a roll right there, but this board seems a more appropriate expression of the shape of my mood, as a mate of mine might say. I place it over the broken pane, then hammer the nails into the frame with a meat tenderiser from the draining board. The wind is downsized from a gale to a whistle. Not too shabby.

For once Mrs Delano is dumbstruck. She sits like a statue, smoke curling out of her fist.

'I'll call a buddy of mine,' I say on my way out. 'Twenty-four-hour lock guy, for your door and mine too. Until he gets here, I'd keep the noise down. You don't want to attract any unde-sirables.'

In spite of my day, I'm smiling on the steps. There's not a word from Delano's apartment. Not a peep.

CHAPTER 6

Before I had more serious things to worry about, I often spent the days leading up to the first transplant session searching my past trying to figure why I wanted hair plugs so badly. Why does a shiny skull prey on my mind so much? I've spent enough hours on the couch to know that these wants often have their roots in my own history.

I could never come up with anything. My father was dead before he got the chance to go fully bald. No bald guy ever beat me, or humiliated me that I can recall. I don't have any hairy heroes that I want to be, or hairless guys that I don't want to turn into.

It's in the subconscious, Zeb informed me one night in the park. The two of us were sharing a pint of Jameson after the bars closed. A hefty ox like me squashed into a child's swing, chains cutting off the blood flow to my feet. I must have been drunk.

Believe me, Dan. Something happened.

I know what happened. Zeb offered me a good deal, started showing me pictures, got my vanity stoked.

If you got hair, then maybe you ain't so old and your life ain't so over.

Zeb could sell shit to a sewage plant. Zeb is such a good salesman that he can literally charge a guy to inject him with the fat that he just sucked out of his ass.

'Bloody bastards. This is a sterile environment' were the first words Zeb ever spoke to me, and I knew straight away by the scout boots sticking out of his scrubs that this guy was Israeli army, something Sergeant Fletcher was too busy to notice as he had a finger jammed halfway up his nose.

'I got this bump in my nose, see?' he said, voice muted by the digit in his nostril. 'Makes me snore something terrible. I need you to fix it.'

The doctor looks a little like the Bee Gee who married Lulu, if he had just run into a sheet of plate glass. You either get that or you don't.

He finished injecting the unconscious guy's penis and petulantly threw the syringe into a metal sink.

'Come on, guys. I'm doing dick fat here. It's touchy work. This man is a big shot in some militia or other.'

I have to say, I was a little surprised. Even for Mingi Street, an underground cosmetic surgery was pretty radical, though I had heard of a place in Sudan that did organ transplants. You'd be amazed how quickly a matching donor can be found. This Israeli guy was a real entrepreneur, especially since ninety per cent of the locals would have no hesitation sticking him with every one of his own needles. I guess you get a pass if you provide a valuable service.

Fletcher withdrew his finger. 'What about my nose, Doc?'

'Does this look like a Swiss clinic? Injectables only,' said the man I would later know as Zeb. 'No rhino.'

'Who are you calling a rhino?' said Tommy, and shot Zeb in the kneecap.

Okay, that didn't happen, but I can dream.

I don't sleep so well after my run-in with Mrs Delano. Probably has something to do with me realising that my upstairs neighbour is beautiful-ish in a psycho kind of way, though all the dead and dying, Connie especially, has put a dent in my libido. I feel a little treacherous that I'm not mourning Zeb yet, but I haven't seen him on the asphalt so I'm nursing a spark of hope.

Not feeling safe is the main thing keeping me awake, even more than the morning sun, though I reckon the hoods won't be making the rounds till noon at least. These Celtic gangsters are whores for the Jameson and Coke. But once the sun crosses the yardarm, Mike Madden's boys might pay another visit, see if they can't find a few more things to break. I cover the door with a wardrobe. If any arseholes come through that, they'll think they're in Narnia. I hang a *Joshua Tree* poster over the window. Not bulletproof, but a puzzler. It's all misdirection, which only works if the misdirected are somewhere in between dumb and smart. Many of the best soldiers in the world have shit for brains and a photo of their target.

How did they find me anyway? Does Irish Mike have something specific, or just a list of known associates?

I puzzle on this, as eventually my mind sinks down into the black rings of sleep. Trust in Bono.

71

Thank God. Nearly there. Some rest finally.

Then, wouldn't you know, a thought occurs to me. One of those notions that banishes sleep, like a stiff wind blowing away cobwebs.

Kee-rist almighty.

That's what Delano said. *Kee-rist*. Not plain old Christ. Now where have I heard that recently? Yesterday. The day before.

And suddenly I'm bolt upright in my bed. That guy, with the Styrofoam hair. The licker, what was his name?

I have it even before I pull the card from my wallet.

Faber, the attorney. With all the rioting in the club that night, this guy Faber completely slipped my mind.

Delano repeats what she hears, and she heard *Kee-rist*. Faber was here, and he trashed my place.

I'm on my feet, pacing around the room, punching a fist into my palm, which I stop doing when I realise how drama queen it feels. There's no sitting this out even if I wanted to. Faber knows where I lay my head and he's obviously got back-up. A runt like him didn't do this damage on his own. That arsehole couldn't even lift the microwave.

This is not about Zeb, this is about Connie. Faber killed her and he's looking for me.

That's it. It must be. Christ, surely nobody kills anybody over an arse-licking? I witnessed Faber's beef with Connie and I broke it up. Could it be that straightforward?

Everyone wants to kill me lately; it's enough to make a fellow paranoid. As Dr Moriarty often quipped, *You know something, Dan. Just because everyone really is out to get you doesn't mean*

72

you're not insane. I always thought that sentence had a couple too many negatives.

Three hours later, I'm still awake, thinking. The old grey cells keep churning out the theories, which I hammer out with Ghost Zeb.

Faber killed Connie.

Possibly.

And you know this how?

Because a crazy lady used his pet phrase.

That is pretty fucking thin, as Riggs and Murtaugh have been known to say.

The world is built on thin. Ask George W.

So, assuming it was the guy Faber. Why?

Because Connie slapped him. Because he's a psycho.

Pretty harsh revenge for a slap. And Faber did not seem like a weapons guy.

What about his help? You don't know who's carrying steel for him.

Good point.

Thank you.

So, we're going to the police.

There's no we, just me. And I do not want the police poking around in my business.

Because of the whole killing-a-gangster thing.

Exactly. So what should we do next?

There's a we now?

I flash on Tommy Fletcher. At this point he is back to being a corporal, following an incident where he doused a sheep with gasoline, set it on fire then actually ate a large portion. There was quite a lot of home-brewed hooch involved. Tommy is belly down on a bluff overlooking no-man's-land, loosing rounds from his FN at rangy wild dogs.

'You shooting mutts, Corporal?' I ask him.

'Nah,' says Tommy, grinning. 'I'm shooting close to the mutts, watching 'em jump.'

I close my eyes and feel sleep rolling over me like a wave of thick fog.

Shoot close and watch them jump. That's more or less doing nothing. It's aggressive passivity.

Simon would be so proud.

I met Zeb for the second time when I was doing my time on a door in Brooklyn. It was a club called Queers, which was trying to attract the pink pound but was pulling in the irony-loving New York arty-farts. This was not my finest hour, as the boss had his bouncers in spangly waistcoats and mascara. Any photos from this era would not be going on my website, if I had one. It was a brief era anyhow, I lasted about a week before I got a rash on my eyelids and decided it was either buy some hypoallergenic make-up out of my own pocket, or quit. I chose the latter.

So I was on the door on my last night at Queers, figuring the shit quotient went up roughly two hundred per cent when the doorman was wearing mascara, when this guy rolls up off his face on just about whatever he could stuff in there. I did the five-finger spread on his chest, just so he'd know right off how big my hand was.

'Sir, don't even ask. You are not coming on the premises.'

Something about this guy struck me as familiar. He looked a little like one of the Bee Gees after a rough couple of years.

'Come on, man,' he whined. 'I got the cash, plenty. You wanna see?'

I did not wanna see. You bring cash out in the open air for more than five seconds outside a club and someone is gonna start a fight.

'No, sir. Keep it in your pocket.'

The man ignored me, as was to become his habit, flashing a roll of fifties that could have plugged a rat hole.

'You know what this is?'

I put a little pressure behind my fingertips, enough to back the man up a step or two.

'I know what it is, sir.'

'No, sir. You do not. You think you know.' The drunk tapped his nose like there was a great secret stashed up there. 'This here is a couple of silicone boobies and a tummy tuck. Sweet job too. If you let me in, I'll give you a grand. How about that? One thousand dollars just to step aside.'

I stood my ground, not because I couldn't be bought, but because this guy thought he could buy me, if that makes any sense.

'Sorry, sir. Put your money away.' And then the guy looks me in the face, possibly to plead or up his offer, and something pings between us.

'Hey,' he said, wagging a finger. 'I know you.'

And then I had him. The pasty complexion, the eyes a little shiny. The doctor guy, from the Lebanon.

But what I said was, 'No. I don't think we've met.'

Zeb stood back and spread his arms wide like a ringmaster introducing himself.

'Hey, it's me. Dick-fat guy.'

He kept talking like I didn't have enough information. 'You know, that militia man, his cock exploded in battle. I'm a national hero.'

Which is about the strangest collection of statements I've heard before or since.

I sleep till four in the afternoon and roll out of bed feeling surprised and grumpy, which is a hard combination to keep going. Four o'clock. The day is dying and I don't even have shoes on. *And* this room is a shithole, *and* why did I not do some tidying up all that time I was lying there thinking? Shaving calms me down as per usual. Eyes open is often a bad time. A moment's blissful ignorance, then life comes crashing in. And today, life is about as bad as it's ever been.

I nick myself with the blade and watch a blood bead roll down my neck.

Connie, I think. *No more weekends. No more you.*

After shaving, I take some of my anger out on the wall, using a breeze block that was part of my shelving unit to bash a hole in the Sheetrock. I pull out a Kevlar backpack wedged between the joists. My weapons bag, four years behind the plaster. Dust flakes stick to my sleeve, I brush them away and head for Chequer's Diner, which is becoming my unofficial HQ. Dust flakes I'm noticing now? I must have too much time on my hands.

*   *   *

The sun has faded from red to white and I'm having a lord's breakfast. Pancakes, bacon, sausage, stack of toast and six cups of coffee. I'm awake now, let me tell you.

The waitress, Carmél, comes over with my change and is a little surprised by me asking for yet another refill. She bumps my elbow with her thigh.

'I had you figured for a fitness guy, Dan. You lose a competition or something?'

'Life's too short,' I tell her. 'Maybe I'll take up cigarettes too.'

Carmél laughs. Sounds like a motor turning over. I'm guessing she's a cigarette gal herself.

I have a plan of sorts.

You gonna save my life? asks Ghost Zeb.

No. You I'm gonna put on ice for the time being, but this guy Faber, I need to do something about him before he makes a hole in my forehead.

Ghost Zeb is sulking. *Yeah, maybe if we'd spent a weekend in the sack, I'd be top of your list.*

It's a fair point.

So, the plan. I phone in an anonymous tip, something vague about Faber and his little run-in with Connie, then I watch and see how the attorney jumps when they question him.

Ghost Zeb is incredulous. *That's it? That's your entire plan? Why don't you just wish upon a star while you're at it?*

Ghost Zeb is turning out to be as much of a pain in the arse as his corporeal self.

Corporeal. This one rookie in the barracks used to confuse it with corporal ten times a day, until someone explained the difference.

I suppose it doesn't matter how you come by information as long as you remember it.

Oh. And no one gets hurt. Too badly.

No one decent at any rate.

I slide a couple of dimes out of my change and head for the phone booth in the corner.

Ghost Zeb is so pissed that he almost stays at the table without me.

I dial the CDP desk from the booth and ask for Detective Deacon specifically, because Goran is sharp; she'd nail me in a second.

'What?' snaps Deacon when she picks up, like I'm interrupting her conference call with Commissioner Gordon.

'You working the DeLyne case?' I ask, doing my best Nu Yawker.

'The *what* case?'

'Connie DeLyne. The Slotz hostess.'

'You mean that stripper?'

'They ain't no strippers up in there.' My accent is gone down south, last century too.

'Yeah, that *hostess* is one of mine? Who is this?'

'This is by way of a 'nonymous tip-off, which I believe is police vernacular.'

I'm playing around now. I shouldn't. A friend is dead, another missing, but in times of stress I can't help myself. Sometimes I giggle like a girl. It's embarrassing.

Deacon sighs, writing the call off. I bet they get a hundred cranks a day. 'Do you have information pertaining to the DeLyne case, sir?'

'I got something good for you, miss.'

'That's *Detective*.'

'They let ladies be detectives now? That right there explains a lot.'

Come on, Sergeant. You don't have time for this. Pull yourself together; this is not a sixth-grade prank call. Seymore Butz? Anyone?

I hear something creak. Deacon must be squeezing the phone pretty tight.

'That's a poor attitude you have there, sir.'

I disguise my giggle with a cough. 'Take it easy, Detective, only trying to help.'

There are a few moments while Deacon pulls herself together; she's probably whispering *you're a professional* over and over. 'So help. I'm getting old here.'

'I was in Slotz a few nights ago, sir . . .'

'That's *miss*, motherf . . . Remember? Detective, female.'

'Sorry. You got kind of a deep voice. I like that personally.'

Deacon breathes deep through her nose. 'Do you have any pertinent information whatsoever, sir? Hold up, is this Randy? Are you dicking me about, Randy?'

I don't know who Randy is, but I'd love to meet him.

'I ain't no Randy. You want this information or not?'

'Yeah, give it up. But if this is Randy, I'm gonna have your balls in a sling . . . sir.'

'Okay, miss . . . if you is a miss. I was in Slotz and I seen Connie beefing with this guy.'

'What guy?'

'A lawyer guy. Name's Faber. Jerry Faber, or maybe Gary.'

I hear scratching. Deacon is writing this down. 'You over-hear anything specific?'

'A little. How he was gonna kill her. She was gonna pay. Stuff like that.'

Deacon is taking notes now, you bet she is. 'You heard him say he was going to kill Connie DeLyne? Those exact words?'

'Yes, sir . . . miss . . . Detective . . . He said it all right. More than once.'

'Will you testify to this?'

'I'm testifying right now, ain't I?'

'Yeah, but I need you to . . .'

That's when I hang up, smiling as I imagine Deacon shouting abuse into her mouthpiece.

Poor Randy, I think. *He's going to need a jockstrap.*

Step two of my dodgy plan: stake out Faber's office.

I take the 14 bus across town to the financial district, where Faber's card tells me he operates from. Maybe district is too grand a term. What we have in Cloisters is a financial block, couple of office buildings with a Bennigans and a Cheesecake Factory thrown in for the lunchtime crowd.

The Bennigans is across from Faber's lobby, so I order myself a Turkey O'Toole I don't want, and spy across the plaza through a window tinted streaky green by painted shamrocks.

Turkey O' Toole. Jesus.

I don't have to wait long. Fifteen minutes later a police sedan pulls up in front of the hydrant, idles for a few seconds, then drives off to a space further along the pavement.

I smile behind my sandwich. Deacon wanted to park at the hydrant, but Goran made her move along. Interesting. What would Dr Moriarty make of that?

Maybe Deacon was beaten up by someone dressed as a hydrant, or maybe Goran lost her puppy in a fire.

Psychology. Anyone can do it.

Another ten minutes and Faber comes out, shooting threats with his six-shooter fingers. Goran and Deacon trail behind him with glazed eyes. I know that look. That's the face you put on when some sergeant major is screaming the skin off your forehead. I'll bet that Faber is crying persecution and calling the chief of police by his golfing nickname. Goran taps Deacon's forearm with two fingers.

Calm down, the touch says. *We do this right.*

Faber is practically dancing now; from across the square I can see his ginger fuzz vibrate.

It's funny, except that maybe he killed Connie.

Detective Goran's lips are moving now and I fill in the blanks.

Take a walk, Mister Faber, but not too far. I'll be dialling your number.

So now the cat is among the pigeons.

Which one is the cat? asks Ghost Zeb.

I'm not sure. That particular saying has always confused me.

Faber beeps a new Mercedes down the block with his key fob and the cops traipse back to their beat-up sedan, probably thinking that they're in the wrong line of work.

Now what, genius? Everyone has a car except you.

Ghost Zeb is getting to be something of a fixture in my head. You're like my spooky sidekick.

Screw you.

Charming. I need to get myself an actual live friend that I can leave in another room.

Anyway, the transport thing is covered. There are city-bike rails all over town, part of the mayor's *A Better, Cleaner Cloisters* platform, along with dogshit-bag dispensers and zero tolerance for wino shacks.

I hurry outside leaving the turkey unexplored and swipe my Visa in the bike rack. Evening traffic the way it is in every town from here to Atlantic City, I shouldn't have to break a sweat keeping up with Faber. He might have a problem keeping up with me, if he ever decided to do that. A big part of me is hoping he will. That would make things nice and simple, law of the jungle.

I'm still tucking my pants into my socks when I notice that Deacon has pulled a lazy U-turn. The blues are on Faber's tail too.

We got a great big convoy, sings Ghost Zeb.

I nod, swinging my leg over the bar. Always liked that song. Appropriate, too.

Riding a bike didn't used to be this dangerous. I almost get flattened three times crossing town to the strip. Three times! I've led patrols through hot zones with less aggravation than this. Eventually some redneck pick-up Jim Bob forces me to actually dismount and pound his hood to make him keep his distance.

Lucky the blues are focused on Faber's car or they might

have spotted my antics. As it is, they pull around the corner on to Cypress with barely a blink of the brake light.

I give Jim Bob my best stone-cold stare and pedal after them.

Not easy looking tough on a pushbike, sympathises Ghost Zeb.

He's got that right.

When Faber pulls over, I brake and ditch the city-bike behind a debris mountain heaped against a derelict two-storey that once housed a Chinese restaurant, judging by the smell of the trash.

The Lotus Blossom. Remember those spring rolls?

Yeah. I got it now. They closed that place?

What do you think?

Ghost Zeb is getting a little strident. It's like I'm giving myself a pass to be a lunatic.

I climb on to the knoll, which stinks of prawn crackers, and check the street with an old Vietnam-era Starlight scope I bought in a Hell's Kitchen pawn shop.

Still works okay in spite of a few years in the bag. It's pretty dark already, but the scope amplifies the streetlight a couple of thousand times and gives me a good view of the bar Faber is striding towards. It's an upscale joint called The Brass Ring. A place I probably would never make it past the door, unless I decided that I really wanted to go in. Faber flings his keys at some poor schmuck doorman and bulls straight past. I know how the schmuck feels.

Goran and Deacon back into an alley and quickly settle into stakeout positions. Slouching down, cracking open the windows.

Two minutes later, smoke curls from both sides. Give it another fifteen and Deacon will make a coffee run.

Their plan is as dumb as yours, Ghost Zeb points out. *What happens now? We sit here wasting time?*

You're not here. I'm not arguing with you.

Real mature.

I whistle a few bars to distract him.

What is that song?

Come on. What are we doing right now?

Ghost Zeb's chuckle whines through his nose, my mind displaying its attention to detail.

Elvis Costello. 'Watching the Detectives'. Very good.

And that keeps him quiet for a while.

The blues call it stakeout and the army call it reconnaissance but it amounts to the same thing. Waiting and watching.

Two hours later and Faber is still in the club, and I can't seem to find a position on the spicy mound that doesn't involve a rock or root poking my groin.

Maybe you like having a root stuck in your groin.

I don't dignify this with a reply.

Goran and Deacon are feeling the strain. The junior detective is out of the car stomping her feet against the cold and mouthing off. Goran wears a put-upon-mommy expression, riding out the tantrum.

With the Starlight I can almost read lips, and what I can't make out, I make up.

Come on, Josie. Let me go in there, see who Faber is talking to.

No. We do this right. Hang back, make a case.

Fuck that. This is our man. You see how he freaked out? Started threatening us and shit.

We hang back, Detective.

Something along those lines.

Or maybe not.

The seriousness of the situation escalates suddenly and alarmingly. Deacon turns her back to her superior, shoulders hunched, agitated cigarette hand tracing jet trails in the air.

Jet trails? Not bad for a doorman.

There is no time for a back-and-forth with Ghost Zeb. Goran has slipped quietly from the passenger seat and drawn a pistol from her ankle holster. A throwdown. Shit.

I could be wrong. Maybe I'm misreading the situation.

Goran pulls a silencer from her handbag and casually twists it on to the barrel, all the time her lips moving, keeping the conversation smooth, no warning signs.

Warning signs or not, Deacon turns around and finds herself down a deserted alley in a bad part of town with the black eye of a silencer staring unblinkingly at her.

I'm not misreading anything. Detective Goran is about to execute her partner.

Pack up and go, says Zeb seriously.

This is the best advice of my life and I know it, but I've got this whole protection thing pulling at my psyche.

Go, now.

Cops shooting cops. There's no way to get in the middle of that sandwich and not get bitten. Ultimately, though, I'm not an animal, so what choice do I have but to help Detective Deacon.

The backpack hasn't been out of the wall in years. It was never supposed to be in that building for so long. Neither was I. Nothing is going to work. How could anything work? Not a spray of oil on the guns, not a rub of a rag for the bullets. The walls in my apartment are like sponges.

Through the sights, I see Deacon going through the stages. First her eyebrows knit in confusion.

What the hell are you doing?

Then realisation drags at her features like thirty years of hard living. This is followed by denial, and finally bravado.

Deacon is presenting her chest to Goran now, thumping it with a fist, cigarette sparks flying. I actually hear her challenge from across the street.

'Come on, bitch, shoot me!'

It doesn't sound real. It's what a Hollywood cop might say.

All the time, I'm tugging on a pair of disposable gloves from a box in the bag, then searching for my rifle, which of course is in pieces. We were trained in this kind of thing in the army: assembling your weapon blindfolded, in the rain, some guy shooting blanks by your ear, getting pissed on by a group of privates. Okay, maybe not that last bit, but regardless I was always useless at the blindfold assembly thing. Generally it took me about an hour and I ended up with a piece of modem art that would look stunning with the right lighting, but couldn't shoot worth a damn.

I spit a string of swear words and lay down the scope. Across the street, Goran is delivering a lecture before she pulls the trigger. Thank God for grandstanding killers. Back home, my squad were once brought in to hunt for an IRA kidnap squad who had crossed the border. We only caught them because they delayed a scheduled execution so they could film it from a couple of angles. Everyone wants their moment.

Now that I have two eyes on the job, the Custom Sharpshooter seems to assemble itself, jumping out of the Velcro straps. The collapsible stock bolts on behind the trigger guard. The stainless-steel barrel screws in smoothly. Feels a little damp. Could be I'm imagining it.

I tear open a box of shells with my teeth and thumb one into the breech. Safety off, Starlight snapped into its bracket. The smell of soy sauce is really putting me off.

Time for one shot, maybe. Not a moment for adjustments or to figure consequences.

Goran is still talking, thank Christ. Maybe she's warning Deacon; maybe there's no need to shoot.

The younger detective sinks to her knees in the filth of the alley, tears streaming down her face.

Final stage, acceptance.

That's a helluva warning.

Goran circles behind her partner, never allowing the barrel to droop. No room for Deacon to make her move. To her credit, she tries anyway, and gets a pistol-whipping for her trouble.

Goran is one cold customer. I had these two figured all wrong.

Deacon's head nods; maybe she's praying, or maybe she's reacting to the gun barrel pressed to the crown of her skull.

Through the eerie glow of the Starlight, I see that Goran's face is almost blank except for a little shadow of pain, like she's lost her keys. The dirty detective cocks her revolver.

I pull my trigger . . .

. . . And surprise the hell out of myself by actually hitting what I was aiming for. Up high, right shoulder. Goran spins like a gyroscope and pitches face down into a bum-shack. Looks like the mayor missed one.

Detective Goran will live, but she won't be aiming any guns with that arm for a while.

I am midway through breaking down my rifle and rehearsing a smug little Clint Eastwood movie reference for Ghost Zeb when Deacon realises that she hasn't been shot. And after a little white-hot pain and a bout of coughing that would pull a couple of lungs free from their moorings, Goran is alive enough to realise that she is not dead.

Nice move, idiota, says GZ. *Now we got a shootout situation.*

Idiota. One of four Spanish words Zeb bandies about. The second is *puta,* the third is *amigo* and finally there's *gringo,* which he loves to throw at me even though Zeb himself has a complexion like cottage cheese dropped on to a pavement from a tall building.

Deacon sees her partner roll over, coming face-up with her police special cocked, spluttering blood-bubbled curses. Deacon ducks under a wild shot, scrabbles in the trash for Goran's throwdown and puts half a dozen shots into her partner's upper body.

Ex-partner, I guess.

It takes me a moment to process. Someone who was supposed to be winged is now dead, and approximately fourteen per cent of the bullets in the corpse belong to me.

PLUGGED

That was self-defence, I tell Zeb. It's a tough report for Deacon to write up, but self-defence all the same.

Go now, says Ghost Zeb. *You don't get to write up a report.*

This time I listen.

CHAPTER 7

Zeb waited around Queers that night until I knocked off. I say *waited*, but a more accurate description would be *passed out* in the all-night pharmacy across the street. He was more or less hurled into my path by the proprietor as I walked home.

'And keep your prick away from my customers!' was the farewell comment.

Obviously Zeb had been up to no good just before passing out. Perhaps the two were connected.

I was in a pretty crappy mood, having just told my boss where he could shove his mascara pencil, but something about the sheer wretchedness of this figure at my feet dissolved my gloom, and I picked the little guy off the ground and frogmarched him a couple of blocks to Kellogg's diner on Metropolitan.

He came to a little after a jug of coffee, and greeted me like a lost comrade.

'Hey, Paddy O'Mickster. Where are we? What happened?'

'You were trying to inject some dick fat into a customer, apparently.'

It took Zeb a minute to process this, then a slow grin lit his features. 'Funny. You're a funny guy, Irish. I didn't get that sense when you were in uniform.'

'The name is Daniel McEvoy,' I say without extending my hand. 'Paddy O'Mickster was my mother's second choice.'

Zeb actually slapped the table. 'More with the funny. I love this guy,' he announced to the diner's five patrons. 'So, Daniel McEvoy, you gonna admit me to Queers tomorrow night? Now that we've broken the ice?'

In response to this, I explained how I was off the Queers door because of a make-up disagreement.

'I am surprised,' said Zeb. 'Why would anyone quit over a little mascara? Hell, I'm wearing women's panties right now. You never know, right?'

At this point I was half amused, half thinking of leaving. This guy was despicable, but he had a certain sleazy charm.

'So, anyways, Daniel O'McEvoy. You're out of a job and I got a job with no one in it, so what do you say? You wanna work for Zeb Kronski?'

This was about the vaguest employment offer I had ever heard, and considering the man before me was wearing women's panties, I thought I should ask for a couple more details.

It turned out that since Zeb didn't have a licence to practise in the US, he was doing the Botox party rounds on a cash-only basis and had already been ripped off twice. He could do with someone to hump the wad, as he put it.

Once he explained, I signed on for a week. Provisionally. See how things panned out.

'Provisionally,' said Zeb, rolling the word around in his mouth. 'Yeah, I like the sound of that.' He pointed at my forehead.

'Say, you're getting a little thin on top, my Paddy friend. I got a procedure make you look like Mister Tom Cruise. What do you think of that?'

I thanked my new boss politely but told him no. No needles in the head for me. I held out for six years before he persuaded me otherwise.

I'm gone before Deacon has time to wonder who gifted her a second shot at life. Not that I'm expecting roses and a sloppy hug. A person with her disposition might not even be grateful. I've seen it before. Some blues are so butch that needing to be saved is a sign of weakness. Deacon is pretty butch.

It's a pity to say goodbye to my beautiful custom rifle, but holding on to it is akin to leaving a trail of crumbs from my backpack to the crime scene. No doubt there are already a forest of fibres on the Chinese knoll; no need to give the forensics boys my identity tied in a velvet ribbon. I break down the weapon and pedal around the west side, dropping off pieces into various drains. The bullets go too, plinking through the bars. I hear there's some test that can match one slug to a batch, but Jason informed me of this fact, so it could be standard doorman bullshit. Jason once swore to me that his daddy had eyes in the back of his head, *actual fucking eyes in the back of his actual fucking head*, so not everything my comrade says can be taken as hundred per cent gospel.

I drop the bike at the bus station and deposit my backpack in a locker. Whatever investigation is coming, you can bet your last pair of shorts that I'm going to be pulled in for questioning. Being in possession of a big bag of weapons is not going to swing any votes my way. I hold on to a little Glock 26, though, in case of an emergency, which seems pretty likely the way things have been going. It's not a question of if. It's a question of when, who and how many. Three questions really.

It doesn't take a Napoleon to figure out my next move. A quick trip home to gather a few necessities, then up sticks to some cheap motel where I can figure my next move but one.

You're leaving me to die, says Ghost Zeb accusingly.

You are dead, most likely. And I'm not leaving you; I'm moving a little further away from Irish Mike and the po-lice, that's all.

You're leaving me. Some goddamn friend. Irish prick.

A sulking ghost, that's all I need.

My street seems pretty quiet, exactly the way it would seem if a couple of experienced gangsters were staking it out. Could be the blues are here too. Maybe the interested parties will stumble across each other and spark off a bloodbath.

Fingers crossed.

I start three blocks out and work in decreasing circles, sweeping every street. Checking parked cars, searching for the telltale bulletproof symbol on the windscreen. You find that little triangle and you know it's good guys, bad guys or maybe a rapper praying someone will shoot at him.

Nothing. No sign of anyone watching my apartment. I try to kid myself that it makes sense. Goran wasn't killed with my bullets and Faber has no need to keep the cat in the bag any more. He's already under investigation.

There's a fire escape bolted to the side of my building; it

zig-zags along the brick, camouflaged by rust, and looks like it hasn't been used in decades. You'd think it would make a hell of a racket if a person were to crank the ladder, but you'd be wrong. For years I've been keeping the hinges oiled in case a quiet getaway is called for. In the dead of night, with a pillow over my face and a torrent of insults spilling down from above, I often imagined that I would finally crack and strangle Mrs Delano. Once there was blessed quiet, I could sleep for eight hours then pull my bag out of the wall and climb down my greased fire escape.

Tonight, I'm climbing up. Five fingers brushing flakes from the rail, the other five concealing the baby Glock in my palm. It's risky coming back here, considering the size and complexity of the shit pile I'm in, but it will only be for a few minutes. Ten max. I'm stealing in the back way to cut down my chances of being seen; also I don't have the key for the new lock yet. In and out, then Daniel McEvoy is history and anyone trying to find him better be invisible or bulletproof.

The fire escape doesn't stop at my window, but it's close enough for me to perch on the railing and rest an elbow on the sill. And while I'm up there, precariously balanced on a couple of toes, I realise that I forgot to take the beeper out of my pocket.

The window beeper is a little gadget I'm especially proud of. Just a remote linked to a tiny motor, but it lets me sneak into my own apartment without leaving the window open.

Moron, snickers Ghost Zeb.

I cannot tell you how badly I want him out of my head.

I'm right here, you know. I can hear you.

Good.

It takes a bit of contorting and there's a long moment when I'm teetering on the tip of one shoe, but I fish the remote from my trousers and beep myself into my apartment.

Tumbling across the sill, my stomach sours at the thought of the devastation inside. For the first time in my civilian life it occurs to me that maybe I should have tidied up a bit before going out. My hand crabs across the floor, expecting to brush against splinters of my speakers or tufts of hard foam from the disembowelled settee, but there's nothing but rough carpet. Strange.

The simplicity of a security man's lot is looking pretty attractive right now. Keep the peace, remove those who would break it. No moral dilemmas involved. My life has been growing ever more complicated since people started dying around me . . .

Since you started killing people . . .

I wounded Goran, Deacon killed her.

What about Barrett?

Self-defence.

Yeah, because he was doing that shuffle. Tell that to the judge.

I don't think Irish Mike uses judges.

I switch on the lamp, which works; very surprising, since the last time I was here the bulb lay like cracked eggshell on the rug. Have we gone back in time, or has somebody tidied up?

Option B, I think, though A would be nice.

So, who?

I think I know, says Ghost Zeb.

Me too, and it's an alarming thought.

The apartment is still pretty battered, but no worse than your average student accommodation. Surfaces have been swept and the gloss of polish shines on the table, which sits legless on the floor. Three jumbo trash bags are propped by the door, fat sentries.

This is an extra dimension to my life that I do not need.

Into the bathroom I hurry; my duffel bag is in the airing cupboard ready for packing. With one hand reaching for the door handle, I catch sight of myself in the bathroom mirror.

My eyes are distended ink blots, with forty years of wrinkles hanging below them like sagging power lines. The black watch cap has rolled back, revealing an expanse of forehead and a buckshot spatter of transplanted hair.

It's growing in.

You think so?

Absolutely.

Isn't it supposed to fall out before it grows in?

Let's talk about this later.

Did I look this old a couple of days ago, before all the mayhem? Being a doorman never weighed so heavily on my face.

I blink a couple of times, suddenly tight across the chest. Just when did I start worrying so much about getting old? Some nights in the Lebanon it felt as though I couldn't wait to die. Or if not that, then at least the idea didn't upset me. Just make it quick, that was my only requirement. Most of us had kill pacts. Anyone in the pact takes a mortal wound, the others toss a coin and finish him off. Sounds brutal, but kill pacts were very popular. I made some real friends. I still drop them a line every now and then, make sure they know the pact is off.

I notice something else in the bathroom besides my own

haggard face. The toilet rolls are stacked in a diamond shape. This is uber-freaky. I skirt the sculpture like it might suddenly come alive and start dispensing Zen advice.

Why would a toilet roll sculpture dispense anything but paper? Where does that thought even come from?

I know who built this. There's only one person who would.

Sweat gathers at the base of my neck. In spite of my therapy sessions, I feel woefully ill-equipped to deal with someone who builds toilet roll diamonds.

My bag is where it should be, and I quickly locate the toiletries that were strewn around the floor by whoever trashed the place but are now lined neatly along the green plastic sink top.

I stuff them into the bag and collect one last essential. I keep ten years of savings, almost fifty thousand dollars, stashed in the sink drain for emergencies, and if this isn't an emergency, it's doing a good impersonation. I screw off the pipe and shake loose the sealed bundles of cash. Usually having this much money on my person would make me nervous, but I'm already as nervous as a person can be without short-circuiting his brain. I pocket the cash and head for the door. In retrospect, I should have gone back out the window.

Deacon arrives outside the door of my apartment just as I tug it open. Her gun is out and there are shoals of blood spatter on her blouse. I search her eyes briefly for signs of gratitude and love.

No luck.

I think about reaching for the Glock inside my jacket; maybe I could make it, or maybe this young, trained and fit officer would put a dozen slugs in a nice smiley face spread through my heart.

Deacon's cheeks are wet and her eyes are wild. A couple of hours ago she was the embodiment of the law, and now she's gunned down her partner with no idea why her partner was about to gun her down. She has no idea who to trust or who to blame.

'Police,' she says, and taps the badge on her belt.

'Ooookay,' I say, interested to hear what's coming next.

'Was it you?' she demands, and her gun is in my face. Shaking. Give me a steady weapon over a shaky one any day. Shaky guns tend to have shaky fingers on the trigger.

'Was it me *what?*'

Deacon screws the barrel into my forehead. Feels like a Life Saver mint, only not so cheery.

'Don't fuck with me, McEvoy. Was it you, *soldier boy?*'

The shaking gun is wiggling my eyebrows.

'You trying to be funny? You making faces at me now, McEvoy?'

'It's the gun,' I say helplessly. 'I'm just standing here.'

Deacon is on the edge; it's in her eyes, in the grit of her teeth.

'One last time. Tell me it was you.'

I don't think there's a right answer to this question.

'Okay,' I admit. 'It was me.'

'It was you *what?*'

Jesus Christ. Is she kidding me?

She cocks the weapon. Not kidding then.

'It was me everything. I set you on Faber's trail, I winged Goran and I watched you finish her off.'

Deacon expected this answer, but still she's stunned. On a positive note, her weapon drops to her side.

'It . . . it *was* you.'

I nod warily. Not out of the woods yet. Deacon's eyes are glazed and her hands are twitching. My guess is she's in mild shock. You face the void and cut down a friend all in the same evening and it's bound to have an effect.

In my experience this can go one of two ways. Either Deacon dissolves to a shuddering heap, or her heart hardens and she shoots me, because at least it's a positive action.

Better to make a move now while her guard is down, but I barely get my fists balled when she comes at me full tilt, hand flat on my chest. This is confusing.

Back into the room we stumble, her fingers ripping at my shirt like it's on fire. Then the flat of her hand is on my heart, searching for the life inside. Her mouth is up, snarling, wanting the kiss. So I kiss Detective Deacon, feeling a premature post-coital regret that should warn me off but doesn't. We trip as one over the remains of the couch on to the Caucasian rug I got from a Lebanese market. It occurs to me that what we're about to do on this rug is probably a sin in several religions.

Not that this gives me pause. I'm feeling pretty tense myself, and this is as good a way as any to let it all out.

I guess there was a third way this could all go. I never came across this option in the army.

Very early the next morning, we find ourselves mashed up against the wall, half covered with a few sofa cushions.

The next morning?

I know. I always hated that: you're watching a movie or reading a book, finally the steamy scene is on the horizon and suddenly it's *the next morning*. How does that make you feel?

Cheated, that's how.

So . . .

It's not like I'm a prude, but this roll on the rug was definitely weird. Deacon bounced me around, pawing at my person. I'm surprised, given my low self-esteem issues, that I was able to perform at all.

Go on, encourages Ghost Zeb.

That's all the detail you need. Anyway, you were there.

Yeah, but I like the way you tell it in your Oirish accent.

You are a sick little imaginary friend, Zeb.

I gotta say, these conversations with GZ are tiring. Even though I know he's just a greatest hits tape cobbled together by my memory, I am starting to think stuff quietly in case he hears me.

I heard that, dickhead. Think quietly? What are you, a lunatic?

I decide not to answer that question.

So, in the morning we're wedged into the corner like two corpses that have been tossed there, neither with a clue what to say.

I regain consciousness first and use the minutes to examine the lady I've just had some kind of relations with. Usually I do the examining beforehand, but there's nothing usual about this encounter. Everything about Deacon says strength. Wide brow, strong nose, full lips, skin the colour of polished rosewood. Her body is lean and muscled like she beats suspects a lot, and there's a welt on her upper arm looks like a bullet wound.

100

I touch the scar gently; feels like there's a marble under there.

'Nine millimetre?' I ask. Mister Romance.

'Branding accident,' Deacon grunts, still half asleep.

I have a feeling we're never going to send each other perfumed letters.

She shrugs her shoulder to dislodge my hand and her bracelet rattles. It's unusual enough for me to notice, snaking around her wrist a couple of times, laden with various charms. Washers, bottle tops, coloured glass. I've seen these before in Africa. Memory bracelets, the story of your life's journey worn on the wrist.

I try for some confirmation. 'Memory bracelet?'

Deacon grunts again.

Most of the charms seem standard enough, but there's a wizened sphere like a shrunken golf ball.

I tap it with a fingernail. 'What's this one?'

Deacon's voice is sleepy. 'Guy kept asking me questions,' she slurs. 'His left nut.'

Okay. No more questions. Maybe I'll just take forty winks; after all, I've got protection.

Deacon's skin is smooth against my chest and I try to pretend she's actually fond of the person behind her. Maybe after a couple of years together Detective Deacon will develop a grudging respect for me and we can have a series of adventures.

Unless she does a sideways shuffle and you have to kill her.

I'm starting to realise that tuning out GZ is next to impossible so long as I have a single brain cell that is not distracted by life.

I attempt to distract myself by wondering how Deacon is going to keep herself out of prison. Obviously she hasn't come clean about Goran, or she'd be filling out a million forms in triplicate and holding staring contests with Internal Affairs.

'They must have found Goran by now?'

Deacon stiffens, and I think that maybe she had been trying to distract herself with all the tough talk. 'Not yet. I put her in the trunk.'

This is not good news, as Deacon's trunk is at the back of her car, which is probably parked outside my door.

'Goran is in your trunk? Hard to explain that to IA.'

Something like regret flits across the side of Deacon's face; maybe there's a human heart beating inside Robocop. 'Explain to IA? You're kidding, right? You screwed my career, McEvoy, and I was a good cop too. Twelve years in. Youngest black detective in the state.'

I feel I should stand up for myself. 'You'd prefer to be dead?'

'It's funny,' says Deacon, and I'm guessing tragi-funny not funny ha-ha. 'People always think I'm dirty cos of my attitude. Typical. A hardball boy cop is a maverick, doesn't play by the rules but gets the job done. You get a girl with some balls, then there must be something wrong with her. I was never dirty, until now. I'm finished. I'll be lucky to get off with manslaughter.'

I sit up to ask the obvious question. 'Why didn't you call it in? It was a righteous shoot.'

Deacon slumps even further into the corner, suddenly dead tired. 'I should have. All night I've been asking myself that question. I guess I panicked; is that what you want to hear, soldier boy? My partner and superior tried to murder me. I didn't know who to trust apart from the guy with the sniper rifle, which I figured had to be you. I hoped you might be able to tell me something. But you know shit, right?'

My time with Simon suddenly comes in handy. 'There is a very strong case for post-traumatic stress here.'

'Who are you?' says Deacon. 'Sigmund Freud? I'm a cop, man. I know how we think and I wouldn't buy that psych bull-shit for a New York minute.'

I forge ahead. 'No, listen, Deacon, it's true. Your partner tried to kill you. You had no idea how high the conspiracy went. You panicked, loaded up the body and went somewhere safe. There are a few holes, sure, but the basic truth is you acted in self-defence. Believe it or not, you are in shock.'

'And you took advantage.'

Yeah, it's a dig, but she's going for the cover story. It's a good story because it happens to be mostly true. The only detail she has to omit is the bald Irish one. I can see her eyes lose focus as she imagines how it would play out back in the precinct. There is a way out.

Then Deacon's phone beeps and she rolls into a crouch, instantly alert. I see the curve of her spine shining like a samurai sword.

She shakes her trousers until a phone falls out, and checks the text message. Her posture was pretty tense, but now it cranks up another few notches. Tendons stand out like piano wire behind her knees.

Not good news.

Deacon bends low, snagging the Sig with her trigger finger.

'You're a knife man, right, McEvoy? That's what it said in your file.'

I don't like the sound of this. What's the word?

Ominous? suggests Zeb.

Yeah, thanks.

'So what? I'm a rifle man too, you probably worked that out.'

'I figured that one,' says Deacon, twirling the pistol. 'But now I got this message from the County Coroner's office telling me that Connie DeLyne was killed with a blade.'

I sit up pretty quick, wishing I had some pants on. At this point I'd settle for a napkin to cover myself. 'It's barely dawn; what kind of coroner works this early?'

'One who owes me. So what about this blade?'

'That was a bullet hole. What kind of knife makes a hole like that?'

'You tell me, knife man.'

Deacon looms over me, tapping the barrel against her thigh, and I feel bald and naked, which I am. Twice a week I suffer nightmares that look pretty much exactly like this. It occurs to me that Simon Moriarty's number is still in my wallet. I really need to call that guy.

'Come on, Deacon. I saved your life. I put you on to Faber.'

'It's you-you-you,' says Deacon, levelling the weapon. 'Whatever happens, Daniel McEvoy is involved. There is definitely some shit you are not telling me.'

I feel myself shrink. 'You want to aim that gun somewhere less sensitive? My heart maybe.'

'No. I think I'm aiming at the right spot.'

'Think about it, Deacon. We're in this together. You need me to back up your story.'

Deacon closes her eyes for half a second. 'I do need you, but I need time to get my ducks in the goddamn basket or whatever. I gotta talk to a few people, weigh up my options. The Goran situation needs to be wrapped up right before I turn myself in.'

'That's all good. You're making perfect sense. We need to find the connection between Faber and Goran.'

'There's no *we*,' says Deacon. 'Just me.'

Zeb sniggers. *No we. See how that feels.*

I lose it for a second. 'Shut the hell up. Now is not the time.'

Deacon frowns. 'Now is not the time? What the fuck're you crying about, McEvoy? You get emotional after screwing, is that it? And what's up with that hair?'

I briefly consider explaining who I was actually talking to, but there's no way to present Ghost Zeb and not sound a little unstable.

'Okay. Calm down for a minute. Think things through . . .'

Deacon cocks the gun, resplendently naked, not a self-conscious atom in her body, whereas I am very self-consciously naked.

'I'm gonna think things through. That's it exactly. Cuff yourself to the radiator, McEvoy.'

Cuffing myself would not be good.

'Listen, Deacon . . . Come on, what's your first name?'

'Detective,' says Deacon, tossing me the handcuffs from her belt.

'You don't want to do this.'

'You're a mind reader now, McEvoy? Those needles on your head some kind of antennae?'

That's two hair jokes. I'm counting.

'There are bad people after me, Deacon. You leave me here in restraints and I'm dead.'

Deacon shrugs and her breasts wobble, which some part of me can't help noticing.

'Don't shrug. I'm fighting for my life here.'

'You're losing. Nice and tight now.'

Her eyes are golden and steady; she's not changing her mind.

'At least let me have the hat.'

Finally a smile; not the happy kind.

'Look at you, McEvoy. Big sharpshootin' soldier going to pieces without his hat. Didn't seem to bother you earlier.'

'Earlier, I had distractions.'

I swear her smile softens a degree; could be my imagination.

'Yeah, distractions.' Then the ice is back. 'Now cuff yourself to the goddamn radiator or I will hobble you with a leg shot.'

I hate that word. *Hobble*. Halfway between hobbit and gobble, which for some reason does not conjure an appealing picture.

'You're not going to shoot me. We just . . .'

Deacon's finger creaks on the trigger. 'We just what? I shot Josie and I've been sleeping with her for eight months.'

I pick up the cuffs but never get the chance to fasten them on my wrists.

Deacon is multitasking when Mrs Delano comes through the door holding a steaming tray of lasagne. The detective has her gun on me and one big toe through the band of her panties. It is without doubt the most surreal moment of my life.

'I hope you don't mind me calling so early, Mister McEvoy,' chirps Delano, made up like Cyndi Lauper circa 'True Colours'. 'Your friend, the nice repair man, gave me your new key, so I did a little cleaning up.'

This is not the Mrs Delano I know. This person is actually smiling; there are teeth involved. The outfit has shoulder pads you could launch a jet from, but nevertheless she's wearing outdoor clothing. For a moment I think that Delano has taken a beating, but then I realise she's been a little liberal with the mascara. She looks like a crying stripper, but there's light in her eyes. And not the usual death lasers; a warm light.

My neighbour doesn't notice anything off for a minute. She has her downcast eyes/bashful face on and is smiling a teenager's lovesick smile. Fixing the window, that's what brought this on.

'I know you eat at the club,' she says. 'But I thought we could watch a movie later this evening, Daniel, maybe split this lasagne. I baked it myself, we can reheat.'

Deacon freezes, one leg up, arse to the door. God help me if I laugh now.

'What do you say, Dan? You want to spend some time with your best girl?'

'Absolutely,' I reply. Why, I have no idea.

In the fraction of a second left before someone gets hurt, I play out a dozen possible outcomes to this ridiculous situation. In the best-case scenario, I get shot in the dick. In the worst, I get shot in the dick and one of my balls.

Mrs Delano's eyes land on the naked policewoman in my apartment. There is a beautiful Kodak moment of silence, then everyone starts yelling at the same time.

'Hold on now, ma'am,' says Deacon. 'Police business.'

'Get down, Delano,' I shout. 'On the floor.'

Mrs Delano's cheeks pump up and turn crimson. I half expect flames to shoot out of her ears.

Deacon has got it covered; she's a professional and her feet are planted in a wide stance now, but Delano throws her with:

'I stacked your toilet rolls! Bastard!'

Deacon rears back like she's been bitten on the nose, and she shoots me a glance that says *what the hell have you and this crazy lady got going on?*

The glance is her mistake, because Delano attacks, steaming lasagne borne aloft.

I cover my balls, because melted cheese sticks. Tough as Deacon is, there isn't a naked person on this planet who isn't scared of hot pasta, so she gives Delano her full attention and shoots the dish right out of her hands. There's a béchamel explosion, minced steak spatters the wall like buckshot and I make my move.

I get off the floor fast, pistoning my legs like I'm coming out of a squat. Deacon already knows what's happening, but she's not fast enough to get the gun around. She screams in frustration, then I have her against the wall, cuffs snicked over her wrists, gun smothered in my fist.

'This is kidnapping,' she spits. 'I am a friendly with a badge. Do you really want to throw that away?'

Friendly? Most of my friends don't aim their weapons at my privates. Most.

Delano is still coming. She's screaming too, something about me being just as bad as all the others, which wouldn't be so bad except for the glass shards she's swinging with every word. Deacon isn't calming down either; she's bucking like there's a scorpion on her back, and trying her damnedest to get a heel into my crotch.

I have no alternative but to play into Mrs Delano's fantasy.

'Thank God you're here, darling,' I say, hoping she's too far gone to notice my atrocious acting. 'This woman tried to assault me. You saw the gun. Look, handcuffs.'

Delano's eyes fog over and she stutters to a halt, gobs of lasagne dripping from her hands, splatting on to my good rug. I wince but don't mention it.

'Handcuffs?'

I push Deacon's head into the wall as gently as I can, covering the side of her face with my palm. I've had relationships go wrong before, but never this fast. 'Yeah. Can you believe it? I woke up to find this crazy lady holding a gun on me.'

'Crazy lady,' says Delano slowly. 'I've heard that phrase before.'

'I bet you have, you fucking lunatic,' Deacon says, spitting the words through mashed lips.

'You shut your filthy mouth,' orders Delano, and without hesitation clocks Deacon on the crown with the corner of Pyrex dish in her hand. The blow has surprising muscle in it, and Detective Deacon goes limp in my arms.

'Sorry, baby. Did I catch your finger there?'

Baby? 'Ah . . . no, I'm fine.'

'Do you think we should kill her? Cut her up like in the movies? I have an electric carving knife. Penis looks good, baby.'

I lower Deacon on to the rug, then hurriedly pull on some

pants, very uncomfortable with my penis being mentioned in the same breath as an electric carving knife.

'No. No need to kill her. She's confused, that's all.'

Delano winks at me, or maybe it's just hard to keep that eyelid open with all the mascara trowelled on to it.

'Maybe she heard about Mister Pee-Pee and came to see for herself.'

'M . . . maybe,' I stutter. 'Whatever the reason, this woman has problems. We need to be compassionate, show understanding.'

'Or slice her head off. I have plastic bags.'

Sure. We could toss her in the car beside her partner, then drive to the mall where I dumped Macey and line up all three bodies together in the Lexus. Hell, why not steal Connie's corpse from the morgue to complete the set?

Mrs Delano squeezes my arm.

'I'm kidding, Dan. It's my crazy sense of humour. That's why you love me.' Her face is glowing. She looks young. 'Remember that time you fixed my window? That was when I knew.'

I am not qualified to deal with this. Why does everyone I meet seem to have mental problems?

Ah . . . but did they have mental problems before meeting you? Who's the common denominator here, Dan?

I do not have mental problems! I say to the voice in my head, perfectly aware how damning it would sound were I to say it aloud.

Deacon's pulse is steady, but she's got a glowing bump on her noggin which I doubt will improve her mood any, and she was pissed enough *before* Lasagne Lady popped her on the skull.

Deacon moans and mumbles something that sounds like:
Hill view utter trucker.
But which is probably:
Kill you, motherfucker.
And with this in mind I pocket her gun. At least this way, she will have to bludgeon me to death with her fists.

I cannot honestly say that I am protecting either of these women; so much for my psychosis. It pains me, it really does, but I have to protect myself in this situation, and sort out the women from afar. Opting to stay here and nurse Deacon would surely result in hosepipes, frame-ups and jail time. Not necessarily in that order.

I pull on my clothes and mentally cobble together a story for my new girlfriend.

'Are you speaking to me, baby?'

'No . . . I don't . . . Was I?'

Mrs Delano is concerned. 'Well you were kind of mumbling, and looked like you were playing an invisible piano too. Everything okay?'

Two of my stress tells: thinking aloud and conducting. Simon Moriarty pointed those out to me. I really have to call that guy.

'Just thinking. You need to be safe, Mrs Delano.'

She walks her fingers up my chest. 'What are we? Strangers. Sofia, please.'

I clear my throat. 'It's dangerous for you here . . . Sofia.'

Delano puts her cheek against my heart. 'Remember when you first called me Sofia, baby? That night in Coney Island. I'll never forget it, Carmine.'

Carmine? Now I'm somebody else. Is that an improvement, I wonder?

Mrs Delano's make-up leaves a face print on my chest when I peel her off.

'You need to go upstairs now, Sofia. Go up and wait for my call.' I flash on the rows of pill bottles in the upstairs kitchen. 'Do you have any medication you should be taking?'

Sofia Delano frowns. 'No more pills, Carmine. They make me stupid.'

'How about one? Just one to help you relax until I call?'

'Maybe just one for you, baby.'

'Good. Good . . . baby. You promise?'

'Sure.'

'Say it. Promise me.'

Delano pouts and suddenly 'Girls Just Wanna Have Fun' starts playing in my mind-pod.

'I promise. Happy now?'

'Yeah. Happy now.'

I steer her towards the hallway, but she stops at the door, planting her back against the frame. Her chest is heaving and her eyes are bright.

Carmine was a lucky guy, I think. *What did he do to you?*

'Kiss me, baby,' she moans. 'I've been dreaming so long.'

After all this time I get lucky twice in one day. Pity about the blood-sodden circumstances.

'Come on, Carmine,' says Sofia, her voice sulky and impatient. 'No kiss, no pill.'

So I kiss her. She grabs a fistful of my neck hair and pulls me in deep, and it's like a movie kiss, long and languorous, and after a year or so I start wishing my name was Carmine.

We come up for air and Sofia's eyes are wet. Blue mascara flowers on her cheeks.

'We still got the spark, Carmine.'

I'm feeling a bit emotional myself. 'Yeah, Sofia. That was something.'

Her nose crinkles. 'But what happened to your hair?'

I hustle her up the stairs with Ghost Zeb chuckling in my ear.

I shut the door behind Mrs Delano, then take the steps three at a time back to my apartment. Deacon is up and about, stumbling around head in hands, swear words drooling from her lips. She's not fully conscious yet, but any minute now.

She spots me with one rolling eye, and lurches in my direction like an extra from *Day of the Dead*.

'Easy there, Detective Deacon,' I say, gallantly steering her to the remains of the sofa. She plonks down, deep into the butchered cushions. Her entire midsection disappears, from boobs to knees. On any other day you'd have to laugh, except maybe yesterday or the day before that.

'How you feeling, Detective?'

'Screw you.'

'We did that, remember.'

'Did we? I didn't notice.'

'I have it on very good authority that I have a lovely pee-pee, so lay off.'

Deacon's eyes are clearing up now. I can see craftiness in the corners.

'Okay. It was wonderful. You were like a stallion, Daniel.' She rattles her cuffs under my nose. 'So let me go.'

I nod slowly. 'You put together a good argument, me being like a stallion and so forth. So okay.'

I slip off one cuff just long enough to attach it to the sofa's exposed metal frame. Deacon does not bother yanking her chain.

'Bastard,' she sighs, rolling her eyes.

'It's temporary,' I assure her. 'Just until I can figure out what to do with you.'

'You could stick a knife in my forehead.'

I mull this over. 'Tempting. But no. What if I winged you, then you shoot *yourself* half a dozen times?'

'That's not funny, McEvoy,' says Deacon, throwing a futile kick in my direction.

'Exactly.'

I finish dressing, hang my jacket on a nail and run the kitchen faucet over my head.

'Why did Goran want to kill you?'

Deacon hawks and spits on my floor. 'Blood. I bit my tongue. I'm going to track that crazy bitch down, no doubt about that.'

'It was because of Faber, right? For some reason she didn't want Faber investigated.'

'I don't care where she hides. Nobody takes a swing at Ronelle Deacon and gets away with it'

I clap my hands triumphantly. 'Ronelle! Well hello, Ronelle.'

Deacon scowls, disgusted. 'People call me Ronnie. Good for the straights and the gays.'

I nod. 'Ronnie. Yeah, that would work. Cute or butch, depends on how you look at it.' I dry my head gingerly, zip my bag and throw it over my shoulder. 'Well, Ronnie, you ready to cooperate?'

'You are a wanted man, McEvoy. Surrender yourself into my custody and I'll see what I can do.'

'Come on. You got a body in the trunk.'

'You're the only one who knows that. And you're a fucking knife killer. What kind of credibility do you have? If I was as bent as Goran used to be, I bet I could come up with a scenario where you killed my partner and held me captive.'

I am not liking the sound of that, or the glint in Deacon's eyes when she says it.

'I think I'll turn you in and take my chances.'

Deacon shakes her head. 'I don't believe you. One of those bullets in Goran's shoulder is yours. Maybe you killed Connie DeLyne, then you shot down the investigating officer. I bet my superiors would go for that.'

She's right. So I say: 'Ronnie, when you're right, you're right.'

'You got it, *Daniel*. All I need to do is put a bullet in your brain and then cry at Goran's funeral.'

She sneers *Daniel* like it's a fake name that might fool others but it won't fool Ronelle Deacon.

'You, cry? I'd pay money to see that.'

'You already saw it, asshole.'

The lady is right again. Last night, coming in the door, there were tears on Deacon's cheeks.

'You're not going to kill me, Ronnie.'

She shrugs. 'Not without a gun. Unless you want to fight like a man.'

'I gave up being macho for New Year's. Bad for my health.'

'Pussy.'

'No thanks.'

I turn my back on the exchange because it's giving me a headache and duck into the bathroom to use the facilities and check my hat. I talk while I work.

'Here's the plan, Ronnie. I'm going to stash your car somewhere safe. You know, the one with the dead detective covered in trace in the trunk. I'm also taking your blouse with the blood spatter that I'm sure the forensics guys can read like a book. Then I'm coming back here and we can work this out. You want a career and I want you to have a career.'

'Blackmailing motherfucker,' Deacon calls from behind the sofa. 'Maybe I should just throw you out the goddamn window. You could land on the car.'

'Bring it on, doll head.'

My headache spikes behind one eye. Even at a time like this, people will not lay off the scalp.

'I have had transplants, if you must know,' I say, a little touchy, striding into the living area. 'This bald thing is temporary.'

Deacon is standing by the window, cuffs on the floor, her gun in one hand, mine in the other.

'For you, Dan,' she says, 'everything is temporary.'

If I had the time and the flexibility, I would kick myself in the arse, not a glancing blow either.

'You had a key on the memory bracelet, right?'

Deacon smiles like a wolf. 'That's right. One of my fondest memories is a little handcuff session a couple of years ago. Now take your hand out of your pocket, kneel down and say *please, please don't shoot me in the balls, Detective Deacon.'*

I give her my best doorman dead eyes. 'I only kneel before the baby Jesus on Christmas morning.' I glance over her shoulder. 'Why don't you ask my friend?'

Deacon closes one eye, like she needs to take careful aim. 'Yeah, sure. I'll ask the guy behind me. Kneel the fuck down, McEvoy.'

I press the remote button in my hand and the window buzzes open, swatting the detective on the butt.

Deacon puts three shots into the pane and I'm out the door before the glass stops tinkling.

I have a ten-second head start, and I can add a couple of minutes to that unless Deacon is crazy enough to chase me half naked.

Better pick up the pace.

CHAPTER 8

Army basic is a lot like school. You learn a lot of junk that you won't ever need, and miss out on stuff that could save your life. I've been cracking heads for twenty-five years now and not once did spit-shined shoes or a shipshape locker give me an edge.

Some people learn the hard way that life lessons are the valuable ones, like a certain short-lived Private Edgar English who checked his Steyer for blockages by squinting down the barrel. Others are lucky enough to survive the lesson and bank the information. I know because I was that student of the bleeding obvious during my second tour.

One desert-dry evening, Tommy Fletcher and I were leapfrogging ahead of our patrol in the village of Haddataha when we were cut off by sniper fire. Suddenly the air was alive with buzzing, shimmering missiles. Metal sparked against metal and chunks of building rained on our shoulders. Jaded old men played backgammon on their steps, barely pausing to watch the intruders get shot at.

While I wasted time spouting military jargon and making hand signals, Tommy put his elbow through the window of the nearest car and twisted the ignition tumbler with his bayonet. Thirty seconds later we were safe in the ranks of the UN peace-keepers. And you can bet your grandma's medical insurance that the first thing I did when my heart slowed down was learn how to start a car I don't have papers for.

Different time, same strategy; I would make my getaway in Deacon's car, bringing the evidence with me and leaving the detective without a ride.

I take the steps three at a time to the street, and it doesn't take a genius to spot Deacon's unmarked cruiser virtually abandoned in the vicinity of the kerb. For a start there's a *Police on Duty* card on the dash. Then there's the fact that I followed this crate around Cloisters on a bicycle not twelve hours since. But the major clue is the trail of blood leading from the popped trunk.

Smear, pool, smear is the pattern. Someone crawled, then rested, then crawled.

Goran's alive, says Ghost Zeb in a Prince Vultan voice.

A cop leaking outside my apartment. Deacon will have me on death row for this.

I check the trunk to be certain that Goran isn't in there, but the only thing I find is an In & Out Burger carton run aground on a metal ridge in the congealing crimson lake. No one with that much blood on the outside of their body is crawling very far.

'What did you do, McEvoy?'

Deacon is beside me, her coat belted tightly at the waist. Pallor shines beneath her dark skin, like a ghost behind a window.

'Not me,' I say. 'I just got here.'

119

Deacon jams her weapon into my kneecap, and I can see she's got the *hobble* word on her mind again.

'There are people on the street,' I point out, but she's beyond caring.

Enough of this.

I grab the gun and twist it clean out of Deacon's hands. A move every doorman knows well.

'Oh yeah?' says the detective, and I glance down to see a small snub-nose tickling my kidney. Her ankle gun. Cobra .32 maybe.

This is insane. I need to eat something and sleep some more. A massage would be nice, and I hear body wraps are good.

It's just gone sunrise and I'm wrestling a blue on the front porch.

'You can't just shoot me, Deacon.'

The detective shrugs. 'Fuck it, McEvoy. I'm just staying alive until someone kills me.'

I know this fatalism well. There were nights in the Lebanon when death and life held more or less the same appeal.

'We need to find Goran, Ronelle. It's the only way out of the tunnel.'

Deacon dips a painted nail in the blood. 'I put a full clip into her,' she says, staring at her fingertip.

'I carried a survivor out of a bomb crater once, and saw another guy killed by a bee sting. You never know.'

'Jesus Christ, McEvoy,' says Deacon, snapped out of it by my dime-store philosophising. 'Bee sting? You on some kind of drugs? Any more crap about bees and I *will* put a slug into you.'

This is the Ronelle I am comfortable with.

The blood trail meanders across the street, along the kerb for a couple of gouts, then down a basement stairwell.

Deacon snatches her gun from my hand. 'What do you think, Hawkeye? She at the bottom of the stairwell? Or maybe all that blood is from some guy with a bee sting.'

I am comfortable with this Ronelle; that's not the same thing as happy.

A street sweeper trundles around the corner from Cruz Avenue, its twin revolving brushes scraping the surface of last night's leftovers. We watch the bristles turn red as the sweeper ploughs heedlessly through Goran's tracks. The driver's forehead smudges the glass and he looks like he would need a defibrillator to get him noticing anything.

'Christ,' says Deacon, and I notice the blood on her bare legs.

We splash through the street sweeper's backwash to the stairwell. Deacon swings herself around a lamppost, her coat balloons and I realise she has underwear and a shoulder holster on under there and nothing more.

Something occurs to me. 'Careful, Detective.'

Too late. A bullet punches into the lamppost, sending a church bell bong along its shaft.

I pull Deacon away from the stairwell. 'Did you bother to disarm your partner?'

'She was dead. Why disarm her?'

Detective Deacon is the kind of person who would argue with St Peter.

'Obviously she is not as dead as you thought.'

121

Deacon gets a two-handed grip on her automatic. 'This is good. If I can take her alive, she can put me in the clear. Ish. The trunk bit could take some explaining.'

'Call it in, then.'

'With what? The spy radio in my panties?'

A mailman runs past us shouting into his radio, effectively doing the calling in for us. We have about three minutes before this place is swarming with police.

I lie on my stomach, wiggling my fingers at Deacon. 'Gimme the Cobra.'

Deacon looks at me as though I'm asking her to donate a kidney. 'Give you the *what?*'

'You've read my file, Ronelle. This is what I do.'

Deacon slaps the gun against my chest like it's a subpoena. 'Make sure you shoot the right cop.'

I don't respond. All this wisecracking is more exhausting than the gunplay.

My subconscious flicks through my memories for an appropriate Lebanon flashback, but I force that kaleidoscope of mayhem back down. Now is not the time for dwelling in the past. It would be a shame to take a bullet in the head because I was reliving Operation Green Line.

The basement stairways on my block are pretty uniform: cast-iron railing, eight steps down and a midget door wedged into a concrete alcove. These nooks were not built for someone of my size. I grab a rail and drag myself along the pavement, shirt rasping against the slabs.

There is noise below. Laboured breathing and rustling of material. I sense that Goran is nearly done, but it doesn't take much energy to pull a trigger one last time. I've seen guys fight for half a day, fuelled by nothing more than bile.

I screw my eye socket into the tiny wedge of space between the railing and the pavement.

Deacon tugs on my pants. 'What do you see?'

'I see a leg.'

'Just one?'

'The other one's bent back. I think she fell down those last few steps.'

'Good. You see a weapon?'

I wiggle forward another inch. Goran's hand is flapping like a fish out of water; her gun glints just out of reach.

'Dropped it. Let's go.'

I scramble to my feet, but Deacon is up before me, elbowing past to the first step.

She's fast, but not fast enough. There is just time to register an impression of Goran's battered and bloody frame, slumped like a broken mannequin, when the door behind her opens. An extremely hairy pair of hands reaches out, grabs Goran by the shoulders and hauls her inside. She's gone in a second, like she was never there. The door slams and bolts are shot.

'You see those hands?' says Deacon, stunned. 'Like goddamn monkey hands. Can you believe that?'

I push past her and knuckle the door. It's steel-reinforced.

'Get it open, McEvoy. Use some military trickery.'

I try to *trick* the door with my shoulder. The central panel buckles and wobbles but does not give.

'Got an oxyacetylene torch tucked into your underwear beside that spy radio, Ronelle?'

123

'I'm thinking of a word, McEvoy. Hobble. You remember that one?'

We don't have time for this. Cloisters is a small place and shots fired is big news. Half the police force will be landing on this block any second, and I don't think now is a good time for armed company.

'So, are you waiting for backup?'

Deacon thinks aloud. 'I can't wait. I need to follow the monkey hands.'

'You're getting in deeper, Ronnie. Every step you take makes it harder to go back.'

Deacon has a look in her eyes, like she's squinting at the horizon. '*We're* getting in deeper, McEvoy. Us. Okay, we're on a tangled road now, but it could straighten out.'

I'm not the only dime-store philosopher in the group. 'Yeah. With a couple of bee stings maybe.'

Once again, it's the bee stings that bring Deacon back. 'Screw you, Daniel. We gotta get out of here. I need Goran alive; without her I'm finished on the force.' She stares into my eyes and I glimpse a hopeful expression I haven't seen before; makes her seem at least ten years younger. 'If I bring Goran in, and you make a statement, I could salvage something out of this shitty day. They'll bounce me back to uniform, sure. Maybe even make me take some psych sessions, but I can stay on the force.'

My palm is resting on the reinforced door throughout this speech and I feel a sudden shock wave run through my fingers as vibration from the building transfers through the surface. Door slam.

'They're out the back door.'

'To a hospital, maybe?'

'It must be Faber who's behind this. And I sincerely doubt they took her to a hospital.'

Deacon smiles, and I am reminded of a wolf that tracked me through the Loup Valley once. 'They gotta believe we're on their tails,' she says thoughtfully.

I see where she's going. 'So maybe they'll drive around a bit.'

'Except we know where they're going.'

'Maybe.'

'So we can get there before them.'

'Big maybe.'

Deacon lopes up the stairs.

'Big maybe,' she agrees. 'I've survived worse odds than that.'

Deacon makes me sit in the back seat on the drive across town, which is completely ridiculous as I'm not under arrest and it's not even a secure cruiser. There's no mesh, and if I had a mind to, I could probably get at the shotgun cradled under the passenger seat. I don't have a mind to. Instead I use the short trip to grab a little shut-eye.

Power napping doesn't usually work for me. If I nod off for ten minutes during sunlight hours, I'm groggy for the rest of the day. But in this instance I have no choice. In spite of the few hours' sleep in the apartment, I am so exhausted it feels like my eyes are bleeding.

Daniel McEvoy is not as young as he used to be.

True as God.

Deacon is driving faster than she should, drawing attention

to herself, but I don't mind. All the bouncing is rocking me to sleep. Even the drone of her voice, stringing together long and complicated litanies of swear words, is soothing.

I slide down on the back seat, cradling my head in the safety belt, which smells of marijuana. My thoughts are just dissolving into dreams when Macey Barrett's phone rings in my pocket.

The damn thing is leaking radiation into my ear before I think to check caller ID.

'Hmmph?' I blurt sleepily.

'You bloody AWOL asshole.'

'Hmmph?' I say again, not sure what's going on exactly. The military term messing with my reality.

'Are you stoned, you prick? I warned you about that.'

'No. Not stoned, Major. Just dog tired.'

The voice is not happy with this. 'What the hell did you call me, Barrett? Major? Are you trying to be fucking funny?'

Ghost Zeb decides to help me out. *Come on, Dan. Whose cell phone is this?* And suddenly I'm awake. This is Barrett's phone, and that's obviously Irish Mike on the other end.

'Yeah,' I say. 'That's it. I'm trying to be funny, as per usual, Mikey boy.'

'Mikey boy! Mikey boy?'

'Too much intimacy? We're not that close, I take it.'

Silence for a moment, then, 'Who the hell is this? Put Macey on.'

Deacon clicks her fingers to attract my attention.

'Here we go,' she says, all business, as though we're off to meet our accountant.

I glance out the window. The Brass Ring is closed for business at this ungodly time of the morning, but I bet there'll be business going on inside just the same. I remember Faber's Benz from the previous day's stakeout and see it parked across the road, which pretty much confirms we came to the right place.

'Hello!' shouts Irish Mike. 'Who is this?'

'It's me, your close associate,' I reply deadpan, hoping the FBI are listening. 'What do you want to talk about, Mike? The murders, the drugs or the prostitution?'

Irish Mike is suddenly sweetness itself. 'I don't know what you're talking about, mister. Actually, I'm betting this is a wrong number.'

'Nooo,' I say. 'I recognise your number, Michael Madden. I put you on my speed dial when we were in Brooklyn, setting up the cocaine pipeline. Remember?'

Irish Mike hangs up.

The Brass Ring has doormen to stop undesirables getting in, whereas Slotz has doormen to eject the undesirables as soon as they've blown their wad. It's hard to understand why a man like Jaryd Faber would spend five seconds in Vic's seedy den when he's obviously top dog in this place.

Maybe I'll ask him before I shoot him.

The club is locked down tighter than a nuclear bunker during the zombie riots the media seems to feel are more or less inevitable, with steel blinds rolled down over the door and windows and not one but two alarm boxes bolted to the wall.

Deacon puts the police mobile in neutral and we spend a quiet moment sizing up the joint. While we are sizing up, I wedge my bundles of cash down behind the cruiser's back seat.

It would prey on my immortal soul if Faber shot me and stole my money.

'Pretty impregnable,' Ronelle admits finally. 'I don't know if we can take this place down.'

'Not going through the front door. But they're not going through the front door, not with a bleeding cop in the back seat.'

Deacon nods slowly. Some of her gusto has drained away. Maybe the truth of this situation is dawning on her, i.e. she's chasing a wounded officer into a fortified club with only a murder suspect for backup. The uncomplicated days of being a detective must seem like a rosy dream.

'Okay, so we go around back.'

'We? I really think now is the time for you to call the cavalry. Faber will soon have a dying cop in there, if he hasn't got one already. Nobody will believe a word he says. With any luck, he'll get himself killed during the raid.'

Deacon pouts stubbornly. 'No. The first thing Faber will do when he hears a siren is put the final nail in Goran's coffin. And when I say *nail* I mean bullet and when I say *coffin* I mean head. I need to wrap this up myself.'

'Be my guest.'

'I thought you had a stake in this. Didn't this asshole kill your girlfriend?'

This is true, and I had pushed it to the back of my mind, but even a reference to Connie sets my blood boiling.

'Okay. We go around back. But let me have the shotgun.'

'Not happening.'

I hold up the little Cobra .32. 'I am not entering a building with this toy. I can barely get my finger through the trigger guard.'

We glare at each other like kids with trading cards until Deacon makes an offer.

'I've got a blade.'

'Good for you. Why don't you throw it at the men with guns?'

'I'll take the Cobra and the pump. You take my Smith and Wesson.'

'Any clips?'

'Two on the holster.'

This is not a bad deal. 'What about the blade? You going to use it?'

Deacon rolls her eyes, pulling an ivory-handled flick knife from its home behind the sun visor.

'Anything else, McEvoy? You want my brassiere too?'

I mull this over. 'What size are the cups?'

There's only one obvious way around back, and that's down the same alley where Deacon put half a dozen bullets into her partner. Ronelle moves quickly, keeping her eyes off the crushed bum-shack, picking her way through the black pennies of blood.

Then she changes her strategy, returns to the shack, pulls her gun and acts out the shooting again in total silence.

'I'm dealing with it,' she explains grudgingly, due to the fact that I'm looking over her shoulder. 'By doing it again I dilute the act, making it less powerful.'

'Ah,' I say. 'Freud?'

'John Wayne Gacy.'

I must look shocked, because Deacon half grins. 'Kidding. Dr Phil.'

'Okay. That's much better. I bet you wish you were diluting the act with shoes on.'

Deacon nods. 'Dr Phil didn't mention that.'

There is a small parking lot at the rear of the club which services three or four service entrances for adjacent or opposite businesses. I spot two restaurants and a pet shop that is receiving a shipment of canaries. The little birds sing when their crates are moved. A cacophony of shrill panic.

'That's how I feel,' I comment to Deacon, strategically exposing a sensitive facet of my character that Dr Simon once assured me would encourage a desire to bond.

'That's how you sound too, bitch,' says the detective, who obviously hasn't read Simon's article.

The Brass Ring opens on to the north corner of the parking lot, and there is a guy at the door, checking cars every five seconds, looking like he would dearly love to strangle every one of the canaries.

'They haven't arrived yet,' I deduce, crouching behind a green recycling dumpster that smells like smoothies and reminds me that I haven't eaten. 'That guy is nervous. Look at him, sucking on his cigarette like his life depends on it. They've called ahead, but they're not here yet.'

'I concur, Sherlock,' says Deacon, squatting beside me. 'Look at that moron. Jumpier than Bambi. All you doormen got patience issues.'

All us doormen. I bet we look the same to Deacon.

'I have an idea.'

Deacon does not clap delightedly or otherwise seem impressed. 'You have an idea? That's what my ex said after he tore the last rubber in the pack.'

This is one of those times when I do not want to know what happened next. I sulk a little until Deacon's curiosity gets the better of her.

'Okay, you enormous baby. Dazzle me.'

So I tell her my plan, which sounds stupid when you say it out loud, but all Deacon says is: 'Who gets to do the hurtin'?'

Which makes me wonder just how much of a police officer is left inside this woman, which reminds me of an old joke that has no place in the modern world, except perhaps in County Sligo, where they love a good misogynism.

I stamp on the dumpster brake and put my weight on the push bar. It lurches forward easily, lighter than I expected. Plastic and cardboard only. Mostly. The lot is busy now with staff arriving for work and the pet guys humping birds into the store. There are a lot of cars for the doorman to keep his eye on.

The dumpster trundles noisily across the lot, and I graze a parked truck to make sure the doorman picks up on my approach.

Yeah, a big green dumpster, says Zeb. *I think he might 'pick up' on that.*

Oh, you're back.

I never went away. And I will never go away unless you find me.

The doorman spots my head and shoulders bobbing behind the dumpster.

'Hey, Trash Man. Get off the fucking ramp, okay? I got a car coming in.'

I shout over the tweeting. 'Come on, guy. How many times I gotta tell you people. I am a recycling engineer, not a trash man.'

Ghost Zeb chuckles. *Nice. Build your character.*

Build my character? What are you? Al Pacino now?

'I could give a fuck what you call yourself. Get off the ramp. Or maybe you want me to tear one of your ears off.'

'That's a real specific threat,' I say, trundling closer. 'Sounds like you might actually do that.'

Doorman is proud. 'That's my thing. Specific threats. People don't believe the vague stuff, but you go *specific* on their asses, then it's a whole different thing.'

I stamp on the dumpster brake so it doesn't slide back down the ramp.

'I get it. Specific like I'm gonna open this lid and a big pissed-off cop is gonna put your lights out with the butt of her shotgun.'

Doorman chews this over. 'That's a little bit overkill. You know. Too much information. By the time I get through digesting that, shit is long over.'

'Pre-cisely,' I say in my Moriarty voice.

'Huh?' says Doorman.

'Private joke,' I say, then pull the lever.

Deacon pops up and puts Doorman's lights out with the butt of her shotgun.

So now Doorman is in the dumpster with Deacon and I'm the new doorman. When they come with Goran, me and Deacon

132

are going to take the car. Simple as that. Two of us, ready for action. Maximum four of them, not expecting trouble. It should be stressful, but easy.

Unless someone comes to check on you, says Ghost Zeb, ever the pessimist.

Okay. There is that.

And so long as Faber is not in the car. He knows your face.

Point taken. Now can you let me watch the lot?

And let's not forget the possibility that Goran called someone else, not Faber. You could be in the wrong part of town.

This is a depressing thought and more plausible than Hairy Hands and Goran actually turning up here.

The doorway is a pretty typical delivery entrance, set atop a concrete ramp and flanked by reinforced double doors. From the corridor behind emanate various kitchen sounds and smells as the staff get the food started for the lunch trade, and from somewhere in the bowels comes the dull thump thump of a dance track's bass line. A big screen over the bar, I'm guessing. A couple of kitchen workers pass me with barely a grunt, shoulders hunched against the chill, cigarette smoke trailing behind them like morning mist.

A black Benz with smoked passenger windows pulls into the lot doing about thirty m.p.h. more than it should be. The car whacks its underside on the ramp, shunting the dumpster across the asphalt. I see Hairy Hands gripping the passenger dash.

The dumpster's wheels snag on the kerb, sending Doorman and Deacon flying through the air like a couple of superheroes. I swear Deacon manages to throw me a recriminating look before she crashes through the windscreen of a parked Chevy.

133

Doorman lands nice and neat in the rear of the pet van, sending out an oomph of yellow canaries.

I am stunned. So much for stressful but easy. Canaries? Come on. Are there cameras rolling somewhere?

My great plan is completely blown. The car was supposed to stop short of the ramp, because of the great big green dumpster blocking the entrance. Then Goran's rescuers/abductors would be forced to either move the dumpster or carry their wounded cop to the club door. While they were thus engaged, Deacon would do her hellcat jack-in-the-box bit and I would come in from the flank.

Now, however, Deacon is folded into the front seat of a Chevy and there are four big men getting out of Hairy Hands' car.

Think, soldier. Improvise.

The lot is in chaos now. Screeching birds everywhere, flapping and launching salvoes of shite. A couple of pet shop guys with nets, calling to the canaries, like birds speak English. Car alarms screeching. Big men shouting at each other.

And then here I am, standing like a stone pillar.

Move. Save Deacon at least.

I must admit, it does cross my mind to fade into the background and save myself much heartache and possibly ballache too, but the notion fades fast and I find myself drawing the Smith and Wesson and sizing up the competition.

Drop Hairy Hands first, I reckon. He was the one who rescued Goran and he gets to sit in front. Plus he has the most expensive sunglasses. Alpha male without a doubt.

I put a shot into Hairy Hands' elbow. An accident. I was aiming for the shoulder, but this gun is new to me. The elbow is gonna take years to heal up. Maybe later I'll light a candle for this guy. For now I have his two friends to worry about. In about a second Hairy Hands' buddies are going to figure out that I am not the house doorman, maybe half a second if they're not as stupid as they look.

I get a couple of steps down the ramp when I feel twin jabs in my neck. Either I've been bitten by the world's smallest vampire, or those jabs were the darts from an electric stun gun.

High voltage, sings Ghost Zeb. *Rock and roll.*

Then fifty thousand volts shoot down my spine and send me jittering down that ramp like a monkey with rock and roll in his soul.

AC/DC, I think. 'Highway to Hell'.

Too easy.

There's bacon frying somewhere. I can hear it popping in the pan. It's a cruel thing to fry bacon near a man and not let him taste it. I swear I can smell salsa too, or something tangy, and I am so goddamn hungry.

Garibaldi biscuits. The French soldiers at the off-base observation posts always had Garibaldi biscuits. They charged outrageous prices for them, but I generally paid. Those guys had the best field rations. Stew, lasagne, casserole, topped off with a cool Gitane. I can smell all of those dishes now, and I hang around on the fringe of alertness savouring the memories.

Eventually the dreams evaporate and I come back into consciousness on the tail end of the notion I went out on.

'Vampire!' I shout, straining to jump out of the chair I am taped to.

'Kee-rist almighty,' says a familiar annoying voice. 'Vampire? That Taser must have scrambled your brain, fella.'

I'm awake now but I feel like a brittle husk, as if the stun gun hollowed me out. I cough and spit out what feels like a lump of coal. I'm surprised not to be breathing fire. Faber is bent over, hands on knees, two feet away.

'Faber, you prick.'

'You know me, cop? Do I know you?'

My eyes are heavy and full of sand, but I force myself to blink until my surroundings sharpen up.

I'm in a kitchen. High-class place, all stainless steel and marble worktops. There's bacon in the pan. Thank God. That means I'm not having a stroke. My weapons are gone and in spite of the situation I muster a little self-congratulation for stashing my cash.

'Faber. I am starving. Honestly, man, those stun guns take it out of a person. You think I could have a BLT? Even just a B?'

This freaks Faber out and he does a little dance, clicking and pointing, trying to remember where he's seen me. I use the time to absorb as much of the room as I can.

Six people that I can see. Faber dancing his ginger jig, dressed in something else from his wardrobe of anachronisms. Looks like a beige mohair suit with honest-to-God flares and Captain Kirk boots. Who the hell is this guy's stylist? Engelbert Humperdinck?

Three of his guys are ranged behind him, jackets off, sleeves rolled up ready to do business. One new one, must be the stun gun guy. Deacon out cold, taped to what I presume is a meat gurney like some lab experiment, and Goran shivering on the floor, a pool of her watery blood shining on the concrete.

'Stop pointing at me, man. Or so help me . . .'

Faber does a two-fingered point to show me who's in charge. 'The doorman. Daniel. In Slotz with that hostess.'

'That's right. Connie. You remember her?'

Something in my voice makes Faber take a few steps back. He puts one of his guys between him and me.

'Yeah,' he smirks. 'I remember her. Someone punched her ticket, that's what I hear. You ask me, she got what she deserved.'

I consider throwing a fit. Straining against my bonds and cursing Faber's seed, breed and generation. But I was once a professional soldier and I know any display would only serve to amuse my captors. So I take a few deep breaths and apparently calm myself.

'We all get what we deserve, Faber. In the end.'

Faber steps from behind his man's bulk. 'Really? You think so, doorman? I deserve my drugs, and because of you I can't get them.'

Okay. We're about to get to the nub of this whole affair. There are drugs involved. Goran was obviously involved with these drugs.

Thinking about Goran, I glance over at her. She has stopped shivering and is staring at a point in the air. I'm guessing she sees angels.

'Your pet cop is in a little discomfort.'

Faber doesn't even look. 'Screw her,' he says, waving dismissively. 'She ain't getting up.'

'You're a sweet guy, Faber. I bet your wife tells you that every night, after you fill her in on your day. Dead hostesses, bleeding cops and whatnot.'

Faber helps himself to some bacon, patting it down with a square of kitchen paper. 'What happened, Dan? Did you maybe see a movie where the good guy is a smartass and gets to live?' He rolls the bacon strip and chews it. 'That's not how it works outside your shithole club. Okay, you had the muscle in Slotz, but not here.'

I have to ask, so I say: 'I gotta ask, Faber. What the hell are you doing in Slotz? This is a nice place you've got here. Smells good even in the kitchen. I haven't seen a single roach, for Chrissakes.'

I'm playing for time a little with this kind of small talk, but I would genuinely like to know. Faber is prepared to give me a moment, so long as he gets to talk about himself.

'That's an interesting question, Daniel, and I get where you're coming from. You look at me, wearing a suit that's worth more than you make in a year . . .'

I order my face not to react.

'. . . and you ask yourself, what's a successful, classy guy like Mister Faber doing in a shithole like Slotz.'

'That's pretty much it,' I say, thinking that maybe I'm over-playing the straight face.

Faber checks the buttons on his waistcoat. 'The thing is, Doorman Dan, all day I'm eating lobster with judges and drinking Dom with millionaires, and sometimes when the day is done, I feel like getting down and dirty, you know what I mean?'

I nod obligingly. 'Well, it doesn't get much more down and dirty than Slotz.'

'Yessir, Vic is quite a character.'

'He's the boss.'

The attorney works up the courage to step closer. 'Here, I'm the boss!'

This mood swing is driven home with a backhanded slap across my face. I roll my head with the blow, but honestly I needn't have bothered.

I spit on the floor; no blood, just spit. 'What do you want from me, Faber? How come I'm not dead?'

'You're not dead, Dan, because I need to know what *you* know,' says Faber, jiggling his glasses for some reason. Maybe it's supposed to signify that these spectacles can see into my soul.

'About what? These drugs that you can't get?'

'Keep going, doorman.'

'Goran used to get your drugs. You two had some kind of scam going.'

'And we have a winner. Give that prick a cigar.'

I feel utterly screwed. Somehow, up to this point I had managed to nurture a spark of optimism. I've been in worse scrapes, that sort of thing. But now, with Goran's eyes filming and Deacon strapped to the gurney, I am suddenly devastated. The steel and concrete are too real, and the walls are closing in.

'I don't know anything, Faber. I'm only here because of the girl.'

Faber teases his Styrofoam hair with greasy fingers. 'What girl?'

'Take your pick. You got one dead, one more or less dead and one on the gurney.'

'What? The stripper? That's why you put the cops on to me?'

'She was murdered. And it's *hostess*.'

'You think I killed her?'

'I know you killed her, arsehole.'

Faber paces the kitchen, counting off points on his fingers. 'So you tip Deacon about my fight with Connie. I freak because of this deal we have tonight. Deacon gets suspicious and Goran makes an on-the-spot decision to whack her, which doesn't work out. Then Deacon's whacking also falls a little short. So Goran calls me to come get her.'

Faber is filling in a lot of blanks here. Obviously at this point he doesn't care what I know, which is never good. Being filled in is okay when you're a kid and you need basic information about numbers and poisonous foods and such, but in my world knowledge gets a person dead quicker than anthrax.

'I had a shootout with your boys right outside the door,' I point out to the pointer. 'The cops are going to find us soon.'

Faber is delighted by this observation, presumably because it's way off base.

'No cops, my friend. I own a lot of property, including this entire lot and the basement where we picked up Goran.' The attorney squats to think quietly. 'No,' he says finally, knees creaking as he stands. 'I can't think of a way out. The three of you need to die. It's tough about the product, but you know, sometimes you gotta eat losses.'

You can't just let a statement like this fade without argument. 'Wait a second, Faber. You have heavies. Can't they get your *product*?'

I don't use words like *product* or *heavies*. They sound 2D coming out of my mouth. I half expect them to plop in card-board letters to the floor.

Faber chuckles like he's fond of me. 'What? These dummies? I wouldn't let them pick up my mail. No offence, guys. This whole thing is too complicated without Goran.'

The dummies shrug amiably. No offence taken.

Faber pats his pockets, looking for something, or maybe he's just twitchy.

'This is a big step for me. Cop killing. There's no going back after this.'

The attorney seems genuinely worried, but I feel it's more a logistics thing than anything to do with a conscience, which riles me enough to comment:

'Kill a hostess though, that's okay. No foul as far as you're concerned. Connie had two kids, Faber.'

'Can you get off that, please?' sighs Faber. 'You've got a couple of minutes left. Use it well. Why not beg for your life?'

'You beg for yours.'

Faber does this weird little tap dance with a ta-dah at the end, which his dummies actually applaud. This whole fake-rat-pack thing has gotta be unhealthy. Simon would get a couple of chapters out of the guy.

'Okay, sir,' says Faber, like I'm in the front row of his show. 'I would like you to know that I regret the whole Slotz thing. Something about that sleazy shithole dump appeals to me and I never wanted to blot my card there. There's a lot to be said for getting a cheap blow job at the end of the day without bumping into the mayor. I'm not apologising again, it would be a bit rich in the circumstances, but I do regret the incident. That's all I'm saying.'

Apologising again? I don't remember the first time.

'So, I'm gonna have you three killed. I feel okay about that now, but I suppose I'll probably lose some sleep over the years.'

A single silenced gunshot pops, like a smoker coughing into his fist. Goran spasms, then lies still.

Faber squeaks with fright, then recovers himself. 'What the hell?' he shouts, actually stamping a foot. 'Never when I'm in the room! How many goddamn times? If I don't see it, then it didn't happen.'

It happened. It definitely happened. Maybe Goran was dying, but now she's dead.

'Sorry, Mister Faber,' mumbles the shooter. 'Won't do it again.'

Faber's pointing finger is a fan. 'I know you won't. I know you fucking won't, Wilbur.'

Wilbur? I can't hold in a chuckle. After all this time, done in by a Wilbur.

Wilbur shoots me a venomous look. 'Can I kill him first, Mister Faber?'

'Of course you can. Just wait until . . .'

'Until you're outside the door.'

'Very good. When you hear it click, then fire away. Get rid of the bodies at the smelter.'

Smelter? A word like that makes everything real all of a sudden. So practical.

'Hey, Faber.'

The attorney waves me away. 'Too late, Daniel. I have to be in court in an hour. As the judge might say, your appeal is denied.'

142

Tell him you can get his drugs, suggests Ghost Zeb.

Faber has his hand on the doorknob.

'I can get your drugs,' I say. I suppose you could say I blurt the words. A bit more squeak in the promise than I'd like.

The attorney steps slowly away from the door as if a sudden movement could make the knob go *click*.

'Say that again, Daniel.'

A fly zapper on the wall sparks as some poor insect gets too close to the light.

'I said, I can get your product.'

Faber drags a chair across the concrete floor and sits himself down facing me.

'I suppose it couldn't hurt to talk.'

CHAPTER 9

So now I've got this thing under the leg of my jeans. A security bracelet, Faber called it, quite popular with the celebs. Feels like there's a mutant beetle clamped on to my ankle, waiting to sink its teeth or claws, or whatever weapons a mutant beetle might possess, into my fibula. It's a clever little machine, no doubt about it. I'm surprised they've even got stuff like this outside the pages of a sci-fi novel.

Faber took great glee from explaining its workings to me. He came across like a techno-fool who knows how this one thing works, and bores the bejasus out of everyone passing on his snippet of know-how.

'So what we have here, Daniel, is a little electronic insurance policy. Judge friend of mine gave it to me in payment for my opinion on a statutory case he was . . . eh . . . involved in. Homeland are already using them and there's a strong lobby to snap them on US parolees too, given the percentage of repeat offenders.'

'Yeah? Spare me the lecture, Faber,' I said, playing it cool.

'Okay. Let me give you the specs. It's tamper-proof, naturally;

there's a sensor on there that monitors pulse and blood pressure; it's got GPS that feeds into my laptop, so we know exactly what building you're in at any time. You nip into the john for a quick dump, and the bracelet picks up the splash. But here's the bit I really love. I can remotely inflict electromuscular disruption if you ain't doing what you're supposed to be doing where you're supposed to be doing it. Or to give you the doorman version: I can zap enough voltage up your ass to make you shit your pants. This thing makes the Taser shock seem like a tickle with a feather.'

And then Faber gave me a little taste, just to show me he wasn't kidding. Felt like he popped my brain into a blender; by the time it was over, I was giving serious consideration to the aforementioned pants-shitting.

So now I am Faber's boy. He's got the key to my heart rate. I spend a minute trying to think of some way to screw with him, but it's a foolproof system, and so I settle down in my seat at the back of the New York bus and try to grab a little sleep. Maybe a low heart rate will fool Faber into thinking I'm dead.

I cross my ankles over the canvas bag at my feet. At least Faber's plan involved me catching a bus, so I got to collect my weapons and drop off my cash after I had picked it up from the cruiser.

It takes most of the day to get out to Farmington from New York. First a train to New Haven from Manhattan, then a transit bus. It might speed things up a bit if the driver didn't stop at every corner in Long Island on the way. Seems like everyone knows his name except me. I don't know why I'm fuming; it's

145

not like I'm in any great hurry to get where I'm going. Plus the rocking motion should help me to digest the sack of Taco Bell I bought at Grand Central. I wolfed it down a little quick, my first proper meal in over twenty-four hours. When you're having a crappy week, nothing comforts like Taco Bell.

I have to admit, standing there under Grand Central's famous vaulted ceiling, I did think about nipping to the rest room, sticking my foot down a toilet and putting a few rounds into the bracelet.

How tough can this thing be? Ghost Zeb reasoned, eager to have me back on his own case.

While I was mulling this over, Faber gave me an almost psychic call on Macey Barrett's cell, which I told him was my phone.

'So here's the thing, Dan,' he said, and I could almost hear the air part as he jabbed a finger at his mouthpiece. 'Sometimes distance makes people brave. They start thinking like it's traditional warfare and they can run away. Before you give in to that impulse, I got some information a chivalrous guy like yourself should have.'

Chivalrous? Does everyone know my weak spot?

'Yeah? What's that, counsellor?'

'Your lady friend. The cop on the trolley. If I don't hear from you by nightfall, she goes in the freezer. We just wheel her right in there. And once in, she's not coming out. I had a plate bolted over the safety latch. After that, I set my dogs on you. You shot the cops and my bodyguards shot you. Simple.'

Looks like chivalry might soon be dead along with Detective Deacon. The bodies just keep stacking up like sandbags.

I spend a futile moment wishing that things were normal again. If this were a normal week, I would be meeting Zeb for karaoke later. The little mensch loves the karaoke bar. Barry Manilow is his speciality, if you can believe that.

Oh Mandy, you came and I came, you were fakin'.

I think he might have screwed up the words a little.

Karaoke, says Ghost Zeb into his sleeve, the way he does when he's in one of his moods. *Not likely since you abandoned the search for me to save Princess Supercop. I'm as good as dead.*

Don't be like that. I haven't abandoned you, but I'm on the clock with Deacon. They're going to ice her, man.

That makes two of us, says Ghost Zeb. *Why don't you do something about my problem, since you're just sitting there? Have you even thought of a plan yet?*

I roll my eyes, which must look strange to the old lady in the seat opposite giving me the glare treatment.

I'm a little preoccupied at the moment.

Not so preoccupied that your brain doesn't have a few spare cells to conjure me up.

Okay, okay. I have been thinking about this, as you perfectly well know. Let me make a call.

Make your call, Judas.

Hey, Judas wasn't Irish.

Just make the call.

One call then I'm back on Deacon.

It takes me a minute to remember Corporal Tommy Fletcher's number. I punch it in carefully, big fingers little buttons.

From what I hear, Irish Mike Madden has family in Ireland. Maybe Tommy can do a little recon, get us some leverage.

It's a start, I suppose, says Zeb, unwilling to give up his sulk. *But don't think you're off the hook. If you don't find the real me, I'm gonna move into your temporal lobe permanently.*

Great. Another ultimatum, just what I need.

Tommy answers when I'm on the point of hanging up.

'What the fuck?' he says instead of plain old hello, which is a pretty standard opener for Corporal Fletcher as far as I remember.

'Is that any way to talk to your sergeant?' I ask, half smiling in spite of the whirlwind of crap spinning around me.

'I'm not in the army no more,' grumbles Tommy. 'Especially not at four in the bloody morning. I got a headache and it's nearly bedtime.' Tommy draws a sharp breath as he realises who he's talking to. 'Daniel? Dan fucking McEvoy? Is that the big jackeen himself?'

'That's Sergeant McEvoy to you, Fletcher.'

'Danny, brother. Are you in country? We gotta party. We gotta go crazy, man. You ever see a one-legged man dance? So, where are you, Sarge?'

'I'm overseas, Corporal.'

'Still knocking heads?'

'A few. That's why I'm calling.'

'Something I can help you with?'

Tommy always caught on fast. 'I have a little recon mission for you, if you're up to it.'

There is an uncomfortable silence, then Tommy mumbles, 'Thing is, Dan, I don't really do that kind of thing any more. I got kids . . .'

Now I feel bad. 'Forget I mentioned it, Tommy. I didn't realise . . .'

Tommy cackles. 'Just screwing with you, Sarge. Course I'm up for it. No killing gypsies, though. I had a curse put on me.'

'No gypsicide, honest. I just need you to trace the roots of a certain family tree.'

'What?'

'Find a few people. But be careful, they have dangerous relatives.'

Tommy is unimpressed. 'Shit, my brother has a dangerous relative. Who do you need me to find?'

I give Tommy the details and he promises to get back to me asa-f-p.

I never wanted a phone before, but I'm starting to realise how convenient they are.

Irish Mike is paying for the call too, chuckles Zeb, coming out of his funk. *Nice touch.*

I must have chuckled too, because now the old lady opposite is showing me her can of Mace.

It's early evening by the time I finally get where I'm going in Farmington. This is not the sort of place doormen are usually required. The entire avenue is so wholesome and autumnal that it reminds me of Ireland. Even in these circumstances I can feel the first lilting twinges of the immigrant gene kicking in.

Farmington is even nicer than Cloisters; far too nice, you would think, to have a criminal underbelly, but as I found out only hours ago, the Farmington criminal underbelly is doing quite well. On this avenue especially.

I do the last mile from the bus stop on foot, humping the

weapons bag, and find a bench to rest my weary frame while I finish off my Big Bell Box meal.

The spicy food reminds me of Monterrey, and I can't help wondering how fast I could get there.

Yeah, that's right, amigo. Pack up and leave me to rot.

Calm down. I called Tommy, didn't I? Wheels are in motion. Now piss off and let me think.

You think too much. You need to get out of your head and into the real world.

Irony. Must be.

So I sit on the bench, reining in my aura, trying to look like a member of the community and not an ex-army doorman sent to rip off a steroid lab. I chew my burrito awhile and grudgingly admit that Faber and Goran had a sweet deal figured.

Back in Cloisters, Faber got a little teary spelling it out.

'As an attorney in the city, I represent a lot of drug people. I get to know them, they fill me in on every detail of their operation, and armed with this information, I get them off most of the time.'

I remember making myself pay attention, even though half my brain cells were fried from the anklet jolt and the rest were threatening to break apart and liquefy.

'So a year goes by, maybe eighteen months, these guys have forgotten all about their natty attorney, when one of their labs gets busted by the cops. First through the door is my dead friend, Detective Goran, followed closely by a few of my own humps all rigged out in DEA armour and helmets. They secure the bad guys, load the drugs into the van and that's all she wrote. Our fake police squad drives away, leaving the ripped-off drug merchants hog-tied with PlastiCuffs. Sometimes we load a couple in the van for show, then toss 'em a few blocks later.'

He leaned back on his heels, waiting for me to think it through, appreciate his genius. Which I did.

'So the theft is never reported.'

'What are they gonna say? Is that the police? I'd like to report that you people stole my drugs? Don't think so.'

'And you got a buyer?'

'I represent a lot of drug guys. They figure I'm brokering for another client.'

That was pretty good, so I said: 'That's pretty goddamn good, Jaryd.'

Faber couldn't help preening. 'Why thank you, Daniel.'

'But now you're screwed because your pet detective is dead.'

Pet detective, says GZ. *Nice.*

'And I'm guessing Goran wasn't stupid enough to let you keep the riot gear.'

'Correct. Goran headed up operations in the field; I did the planning.'

'It's a good plan. Sweet, the kids might say.'

'Again, thank you. But much as I appreciate your appreciation, I need more than that before I let you go after my package.'

In Ireland, going after a guy's package means grabbing him by the balls. I think Faber is talking about his drugs again.

'You read my file?'

'No. Any good bits?'

'I have a special skill set.'

'Any of those skills relevant?'

'Shit, Faber, if your *package* was in Fallujah I could extract it.'

Faber licked his lips. *Extract*. He liked that bit of military.

'It begins with an F, but it ain't Fallujah.'

Ten minutes later, Faber had Deacon's computer on his knee and was scrolling my file.

'Kee-rist almighty, Daniel. This reads good. You kill anyone over there?'

'Only the ones that died. What's in this for me, Faber? If I'm gonna be a criminal, I might as well get paid.'

I figured if anyone could understand greed, it would be a lawyer.

'You get my package and I'll give you fifty grand plus your life back.'

He was lying and we both knew it; what we didn't know was if the other person knew we knew it.

What are you, six?

'Okay, Faber. You got a deal. Cut me loose and give me the details.'

Faber called one of his boys over, gave him a set of keys and a few whispered instructions.

'Not just yet, Daniel. I need to make an impression on you first. Show you what a dead serious kinda guy I am. One more taste of electromuscular disruption should do it.'

The house I'm watching is straight out of the opening credits of a suburban sitcom. According to what TV tells us, there should be an overweight dad, a foxy mom, couple of smartarse kids and maybe an in-law down the basement. Work in a couple of catchphrases, like *sheesh, Ma* or *none of you people get me* and next thing you know it's season nine and DVD box sets are topping the charts.

This is the last place you'd expect to find a steroid lab. Nevertheless, according to Faber, this is exactly where I will find one.

'And a lotta security,' he said. 'State of the art. These guys don't skimp.'

Faber is not risking any of his guys on this run, so I'm on my own. No fake police backup. A pity, as according to Faber, Goran had put together quite the strike force. Pro-bars, one-man battering rams, the whole kit and caboodle.

'Think of it as a test, Daniel. You bring home the goods and maybe next time I let you take out some of the boys.'

I should call the FBI, that's what I should do. But once the Feds become involved, the best-case scenario is I live out my days in witness protection; the worst-case is Deacon freezes and I get life without parole. So maybe I put Newark on speed dial, but I don't push the button just yet.

Newark on speed dial? Your thoughts are beginning to sound American.

Zeb is right. I've been here too long. I need a pint of Guinness that's taken five minutes to pour, and a date with a freckled redhead.

The house looks normal, but I squint into the shadows and see camera domes suckered to the eaves. Laser eyes too, on stalks in the garden. The windows are small, with decorative cast-iron bars, and the door is painted to look wooden, but I'm betting on steel. Spotlights on the lawn and roof complete the package. This place is a subtle fortress. There's no chance I'm fighting my way inside.

I circle around back, which is not as easy as it sounds. In modern America's paranoid suburbia, the tendency is to shoot strangers first and ask questions later, if at all. There are stories on the news every day about garbage men getting plugged by panicked housewives just because they were speaking in some language that was not English. Sometimes that's their actual court defence.

He was round back of my house, messing with my trash, speaking terrorist talk. What does he 'spect?

But I politicise.

Luckily, shadows are lengthening, I'm wearing black and I have done this kind of thing before. I nip through the adjoining yard, all ready to lay someone out if I have to. I'm hoping for a male. I could live with socking some stocky gardener, but a slip of a girl might be more than my beleaguered psyche will allow.

Pull yourself together or you'll start making mistakes.

Yeah. That's rich coming from a guy who once tossed back three shots of furniture polish after the club one night. Three shots before he noticed something wrong.

First decent crap I took in months, says Ghost Zeb.

I make it around back through a bricked alley without having to relieve anyone of their senses, and conceal myself in a cluster of evergreens. I peep through branches to the bay window and see the empty lounge of an affluent suburban home with regulation Eames recliner that is too expensive for the kids to ever sit in. Nice garden, though, I gotta say. Plenty of green, nice wild feel to it without being neglected. Reminds me of . . .

Oh, please. Shut the hell up.

Okay, then.

I hear a sudden growling and I realise that there's a dog in the trees with me. Big bastard too, I'm guessing, by the way his breath is in my ear. These are *his* trees and he's pissed. I have maybe two seconds before he clamps his teeth around my face. Faber will notice a hell of a spike in my vitals then.

Please not a Rottweiler. Please not a Rottweiler.

I look and there's a Rottweiler two feet away from me, his sharp head comically bewigged by soft green ferns. He's got his lips pulled back over his incisors and his black eyeballs are on me like target lasers, which kinda takes the comic out of it.

Christ. This is not right. How much more shit can be piled on one person in a day?

The dog lunges and I roll back into the tree roots and shrubs with him, clamping his snout with one hand. I get a fistful of dog snot, but at least those teeth are contained for the moment. I reach down with the other hand and grab the dog's crotch.

Congratulations. It's a boy.

Screw squeamishness. In the words of David Byrne: *I ain't got time for that now.*

The dog is in my arms and he's wriggling like a sea creature out of water. I can feel the animal's fury testing my muscles to their limits. Branches snap around our heads, and with the dusk falling it's like a scene from a horror movie. I half expect some masked creep to emerge from the alley with a mommy fixation and a carving knife.

I give the Rottweiler's balls a squeeze to get him good and

angry, then use every pound of strength I can muster to flip him over the garden fence. I hear the thump and scrabble as he lands awkwardly next door then finds his paws. This is not a move I had ever planned or run through in any of my just-in-case scenarios; it's kind of a spur-of-the-moment thing and could even work to my advantage.

Go, Bonzo, I broadcast at the dog. Give 'em hell.

Next door the commotion is immediate. Bonzo rampages through the drug den's back garden looking for some throats to tear out. I'm betting this particular dog is not used to being manhandled over a fence. They say that hell hath no fury like a woman scorned, but I would argue that a scorned woman would pale and back out of the room faced with a Rottweiler who just got his scrotum twisted.

I peep over the fence. Next door's garden has roughly the same dimensions: a rectangular lawn maybe twenty by thirty, with various immature trees clustered at the end. It also has a freshly laid rear driveway with a pick-up reversed up to a back door, which is obviously reinforced.

There's a guy on the door who doesn't know whether to give Bonzo his tough-guy face or shit his pants.

I may not be able to get myself into this house, but maybe I can make whoever is in there come out to me.

The dog shakes his sleek head like he's disembowelling an imaginary rabbit, then spots the guy at the door and decides to transfer my crimes to him. His growl says, *I am going to eat you alive, motherfucking ball-squeezer.*

There isn't a man on this planet who isn't scared by a Rottweiler coming at him with drool streaming out of his mouth.

156

PLUGGED

I squat to rummage through the bag at my feet. First I pop a couple of earplugs from their plastic envelope, then I select a Steyer Bullpup assault rifle with a 40mm grenade launcher slung underneath the barrel. And to think I almost didn't go for the launcher option, but the dealer sold me on it. *Hey, don't take the launcher model, what do I care, but for a hundred bucks I can throw in two grenades. A hundred bucks! You telling me, Irish, that you can't think of a single situation where a couple of grenades wouldn't come in handy?*

I could think of a couple of situations. This wasn't one of them. Flying dogs and grenades in the suburbs.

I stick my head over the fence and peer through the branches just in time to lip-read the doorman's *fuck this* and see him hurry in the back door. He slams it half a second too late to stop the Rottweiler making it inside.

That is a lucky bonus. I was hoping for the dog outside at the door, causing a distraction, but inside the house itself . . . Should be carnage. Hopefully.

Seconds later the consternation starts. Crashing, tinkling, shouts of surprise. A couple of gunshots.

They're thinking, *What the hell is going on? Where is this coming from?*

Pack up the shit. Pack it up.

First rule of any factory: protect the product.

I pull the assault rifle into my shoulder and flick off the safety, and instantly I am a soldier again. It's the *click*. Once the safety is off, it is no longer a drill.

I strafe the roof, knocking holes in the slates, leaving beams exposed and severing the power lines. If those guys don't have a generator in there, surveillance is down. Even if they do, I have a minute.

Now they're thinking, *Gunfire. It's a raid. We need to move out.*

Gunfire is one thing, but explosions really light a fire under people. I feed a grenade into the launcher, close the slide and pull the secondary trigger, sending a silver 40mm egg of explosives through a hole in the roof. I hope no one was hiding their Christmas presents up there.

The explosion is not Hollywood big but it's enough to reduce the attic space to so much firewood. The sound wave makes reality jump a frame or two, and a cloud of smoke and dust hang over the house, a marker for the fire brigade.

That's all the destruction I need. I stuff the assault rifle back into my magic bag and drop over the fence into enemy territory. Maybe their cameras are out, maybe not. Either way, I have to act.

The pick-up crouches in the driveway like a wild beast. A brand-new Hilux with outsize wheels and probably a lot more than shop horsepower waiting under the hood. This is the getaway vehicle, no doubt about it. Any aggravation comes in the front door, and the steroids go out the back in this beauty.

A guy comes on to the patio, gun in one hand and keys in the other. There's a stripe of blood across his arm and I'm thinking *good boy, Bonzo.* And also *rest in peace, doggie.* I twist the wing mirror so I can follow what's happening, then squat behind the Hilux's grille, and give the situation a few seconds to develop. Maybe this guy has the steroids on him.

Or maybe not. A second man wheels out two large sealed

plastic barrels on a drum caddy. This guy is limping from a leg bite and I'm starting to feel sad for Bonzo.

The men load both barrels into the flatbed, grunting and cursing.

'Get the last barrel,' the first man shouts over the crackling flames billowing from the attic.

'Fuck that,' says junior guy. 'I ain't going back in there.'

Guy 1 brandishes his weapon in a way that tells me he doesn't have a whole lot of gun-time.

'Okay,' says junior guy hurriedly. 'Jesus, Bobby. We just split a tuna melt.'

'It was a nice sandwich, man, and we'll always have that. But I'm the supervisor and I gotta put the tuna aside. So just get the barrel, E Bomb. Shit.'

E Bomb tiptoes back into the house in a way that makes me think that Bonzo is still alive.

E Bomb? Christ, what have nicknames come to? The problem is that these guys are inventing their own names. No one christens themselves Four-eyes, or Shit-breath. One guy back in Dublin, did six months for peeping Tom offences, guys called him Windows 2000. Now *that's* a nickname.

Even though the house is under attack, this guy is so focused on making sure there isn't a dog clamped to his arse that he never sees me coming. I sneak around the driver's side, punch him in the temple. Hard. And catch his keys before they hit the ground. I don't even need to take my slim jim out of the bag.

Thanks, Bobby.

Bobby bounces off the door, belches, then collapses to the

drive. I smell tuna. I am amazed when he shakes his head and gets in a swing at me. A good one that connects with my entire face. I am going to be lit up like a pumpkin in the morning. I am so pissed that I smack Bobby's head against the fender maybe a little harder than I need to.

I beep the pick-up with a Toyota fob and jump inside, slinging my bag of tricks into the passenger seat.

That punch hurt my knuckles. Maybe cracked one.

Could be arthritis, says Ghost Zeb, rifling my repressed memories. *Your father suffered from it. One of the reasons he drank.*

So he said. Didn't stop him beating on us.

The pick-up starts on the first turn of the key. I should bloody think so, all the money those steroid manufacturers spent on it. I yank the gear lever and floor the gas. The only thing between me and the open road is a key-coded gate that looks like it has enough square bars to contain even the Hilux.

Which is why I veer left and go through the flimsy wooden fence. Morons. I mean really, what kind of a tool organised their security? It only took one man and a mutt to reduce it to smithereens.

The last thing I see of the steroid house in my rear-view mirror is Bonzo, loping out of the back door with a hank of something in his jaws. *Good dog*, I think. *Good dog*.

CHAPTER 10

I try to stay focused on the drive back to Jersey, but the smooth ride is comforting and my mind begins to wander.

I keep saying that I'm not big on flashbacks, but whenever my mind blurs, the Lebanon is always there. Sky filled with streaking rockets, mangled shards of metal constantly raining from above. Everything was pockmarked by shrapnel. Everything. Mahogany-skinned old men on their stoops shooting the breeze like it was same-old same-old. Which it probably was.

I remember one French guy whose claim to fame was a dick the size of a baguette. This boast was put to the test one day when we came across a dog fight arena and . . .

Macey Barrett's phone rings and I nearly jump out of my skin when the car automatically picks up its Bluetooth signal and transfers the call to the Toyota's sound system.

'Daniel?'

'Holy Mary!' I blurt, which is a pretty accurate impersonation of a Christian Brother I used to do back in the eighties. Still pops out every now and then in times of stress.

Faber's laughter is distorted by the speaker. 'For you, I'm Holy Mary, God, Jesus and the Easter Bunny all rolled into one.'

I recover myself a little. 'Faber. How's it hanging, Jaryd? Good day in court pointing the shit out of everything?'

Faber's not laughing now. 'I point for emphasis, that's all.'

'You point all the bloody time. It doesn't mean anything you do it so much. It's like a tic. I'm telling you, Faber, that's why you never win anything at the tables.'

Silence for a moment. All I can hear is the discreet growl of the engine and the asphalt joins bumping under the wheels. *The heartbeat of the road.*

Faber gets over his pointing sulk. 'Have you got the product?'

'Two barrels of it. I hope you have secure storage.'

'Two fucking barrels? Where am I going to put two barrels?'

'Hey. I can dump one, no problem.'

'No. I can store it. I wasn't expecting two barrels. A briefcase maybe.'

'This is steroids, Faber, not heroin. There must be half a million doses here.'

Faber whistles. 'Those steroid guys really work for their money. The mark-up would make a crack dealer piss himself laughing.'

'Faber, this wouldn't be you trying to weasel out of giving me my fifty large? Because if that's the case I can drive this truck to any one of a dozen people I know.'

'That would be a bad idea, Daniel.'

'Tell me why, arsehole.'

So he tells me. 'Because your buddy Deacon, she's already gone in the freezer.'

My stomach sinks.

'Okay, dickhead. You watch your little screen and you'll see me coming.'

'I better see you coming fast. It's cold in that freezer.'

I hate this guy and I wish he was dead.

Faber's playing it cool, but he must be sweating over his decision to send me for the steroids. Even with a monitor on my ankle I'm a wild card and he knows it. Greed made him hasty and now he's had an entire day to think about the possible consequences. I bet that pointing monkey just cannot wait to roll me into the freezer beside Ronelle, and start peddling his steroids outside health clubs all over New Jersey.

I drive slow, keeping to the speed limit, with the radio tuned to local travel news, in case there's a pile-up on the motorway I need to avoid. Accidents mean blues, and this pick-up screams drug money.

Traffic is light and there's a sweeping mist scything past the streetlight beams. All those little drops, like half a million twinkling steroid pills.

I drive on without seeing a single cruiser, in spite of our mayor's road-safety drive, and in a couple of hours I'm back on good old I-95, cruising past monolithic Borders and Pottery Barns, past giant empty parking lots and all-night diners. I am envious of the people inside in their cocoon of light, enjoying the simple pleasure of some late eggs or a coffee refill. Not that I'm hungry yet, with the congealed lump of Mexican takeaway melting slowly in my stomach acid.

Christ. When you're inside a diner you wanna be outside and when you're outside you wanna get back in. What are you, schizo?

I'm talking to you, aren't I?

By three thirty I'm bumping my tyres down the Cloisters off ramp and swinging a wide arc into the bus station car park. I have to look hard to find a young hood selling pot. If you didn't know any better, you'd think this sleepy town had no hostess-killing lawyers living in it. I cut across empty spaces in the car park and pull in behind the dumpsters, beside a certain white Lexus that I had hoped never to see again.

No doubt Faber's computer will pick up this unscheduled stop, but he's not going to risk shocking me now with all this junk in the trunk. If he calls, I'll tell him I'm filling up at the twenty-four-hour pumps.

It could be true. Long Island is a long way from New Jersey, and the pumps are fifty feet away.

The engine is still ticking when Faber calls.

'I got my finger on the button here, McEvoy.'

'Come on, boss. I need gas,' I tell him. 'Five minutes' delay. Maybe seven if I grab a coffee. Check your doodad, there's a Texaco here.'

I imagine Faber pointing at the phone. 'Gas? You couldn't drive another four miles?'

'You pointing at the phone, Jaryd?' This pointing thing is a great needle and I am going to work it to death. 'I thought I heard a rush of air. Like a ninja thing. You a ninja pointer, Faber?'

I hear a crackling noise, like Faber's snorting into the phone. 'That little remark just cost your detective friend two degrees

164

of heat. That raincoat won't keep her warm in the freezer, especially since I got it here in my hand. What the hell were you two doing before you came over here? She's only wearing purple panties and a raincoat. Tell me why you really pulled over, Daniel.'

'I've been running on fumes for the past half-hour. The goddamn on-board computer is telling me I have a radius of two miles. So I am filling the hell up, unless you want the real cops to get hold of your steroids.'

'And?'

'What do you mean, *and*?'

'I am sensing an *and* here, McEvoy. Do you want to tell me what it is, or, should I just go ahead and turn the thermostat down as low as it can go? See if we can't freeze Deacon's lingerie right off.'

So I give him an *and*, but not the real *and*. 'Okay. All right. Take it easy. I picked up a few weapons from my locker in the bus station on the way out, and now I'm dropping them off. I bring 'em over to your place and they get confiscated, right?'

The secret to a good lie is to bury it in truth.

'What've you got there?' asks Faber, playing it cool like he could tell the difference between a Gatling gun and a Colt .45.

'I got two phasers and a fart ray. What do you care? You're getting your steroids. Maybe you should take a couple of them yourself, beef up that pointing finger.'

I can't help it. It's a curse.

'Five minutes,' says Faber gruffly, then hangs up.

I squeeze the steering wheel until the leather groans, then laugh a long, jagged laugh that chops at my throat like an axe hacking on a steak. When the fit passes, I buzz down the window and spit into the night.

You okay now? asks Ghost Zeb.

Yep. Fine. Peachy.

Just over seven minutes later, what I had to do has been done and I'm pulling around back of The Brass Ring thinking that the parking lot seems a little placid without canaries and praying I didn't get any blood on my clothes.

One of Faber's guys, Wilbur, is on the ramp cracking his knuckles, and I'm having a little chuckle over his shit-kicker name when I remember how eager Wilbur was to shoot Goran in the face. I'm thinking that Wilbur got teased a little too often in the schoolyard and is taking revenge on the world.

Wilbur throws me a nod that speaks volumes. Not good *hey, McEvoy, let's go grab a Cobb salad* volumes, more *see what I did to Goran? Well you're next* kind of volumes. I've had so many security guys giving me the hard face over the past few days that it's getting kind of comical. I wonder, is that how the world sees me?

Bald and comical, says Ghost Zeb. *That's it exactly.*

Screw you, Zebulon Kronski. Stay fucked, why don't you?

Hey, come on. I'm kidding. Can't a guy kid?

Keep a civil tongue in your head. No more bald cracks after all the money I paid you.

Understood.

It better be.

Wilbur comes down the ramp and is half trotting beside the

Hilux before the vehicle comes to a full stop. I step on the gas a little just to piss him off, then reverse to the ramp.

'What the fuck you doing?' he huffs when I step down from the cab.

'Sorry, Wilbur man. Overshot. Big truck, you know.'

Wilbur rests a ham hand on the wing mirror. 'Where's the stuff?'

That deserves an eye-roll. 'Where's the stuff? You see the two enormous white barrels in the back. What do you think?'

Wilbur pats something. Either his heart or a shoulder holster.

'I wouldn't play smart with me, Irish. I really wouldn't.'

It's too much. I can't take it. So I punch that leaning-over bastard just as hard as I can in the kidney. Something splits inside him and my injured knuckle sings like a saw-fiddle.

Wilbur goes down gasping, wishing it was five seconds ago and he had kept his mouth shut.

'You are a dick,' I say, sparing time for a short lecture. 'And a murderer. Of women. A female murdering dick. That's why I burst your kidney. And also so you won't be able to shoot me later, because of all the pain and internal bleeding.'

Wilbur chooses not to rebut, so I go on about my business.

There is a double drum caddy in the bay, which is handy. I won't even have to make two trips. I roll and grunt the barrels on to the caddy and shoulder them up the ramp.

The club is quiet now. It's a week night, so the entire zip code is still as the grave at this hour, except Wilbur, who's writhing on the ground like an ageing break-dancer. I take a deep breath and wheel the caddy into the club itself, making sure to leave the doors ajar behind me. I trundle down a hallway with red velveteen wallpaper and brass portholes. If Faber was going for the Liberace's yacht look, then he's got it spot on. I didn't notice much about the decor the last time I came in the back way on account of my body being full of all this extra electricity.

In between the portholes, the walls are lined with signed pictures of celebrities. As far as I can make out, these are stock head shots with nothing to suggest that Kevin Costner frequents The Brass Ring. This guy Faber just gets classier by the second.

I hear voices at the end of the corridor and so I trundle the caddy that way. It's either Faber down there or the cleaning staff; I am almost past caring. My entire existence is getting a little dreamlike and I feel bulletproof and doomed at the same time.

I barge through the kitchen door, barrels first, catching Faber in the middle of an anecdote. Two of his guys are gathered round laughing heartily like he's Bill Cosby in his heyday. While I'm waiting for the hilarity to end, I spot an AirPort wi-fi base station plugged into a socket by the door and I nudge it out with the caddy's wheel.

'So the guy gets off with eighteen months suspended,' says Faber, raising his hands for the punchline. 'And I get paid by all parties.' Everybody laughs on cue, and one of those ass-licking goons goes so far as to repeat the punchline and wipe a tear. Shameless.

Faber lets the laughter die to let me know how unconcerned he is by this whole thing. He deals with bigger fish than me every day.

'You finished, Jaryd?' I ask him testily, pushing the caddy to the centre of the room. 'You want to let the lady out of the freezer now?'

Faber turns around, making a big show out of being surprised that I'm even there.

'Hey, Dan. Is that the time? Shit, I've been telling the guys a couple of war stories here, forgot all about our little situation.' He suddenly spots the massive barrels in the middle of his kitchen and claps his hands. 'You brought me a present.'

I keep on pretending that I'm doing this for the money. 'You got one for me? Fifty thousand ones.'

Faber drops a huge wink at his boys. 'Yeah, sure. I got your *present* right here. Why don't we just have a look at my pills first?'

I push the caddy towards Faber's biggest guy and he has to do a nimble little shuffle to save his toes.

'Knock yourself out.'

Faber has his three guys get to work. One covers me with a pistol, another gives me the brisk-frisk while the third tips a barrel from its perch and pops the security lid. The drum's mouth glows and the guy's double chin is swabbed by crescents of blue light.

'Holy fuck,' he says. 'This shit is radioactive.'

Faber digs his arm in deep and lets the pills run through his fingers, like he's a pirate feeling up his doubloons. This is the point where my what I like to call *plan* could have been seriously derailed, but I got away with it. It was fifty-fifty and I picked the right fifty.

'Score,' he says.

'Score,' I say. 'You like MTV, Jaryd?'

I might as well needle him. We both know what's coming. At least what he thinks is coming.

Faber opens his mouth to give the word, then has a thought that disturbs him. 'Where's Wilbur?'

'Why's that, Jaryd? You told him to bring up the rear?'

'I asked you where Wilbur was.'

I shrug. 'I don't know, exactly. Not to the precise inch.'

Faber hurls a handful of pills back into the drum. 'You prick, McEvoy. He better not be dead.'

'Or what. You'll kill me twice?'

The attorney's grin is sly. 'Kill you? Why would I want to do that?'

'Because you better. I know about you and Connie, and I tried the cops once already but it didn't work. Next time I'm gonna do the job myself.'

Faber acts frustrated. 'Why are we still talking about that stripper? Screw it. I'm not wasting my time arguing with a dead guy.'

He walks to his laptop, arms swinging to let me know he means business. The guy is going to shock me again. I knew he would, he enjoyed it so much the last times.

'Why don't you lie down for a while?' he says, which sounds rehearsed, and hits return.

The bracelet's signal is activated, and on cue I fall to the ground gibbering. I feel embarrassed shaking and dribbling like that, but it should buy me a minute.

I feel a powerful urge to sit up and explain to Faber that even a child knows you can't send an internet signal without a wireless transmitter, but I swallow it down and keep spasming.

A good thing too, because a couple of seconds after I hit the floor, things start happening pretty fast.

The first sign of trouble is the elongated whip snap of a pistol shot echoing down the corridor.

That's Wilbur gone to meet his maker, I reckon.

So what? That arsehole shot Goran. Maybe he killed Connie too, so I won't be shedding any tears.

Faber jumps up on his toes like a ballet dancer.

'What the hell was that?'

'Gunshot,' says one of his guys, answering literally what he was asked.

Even though a shell has just popped outside, Faber takes time to turn on his own guy. 'I know it was a goddamn gunshot, Abner. I fucking know that much.'

Abner? Abner and Wilbur? You cannot be serious.

Abner has his gun in a two-handed grip, pointed down between his toes. It's a big gun and he's a big man, but his brow is twisted like a child's.

'I guess you prob'ly did know that, Mister Faber.'

And predictably the pointing starts. 'Go find out who fired that shot.'

Abner scoots out the door, and I am guessing he's not coming back.

I take all of this in from my low vantage point. I'm not bothering to shake any more, but no one notices. I shift my gaze to the freezer and see the needle is way down in the blue.

There isn't much time left.

A couple more shots crack outside the door and the wall thuds and buckles like a rhino ran into it.

That's Abner gone.

Two left now, including Faber. I could probably take them, but then I'd have to take whatever's coming in from outside. Better to move myself out of the equation.

I flip on to my elbows and crawl quickly towards the freezer head down like I've been taught. Faber is shouting something but it's just panic. You would think a lawyer would know to dial nine-one-one, but he's not capable of putting a plan together. I almost feel sorry for what I've unleashed on him.

Footsteps thunder along the corridor outside, moving towards the door, inevitable as a tidal wave. I pop on to my haunches and thumb the thermostat into the red, for all the good that will do. It will take minutes for this old freezer to shake itself awake. But it's better than nothing.

I snap the steel handle open and roll inside through the hiss and steam. Two seconds later, the weighted door clunks shut behind me. The sound makes me wince, but it's for the best. Inside is definitely better than outside for the moment.

Ronelle is strapped on the trolley, white as a marble statue, frosted like a birthday cake, parked carelessly in a forest of frozen carcasses.

So she's a marble statue birthday cake . . . in a forest.

Not now, Zeb. Really.

The buckles holding her down are cold and unnecessary. The detective is alive, but weak as a newborn and vibrating gently with the *thrumm* of deep cold. I throw off her straps and cover as much of her torso as I can with my jacket. Any bits sticking out, I rub briskly with my hands.

'Don't get any ideas, Ronnie,' I tell her. 'Just warming you up. No funny stuff.'

I move around the trolley and bump it over to the door with my hip so I can peek through the window. There is an emergency intercom set into the wall, and I lean over to press the switch with my forehead. Noise floods the freezer like a wave.

The porthole is frosted with crystals and streaked with grease, and it feels like I'm watching the outside world on an old gas-tube TV.

Four men have crashed into the kitchen beyond, securing the room for the arrival of the fifth. These men look good, but not great. Not ex-military, that's for sure. There are holes in their positions that a five-year-old basketball player could dribble through.

Still. In their favour, they have a pretty fair selection of guns between them. Mostly automatics, but I spot a couple of old-fashioned revolvers too.

'We're better off in here,' I whisper to Deacon, who has one eye open and is glaring at me like I'm an alien.

'McEvoy,' she chatters, much to my relief. 'I was wrong. We gotta call it in now.'

Now we gotta call it in?

'No need for that. The cops are coming soon, one way or another.'

Outside, a man trots into the room like he's coming on stage in Vegas. A big guy, face a road map of burst corpuscles, soft cap pulled down over one eye. I know who this is. We've had text.

'Irish Mike Madden,' I whisper to Deacon, who has managed to crank the other eye open.

173

'Where's my gun?' is her response to this news. Reasonable in the circumstances.

'Not here. Be quiet.'

Deacon wants to object, but she's out of energy for the moment and it is all she can do to scowl at me.

Mike Madden does a little shuffle along the carpet, all the time smiling, and comes to a stop with an arm-waving flourish.

'Counsellor,' he says to Faber, who is doing his damnedest not to fall down.

'M . . . Mike,' he stammers. 'Mister Madden. What are you . . . What brings you here?'

I love these guys. Still holding on to the civil façade when there's men dying or dead in the corridor.

Mike taps his chin, like he has to think about Faber's question.

'One of my guys is missing, laddie,' he says finally. 'I sent him on a job to a pill shop and he never came back.'

Faber straightens his tie, breathing a little better. This is all a misunderstanding.

'Mike. I know this is your town, everybody knows it. I would never . . .'

Madden talks right over him. 'I sent him to a pill shop. And here you are with a couple of barrels. Full of pills, are they?'

'Not your pills. Not yours, Mike. How stupid do you think I am?'

Mike sighs, like the truth makes him sad. 'Money makes people stupid, laddie. That's life.'

Faber scoops a handful of blue pills from the open barrel. 'Steroids is all, Mike. Just steroids. Not your territory. No profit in them hardly.'

'Is that so?' Mike dances across to the barrel, casually slapping Faber's final guy on the cheek on his way past. 'Let's have a little look-see.' He tips the barrel, sending thousands of blue pills bobbing across the floor. Faber pulls one foot up, like it's piranha-infested water coming his way.

'Whaddya know. You weren't lying. Just pills is all.'

And suddenly Madden's smile disappears. 'Open the other barrel, counsellor.'

Faber is a smart guy. He gets it then.

'Oh, Christ. I see. There's a . . . I got an explanation for you. Probably . . .'

Mike pulls out his cell phone, navigating through the touch-screen menus.

'So I'm enjoying a late-night bottle of Jameson with my little colleen, when this text message comes through.' He tosses the phone to Faber, who lets it drip through his hands a few times before he gets a grip. 'Read it for me.'

Faber reads it to himself first, and whatever blood is in his face drains out of it.

'Jesus,' he breathes. 'Oh God.'

'Out loud!' roars Mike, suddenly on his tiptoes. 'Out loud, you crooked ginger bastard.'

He clicks his fingers and one of his guys drops Faber's man with a single shot. The man dies quiet, sliding down the wall with no change of expression.

Faber drops the phone and starts crying.

'Pick it up.'

This is difficult for Faber to comprehend. All his life he's been talking people out of trouble, and now suddenly here's this immovable object.

'Pick up the goddamn phone.'

Faber falls to his knees and has to clasp the phone in both hands before he can steady it enough to make out what's on the screen.

'Now, if you'd be so kind . . .'

And Faber reads the message in a hitching voice, filled with fear and phlegm.

'I'm in a barrel at The Brass Ring. Bleeding real bad. Faber did this . . .' The lawyer stops, unable to finish.

'And . . .'

'Please, Mike. I didn't do this.'

'Read the fucking rest of it.'

Faber takes a few deep breaths. 'It says . . . It says . . .'

Mike can't wait any longer. 'It says: *If I die, kill the forker.* That's what it says. *Kill the forker.*' He laughs. 'Forker. Predictive text.'

Faber makes a desperate appeal for his life. 'There's this guy. On the floor back there. Covered in his own shit, probably. He did this. All of it.'

Mike makes a big show of looking around. 'Nope. No shit-covered mystery guy. You're in the dock for this, counsellor.'

'But he was there. You have to believe me. I'm telling you the truth.'

Mike sighs. 'This is a whole lotta hoopla for not much there-there.'

I suppose if you're as powerful as Mike, what you say doesn't always have to make complete sense, though the *hoopla there-there* phrase has a ring to it.

'Open the barrel, lads.'

Two of Mike's men yank on the lid until one of the teeth gives; the rest relinquish their grip and the barrel yawns open like a lazy crocodile. They pat around in the surface pills for a while until Mike grows impatient for his big moment.

'Tip it,' he commands.

'Don't. Please.' Faber is begging. Maybe that should give me some satisfaction, but it doesn't. Staying alive is all I want out of this.

Mike's boys put their shoulders into the barrel and it teeters past the point of no return, bouncing and skittering across the floor, spilling out a fan of pills and the corpse of Macey Barrett. He comes to rest at Madden's feet, pools of blue pills in his eye sockets and mouth.

Faber screams and screams like he's seeing his own death, which of course he is.

'Oh, please,' says Irish Mike in disgust, and suddenly there is a gun in his fist.

Faber holds up his hand to ward off the bullets, but Mike has already pulled the trigger. The bullet takes off Faber's pointing finger, then continues, barely deflected, into the attorney's heart.

Faber clutches his chest, a final scream leaking out of him, takes a step backwards on to the spread of pills. His final act is an ignominious pratfall, then he's dead on the floor.

Mike kneels beside Macey Barrett and is about to touch him, when one of his guys coughs gently.

'Uh, boss. Trace.'

Mike pulls back his fingers. 'Yeah. Good. Thanks, Calvin. Always looking out for me.'

He pockets his gun, then gives the room a quick scan, looking for cameras, I'm guessing. I draw back from the freezer porthole and squat under the glass, just breathing and waiting. Deacon is coming around now, muttering to herself, mostly stuff about me, most of it bad.

I peek through the porthole again and the only people in that room are corpses.

I see dead people, jokes Zeb.

Yep. Me too. Far too often.

You had Mike Madden out there and you never asked him about me.

There's a time and place, Zeb. And that wasn't it.

I feel a sense of victory that I'm not proud of. My plan was full of holes, but nobody fell into them. Two birds with one bullet. Faber has paid the price for murdering Connie and Irish Mike is no longer on the hunt for Barrett's killer. Home free.

That's really great. I'm happy for you.

One thing at a time, Zeb. I still got problems.

One of my problems groans and attempts to sit up. I wedge my forearm under her head and try for a tender smile.

'Hey, Ronnie. How you doing?'

'Who the fuck are you? Joey Tribbiani? And what's that weird look you're giving me?'

I drop the tender smile. 'Let's get you off that trolley, Detective. The bust of your career is outside that door.'

Deacon flaps her palm against the freezer.

'What? The locked steel door?'

178

I sit her upright, pulling my jacket tight around her shoulders.

'Have a little faith, Deacon. It's a freezer, not Fort Knox.'

There's a seal around the porthole, which peels off easily once I get a nail underneath it. Most modern freezers have a safety latch on the inside in case anyone gets trapped, but just as Faber said there's a plate welded over this one.

Still, it's just a door with a basic lock. A lot less complicated than your average automobile door.

I reach down inside my pants.

'What the hell are you doing?'

I pull out the slim jim taped to my leg. 'For your information, I'm gonna jimmy-jang the lock. Thinking ahead, Ronnie. That's the secret.'

'Yeah, you're a regular Nostradamus-seeing-into-the-future-motherfucker.'

This might not be the time to ask for a second date. I think I preferred Detective Ronelle Deacon when she was blue and frozen.

I feed the thin steel band into the door's innards through the slit vacated by the seal. A good carjacker could pop this door in under a dozen seconds, but it takes me half a minute. I feel the latch cord tugging the steel band and I can't resist a wink at Ronelle before I yank it open.

'Show-off,' she says, but she's smiling and I think that maybe there's a future where she's not trying to kill me. Maybe.

Deacon tries to slap me off, but I carry her out into the kitchen. Freezer steam floods out behind us like London fog.

'Christ,' breathes the detective, and I realise that this is probably her first glimpse of carnage. 'Whose fault is all of this? Ours?'

l prop her on a high-backed stool. 'Goran was dealing drugs,' I tell her. 'She had a scam going with Faber ripping off dealers. Faber murdered my friend too.' I clasp her shoulders firmly, making steady eye contact. 'They were always heading towards this. None of it is our fault.'

Deacon does not avert her eyes. 'I think maybe a lot of it is *your* fault, Dan. But I don't know how.'

A siren sounds in the distance. Coming closer.

'Finally, a concerned citizen,' says Deacon. 'I was starting to believe that there weren't any left.'

Bad timing, I haven't had time to drill a story into her.

'Listen, Ronelle. We have shady circumstances here. Very dubious. You have to tell Internal Affairs something they want to hear or both of us will be taking a trip to State.'

Deacon's brow furrows, cracking the ice on there. 'I gotta tell the truth, Dan. There's no other way. I'm still police.'

'There are bullets from your gun in your partner. Who's to say that you're not the bent detective and Goran died trying to take you down? At the very least your career is over for not calling this in last night. At most you get nailed for murder one.'

It makes sense, but will Deacon see it in time? That siren is awfully close.

'What do you suggest?'

Thank Christ.

'You got an anonymous tip about Faber on the DeLyne

murder, which is true. You came over to find a drug deal in progress. They got the jump on you, shot your partner and locked you in the freezer. You got out and made them pay for shooting a cop.'

Deacon's eyebrows go up and snow flutters down her cheeks. 'What? All of them?'

'Hey. You're Ronelle Deacon. You were pissed. I'd believe it.'

Deacon wrings her fingers, getting the blood flowing. 'Okay, lemme think.' She wrings for another second. 'Right, that's the stupidest bucket-of-pigshit plan that I ever heard. You know how long it's gonna take IA to tear that into confetti? What? You hate me, McEvoy. Is that it?'

'Hey, take it easy, Ronelle. I got feelings.'

'So, Officer Deacon, you bust out of a freezer in your French under things, unarmed, and kill like a hundred guys. Jesus Christ.'

The sirens are closer; I think I hear tyres squealing. 'It sounded better when I said it. You're using mocking voices and stuff.'

While she's thinking, Ronelle paws at an automatic in the sink, picking it up with fingers that are still white.

'That's probably loaded, Ronnie. Just so you know.'

She twists her frozen finger around the stock. 'Loaded. Okay. Christ, I hope my spazzy fingers don't accidentally shoot someone.'

I swallow drily. 'Okay. Funny. Now I got to get going.'

The automatic is pointed roughly at my groin. 'I'm supposed to let you walk?'

I try to look earnest and good. 'Come on, Deacon. I'm just a complication. If I disappear, all is right in the world.'

The siren is right out front. Red light swings across the roof through the blinds. I start tapping my foot; can't help it. The foot-tapping jiggles my anklet, so I quickly saw through the strap with a handy cleaver.

'You look like shit, McEvoy,' comments Deacon as I work.

'Guy tagged me when I was trying to save your life for the second time,' I say picking up Barett's phone which I have become attached to.

I hope I didn't overplay the hero thing. Doesn't matter really, because any Brownie points I might have accumulated are about to be wiped out.

'Yep, so anyways, I gotta put you back in the freezer,' I say, stuffing the anklet in my pocket.

Deacon's face says *what the fuck?*

'My plan was fine, until the last bit about you breaking out and going Rambo.'

Deacon doesn't say anything for a moment, and I'm pretty sure she's thinking about shooting me in a vein.

'You're a good cop, Ronelle. I know it. This is your chance to be a good cop again. It might cost you a few brain cells, but you can offer that up to Jesus. That's what we do in Ireland.'

Deacon mulls it over, then hands me my jacket and nods at the freezer door.

'You're right. I gotta go back in, fuck it.'

It really is the only way. If the blues find Deacon strapped to a gurney in a locked freezer, then she is totally clear. She can even claim memory loss.

'It's just for a few seconds; they're right here, and I turned the temperature up.'

Ronelle lets me hoist her back inside. 'Well turn it back down, dipshit. I hope it's not Krieger and Fortz. Those two couldn't find their dicks with a dick-o-scope.'

Dick-o-scope. Nice.

I lay Deacon on the trolley, hoping her frozen marrow doesn't snap, and strap her down just tight enough.

Before I can secure her right arm, she reaches up and catches my jaw with one shivering hand.

'I'm cold, Daniel,' she says.

'It's just for a minute.'

She pulls me down for an icy kiss. I feel our lips stick together.

'Thanks for coming back. I won't forget it. Next time I catch you for murder one, I might break it down to manslaughter.'

'Appreciate it.' It takes a lot for someone like Deacon to say thank you; I expected the barb on the end as soon as she started the sentence.

'You better get out of here before I start warming up.'

Cute.

I am out of there.

CHAPTER 11

I worked for Zeb off and on for a few years, mostly around Manhattan, and I saw gallons of Botox injected into acres of skin. The money was irregular but good, and I have to admit that the perks were exciting; only problem was, the ladies that Zeb had ministered to were not supposed to do a lot of jiggling for twenty-four hours, so things could be a little muted.

We got on okay at first. When I say okay, I mean I never had to ask more than five times for my money, and he never tried to hold back more than forty per cent. On one occasion I was forced to shake him by the collar, but that was as rough as it got. Nobody tried to rip him off either for the first year, which really pissed Zeb off; in his twisted mind, nobody ripping him off was tantamount to me ripping him off, as he was paying me for nothing. I tried explaining that I was a bit like a nuclear deterrent, but Zeb refused to see the sense in this, as it didn't align with how he was thinking. It got so that he started to pick fights with people, daring them to screw with him, or rather with me. Mostly these people were confused housewives who had never heard verbal abuse before that wasn't filtered through the TV, but every once in a while the household had its own security and I took a couple of unnecessary punches because Zeb felt the need to big himself up. It got so he took to strutting down Eighth Avenue like Tony Minero, tossing insults left and right. He barely noticed me, just took my presence for granted. One night I just stopped at the crosswalk and let him go ahead with his *motherfucker* this and *get out of my way asshole* that, until some college kid pounded him a good one in the side of the face. The kind of punch that makes everyone who sees it go *damn*.

We parted company soon after and I upped sticks for Cloisters, but after six months Zeb tracked me down and set up Kronski's Kures in the mini-mall. For almost a year he claimed the relocation was on account of me being his only friend. But one night in O'Leary's, he got so drunk that he forgot who I was and confided in who he thought I was, saying how some pusher's girlfriend in Queen's had a permanent droop on one side of her face on account of the cheap botulism he pumped into her forehead and he was hiding out here in the Styx with the big Mick until things cooled down. But then he started making good green here in Cloisters and decided to stay a while.

I don't work for Zeb any more, though he begs me every day. I just hang around with him for free. It's nice to have a whiskey buddy, plus we have this thing we do with movie references and song titles. Can be lots of fun.

I've been in worse shape, but not recently. Seems to me there was a time when I could take punishment the way a young man takes his liquor; go all night and still function at work the next day. Now I'm grunting with every step, walking like my bones are made of glass. The various tussles with Bonzo, the tuna-melt guy and Faber's goons have really taken a toll, and I wouldn't be surprised if I die earlier than I should as a direct result.

At least the book is closed on Faber, unless he can generate himself a fresh ticker. Whatever his reasons for murdering Connie, he took them to the grave. Maybe when he floats out of the Tunnel, he'll have to explain himself to St Peter. For his sake, I hope he can come up with something better than *she slapped me, Jesus.* I would pay good money to hear that conversation.

The Deacon problem is on hold. But I have a feeling that as soon as Ronnie gets bored of the super-cop tag, she'll be giving me a call. It would be nice to believe that Detective Deacon would be in my corner should I need some badge. I'll make the call if I have to, but I'm not counting any chickens. First and foremost Ronnie is a cop, and she'll uphold the law even if it means hanging her and me both.

Counting chickens? pipes up Ghost Zeb, still hanging on in there. *What the hell are you doing counting chickens?*

Don't you listen? I'm *not* counting chickens.

Counting chickens, not counting chickens, I could give a shit. All these situations you're closing the door on, what about me? I'm out there somewhere.

Probably dead.

Probably, yes. But did you ever think that I could just be maimed? I'm out there somewhere with my dick cut off, I got maybe forty-five minutes to make it to the ER for reattachment surgery.

I can't help wincing.

Okay, Zeb, okay. I'll make a few enquiries.

When?

Soon. Very soon. I just have to pick up my funds at the bus station, then square things with work and Mrs Delano.

I'm bleeding to death and you're squaring things?

If I find you, will you get out of my head?

Not only that, but I'll do all your check-ups for free.

Yeah, see that's how I know you're not the real Zeb.

My apartment should be goon-free now that Faber's breath has fogged its last mirror. Just in case there are any hostile stragglers, I dial a phoney B&E call into the local blues from Mr Hong down the hall and slip upstairs to Sofia's apartment when the cruiser whoops up to the steps.

Sofia Delano pulls open her door before the knock reverb fades and stands before me, chest heaving like she's run a mile to get there.

'Carmine,' she breathes. 'I've been waiting so long.'

I slip inside her lobby, passing close, feeling the breath from her upturned mouth on my cheek, seeing the sheen of her lipstick.

Delano reminds me of someone. Not Cyndi Lauper any more; another eighties icon. Blonde hair, blow-dried big. Striped woollen dress, leggings and ballet pumps.

Ghost Zeb puts his finger on it. *We're the kids in America, woh-oh.*

'My Kim Wilde look,' says Sofia Delano. 'You always liked it, Carmine. Remember that club? The One Eight Seven? Those were good times.'

She looks wonderful, smells intoxicating. If only I could remember the good times.

'Mrs Delano ... Sofia ... I'm not Carmine. I'm Daniel McEvoy, from downstairs. You hate me, remember?'

She takes my face in her hands. 'Not any more,' she says and kisses me hard. Not any more? Does that mean she doesn't hate me any more? Or she doesn't remember?

I don't know, and for a moment I don't care.

And even though I didn't share the eighties with this woman, I do remember the decade. And here they are, coming around again. With sweet chocolatey perfume, shoulder pads, the haze of hairspray and soft red lips. This is more than a kiss; it's a time machine.

I feel Sofia's sprayed hair scratch my cheek, and hear the moan in her throat like all her dreams have come true, and I want to weep. Is this how low I have sunk, making out with a disturbed woman?

I push her gently away, hearing the soft pop as the vacuum seal of our lips is broken.

'W ... wait,' I stammer. 'This is not right. I can't ... we can't.'

There is a bruise of lipstick smeared across her upper lip. 'Sure we can, baby. It's not the first time. But let's do it like it's the last.'

What an invitation. You could sell a movie with a tag-line like that.

'No, Sofia . . . Mrs Delano. This is not me. I mean, I am not Carmine.'

Then something unexpected. She slaps me in the face, hard. I actually rock back on my heels.

'Pull yourself together, Carmine. How many lives do you think we get? I'm forty years old next summer, and this is my last second chance. You going to break my heart again?'

I can't do it. I should, goddamn me, but I can't find the strength.

'Okay, Sofia. Okay, I get it.' I stroke her cheek tenderly. It's easy to do. Natural. 'No broken hearts tonight. I want to do it slow, take things easy. We got time, right?'

She blinks, uncertain, as though offering sex to this man Carmine is all she knows how to do.

'Time?'

'Yeah, time for romance?'

'Ro-mance?' The word hiccups in her throat. 'You *want* romance?'

'Sure. A man can change, can't he?'

'I . . . I guess.'

Whew. A reprieve, though a big, insistent part of me doesn't want a reprieve.

'Good. Great. So, Sofia, you got anything to drink?'

'I got some cough syrup. And some coffee.'

I react to 'coffee' like it's the holy grail. 'Wow. Coffee, that would be *awesome*.'

Definite overkill. I use the word *awesome* about as much as I use the word *bling*.

Sofia stumbles to the kitchen on sea legs, a bewildered smile cutting through the lipstick.

'Carmine Delano asking for coffee. My husband certainly has changed. Maybe you dumped some of that macho baggage you've been lugging around, along with the hair.'

'It's temporary,' I blurt, wanting to please her now. 'The hair. It's growing back.'

Sofia pours two mugs from the machine. 'Hair, no hair. Doesn't bother me, baby. So long as I have you. It's been hours since you left. I was starting to think I did something wrong.'

Hours? More like years.

'I . . . uh . . . I had some business to take care of.'

Sofia pushes me gently to the settee, deep brown leather, squeaks when I sit. A man could get used to relaxing in a promo sofa like this. Smells of Italian food and perfume.

'Business? Like that naked bitch downstairs? Same old Carmine.'

I absurdly defend myself. 'That woman was a detective. She was trying to kill me.'

Sofia eyes me archly. 'Uh-huh. I bet she had good reason. I know what you are, Carmine, all about your dalliances.'

Dalliances. First time I've heard that word since Ireland.

Drinking and dalliances. That's you, isn't it? That's your entire goddamn life in a nutshell.

Mother shouting that at my father, and him laughing. Scratching his chin with one hand and swiping the air with the other, trying to catch an invisible fly.

'Dalliances, eh?' he'd twitter, then do a little mocking fairy dance. 'Was this before or after the croquet?'

Back to here and now, but I'm shaking a little. 'No, Sofia. No dalliances. It's only you. You're the only one for me.'

190

It's easy to say and it would be easy to mean.

Sofia glows; she sweeps her blonde hair aside, eyes down-cast like a twenty-year-old bride.

'You mean it, baby? You mean it this time?'

'I do.' I take her hand and place it on my chest. 'Feel my heart and tell me I'm lying.'

If my heart could speak, it would say that my every word is a lie. Her husband is gone and he better stay gone, because if he comes back I might just have to kill him.

Sofia places her cheek beside her slim fingers. 'It's a strong heart, Daniel. Strong enough to protect me.'

'No one's going to hurt you now, Sofia. That guy, the Kee-rist almighty guy, he's gone for good.'

'Kee-rist almighty beep,' whispers Sofia, then falls asleep just like that.

Kee-rist almighty beep? says Ghost Zeb. *What the hell does that mean?*

I decide to think about that later; for the moment I'm thinking about how Mrs Delano just called me Daniel.

The human mind has layers, Simon Moriarty once told me. *Some of them know what's going on. Some of them don't.*

I really must call that guy.

So I do, call the guy, next evening over a late late breakfast before I head out to work. I've had eighteen hours' sleep and three square meals and I feel like it's time to solve some of my problems.

'Hey, Doc. It's Daniel McEvoy.'

Silence on the other end for a few moments, while Moriarty opens his mental filing cabinet.

'Daniel? Daniel bloody McEvoy. A blast from the past. How are you doing, Dan? Not too well, I'm guessing.'

I allow my gaze to drift out the window. There's a light drizzle coming down silver though the streetlights. Looks nice, like movie rain.

'Well, I'm noticing how nice the rain's looking, if that means anything.'

I hear the sound of a Zippo wheel spinning and it brings me back ten years.

'Noticing rain? You are truly screwed, my boy. Nine out of ten serial killers start paying close attention to meteorology just before they cut loose. By the way, you do know it's two in the morning over here. You're lucky I was up carousing.'

I'm smiling into my phone, a sucker for the old accent.

'Whatever, you arsehole.'

'Gobshite.'

'You sure you have a degree?'

'You called me, Sergeant McEvoy. What's your problem?'

'Problems, Doc. Problems.'

'Okay. Shoot, so long as you're aware I'm billing the army for this.'

Down the street a couple are arguing about something. She's big on the hand gestures, waving like a windmill. Would I find that cute or irritating? Shit, I'm already irritated.

'Okay. I've got this woman in love with me.'

'Well done. Live long, die happy.'

'No. She thinks I'm someone else.'

'Ah ... Well, sometimes secrets are a good thing. I know

that general thinking says holding things in can be damaging, but some things are better kept to oneself.'

'It's more than secrets, Doc. She actually believes I'm a different person. Her husband, I think.'

'And you're not her husband?'

'No. I'd remember.'

'Okay. I hate to diagnose on the phone, but it sounds like she's de-lusional.'

'You think so? Holy shit.'

Simon chuckles. In the tiny speaker it sounds like he's gargling tar. 'Okay. I'm re-membering you now, McEvoy.'

'What can I do?'

'Don't shatter her illusions too harshly. You could do irreparable damage. Play along for the time being, until you can get professional help.'

'That could be tricky.'

'Tricky how?'

'I think Sofia could turn violent. She's been hurt before.'

I hear Moriarty drag deep on his cigar. 'Christ, this is so unprofessional. Look, Dan, if you care for this woman, get her into treatment. Use some pretext or other, say it's marriage counselling.'

'Marriage counselling. Nice one.'

I am about to fold Macey Barrett's phone when Dr Moriarty asks a question.

'And what about you, Daniel? How are you?'

'Cracked knuckle, maybe.'

'Mentally, smartarse.'

How am I? There's a question. I'm carrying around my best

friend in my head. I'm obsessing about my hairline and I am giving serious consideration to entering a relationship under an assumed name.

'Yeah, I'm fine, Simon. Really.'

I can hear Moriarty's pen clicking on the other side of the Atlantic. 'You're lying to me, Daniel.'

'You sure?'

'Yes, I'm sure. It's all Doc-Moriarty-arsehole. Then suddenly it's *Simon*. You're trying to gain my trust by humanising yourself. Textbook stuff.'

'I am human, *Simon*.'

Another chuckle from Ireland. 'Not to me. To me you're nothing more than a few stripes on a sleeve.'

I realise that I like this guy and that it would be good to have a beer and not discuss my various hang-ups, fixations and neuroses.

'I suppose I'm trans-parent to you, Doc.'

'Absolutely.'

I take a deep breath, realising that there is no way to say what I am about to say without sounding a little section eight. 'Okay, Doc. I have this friend.'

'Really? You have this friend who can't get an erection and could I make the prescription out in your name?'

'No. Not like that. I have this real friend whose personality lives in my brain.' Shit, there, I've said it.

'You're just having conversations in your head, playing devil's advocate with yourself; everyone does it.'

'No, it's more than that. He's a real presence. He doesn't follow the rules.'

'You have rules for your imaginary friends, Dan?'

'Hey, I'm pretty sure that you're not supposed to mock your patients.'

'When you send me a cheque, you can be my patient.'

There is no point trying to outsmart this guy; he does it for a living. So I forge ahead.

'Usually these devil's advocated internal conversations happen when I want them to. They're kinda vague and in the background. But this guy, Zeb, is here all the time, distracting me, poking his nose in. Then, when I actually need some advice he disappears.'

'Is he there now?'

'No, Zeb doesn't trust doctors.'

'I see. And what does the real Zeb do for a living?'

'He's a doctor,' I say, smiling.

I hear Simon's pen clicking half a dozen times, then: 'You're not a dummy, Dan, even if you pretend to be. You know this guy Zeb is just a part of you.'

'I guessed as much. So no need for a straitjacket yet.'

'Not so long as you're in control. Lot of your murderers swear the voices told them to do it.'

'Don't worry, Zeb has been urging me to kill people for years. I've ignored him so far.'

'So far. Maybe I *should* write you a prescription. A couple of gentle antipsychotics could do you the world of good.'

I know some vets who took antipsychotics. Every one of those guys thought Tweety and Sylvester were hilarious.

'No thanks, Doc. I think I'll pass on the meds. I need my wits about me right now.'

'Whatever you say, Sergeant. Keep tabs on yourself then, if such a thing is possible, and if you find yourself sawing bodies into pieces on the suggestion of this Zeb voice, then drink a fifth of whiskey, put yourself to sleep for eight hours and call me in the morning.'

'So I'm your patient now. Should I send you a cheque?'

It's Moriarty's turn to snort. 'Yes, that's it, Dan. You send me a cheque.'

I hear another voice in my ear. A bed-rumpled female.

'Come on, Sim-o,' says the woman, not a patient, I'm guessing. 'You can't stop in the middle.'

'I better let you go,' I say.

'One of you better,' says Simon, and hangs up.

Ghost Zeb comes out from beneath the synapse bridge he was hiding under.

Shrinks, he says, and I can feel his shrug like a cool bottle of beer rolled across my forehead. *Witch doctors, every one of them.*

Cloisters' seedy street isn't too obvious as these places go. On New York's 8th Avenue you know exactly what kind of street you're walking. The flashing billboards and windows stacked high with lingerie-clothed mannequins never let you forget it. The smell of lust rises from the pavement and the door handles are coated with grease and guilt.

Cloisters doesn't have so much in the way of billboards and guilty handles. We have three gentlemen's clubs that you wouldn't know were there unless you knew they were there, with nothing but a small neon sign, square of red carpet and a velvet rope to drop a wink to those on the lookout. There are eight casinos in Cloisters, each one marked by a sign that city regulations restrict to a size slightly larger than a pizza.

After my transatlantic phone call, I take a brisk walk through the rain to the bus station to pick up my savings, then cross town to the strip and announce myself at the casino door.

'Ta-dah,' I sing, spreading my arms wide.

Jason gives me the diamond-fang smile. 'Hey, Dan, buddy. Where the hell you been? Fucking Ireland or some shit? Seriously, Victor lost his nut here yesterday. Fired your ass in absentia.'

This is bad news, but I was expecting it. You don't pull a no-show on Victor Jones and expect him to let it slide. Victor never lets anything slide.

That fucker wouldn't let anything slide at a baseball game.

I chuckle. Zeb made this pronouncement one night after Victor cut off his tab.

Jason is not expecting a chuckle in response to his litany of doom. 'I respect your balls, Dan. Chuckling and shit, showing up here like it's business as usual after missing a shift, but you're gonna have to pull some hocus-pocus outta your hat for Victor. You feel me?'

I envy Jason his ability to confidently use phrases like *you feel me* or *off the hook*, another of his favourites.

'Okay. I better get inside and grovel.'

Jason cracks his neck, which always makes me wince.

'Come on, Jason. I hate that. Do you want to give yourself arthritis?'

'Sorry, Dan. I'm aggravated. We got no customers yet, so Vic's rolling a couple of the new girls.'

Rolling the new girls is not as bad as it sounds.

Okay. Maybe it is as bad as it sounds. Just different bad.

Rolling the girls is one of Victor's favourite pastimes, and he's going to keep on doing it until one of the rolled girls goes crazy and spikes his Dom P with rat poison.

This thought brings on a dreamy sigh.

'Hey, Dan, you dreaming about *Oirland* again?'

It's Marco, the little barman, peeking out across the empty bar, smiling but not laughing because I'm a lot bigger than he is.

Then he notices my bruised face and his smile shrinks a few molars. 'Holy shit, man. What happened to you?'

'I was dreaming about *Oirland*,' I say straight-faced. 'And this guy interrupted me, so we had a talk. You should see the state he's in.' I mime drinking through a straw in the side of my mouth.

Marco wipes a glass like he's trying to climb inside it. 'You're a funny man, Daniel. Hilarious. You know I've got a weak heart, right?'

I cut him some slack with a soft smile. 'I know, Marco. Victor's in back?'

Marco wipes harder, not happy with giving bad news to big people. 'Yeah. Doing his favourite *thang*. He said to send you back if you showed up.'

'Those exact words?'

'Not exactly.'

'Give it to me straight.'

'What he said exactly was "If that Irish monkey-fucker shows up, you send him back here for a bitch slapping."'

My eyebrows shoot up to my hairline of old. 'Monkey-fucker?'

Marco almost disappears behind the bar. 'Not my words.' Then he gets brave. 'I would probably have said leprechaun-fucker, to tie in with the Irish thing.'

'Yeah, that's much better. Do me a favour, Marco. Pour me a large Jameson; I should be out in a minute to drink it.'

'You got it, Dan,' says Marco, reaching for the optic. 'I'm gonna miss you, man.'

'I'm getting fired, not dying,' I mutter and head for the back room.

The back room in Slotz is the only original part of the building. Nice little red-brick room with a row of head-height postbox windows. Vic installed a polished wooden bar in the corner that's way too big for the space, and there's an old green baize card table with brass corners wedged into the leftover room. This is where the real money is made in Slotz. The back room has been running a high-stakes game since Prohibition. To hear Vic tell it, you'd think that every New York gangster from Schultz to Gotti had lost a bundle in here.

When I push through the door, Vic is swizzling a green cocktail and treating a couple of teenage girls to a social studies lesson.

'The entire room is living history. This table. *This* exact table is fifty years old.'

The girls are nodding eagerly hoping for Vic's approval; I on the other hand have decided not to beg for my job back. I have realised suddenly that without Connie, this dump holds zero appeal for me. So I do not have to listen to Vic's shit for one more second.

'Fifty years? Back home we have fast-food joints older than that. We have bloody walls older than this entire country.'

Victor jumps. He was so into his spiel that he didn't even notice me coming in.

'What the hell?' he stammers, for some reason grabbing at his purple bowler hat, like that's the first thing a raider would go for. I notice that he's wearing a bandanna under the hat, and another stuffed into his breast pocket. 'McEvoy! You're like a case of the clap. You arrive quiet, then flare up.'

Brandi is in the room, hovering at Vic's shoulder like the spectre of death in heels, so obviously she laughs. Victor's got one of his cousins there too: AJ, a prize moron. Rumour has it that AJ once twisted a model Statue of Liberty up his arse, then tried to tell the ER doctor he sat on it in Battery Park.

'You know a lot about the clap, Vic?'

Victor sees my eyes then, and he knows I'm not here to petition.

'You want to watch what you say to me, McEvoy. I'm connected.'

I am so sick of this man. This is the man who ordered his surveillance discs wiped on the night of Connie's murder, even though there may have been evidence on one of them.

'Connected? Give me a break, Vic. Your fat arse is connected to that chair, that's about it. Your brain isn't connected to your stupid mouth, that's for sure.'

AJ is off his chair, baring his teeth, waiting on the word.

I eyeball him good. 'You better sit down, Lady Liberty, unless you got room for my foot up there alongside that statue.'

Vic waves a pudgy finger. 'Sit, AJ. This man could kill us all without breaking a sweat.'

'Maybe you're not as stupid as I thought.'

My former boss leans back in his chair, steepling his fingers, a cross between Al Pacino, P. Diddy and Elmer Fudd. 'So, what can I do for you, doorman? Before I bar you for life?'

Barred for life. Not much of a threat.

'You can pay me. It's the end of the month.'

Vic is delighted; he pokes the table with a finger. 'Yesterday was the end of the month. You didn't work the full month, McEvoy.'

Typical. 'Listen, Vic . . . Mister Jones. I had an emergency so I missed a day. And okay, I didn't call. So dock me for the time I missed and pay me the rest.'

It's not really the money. I have fifty grand plus on my person, but this piece of slime owes me and he is going to pay. One way or the other.

Vic affects a pout. 'I would love to pay you. Sincerely. But I got all my disposable cash tied up in this game with these lovely ladies.'

One of the lovely ladies simpers, like Vic's doing them a favour taking her money. The other one knows how much trouble they're in. She is pale and her fingers grip the table's edge like it's the railing of the *Titanic*.

'Open the safe, then.'

'What safe? I don't have a safe, doorman. Anybody know anything about a safe?'

I pinch my nose and breathe heavily. After everything that's happened, I am not about to be messed around by a small-time big-time wannabe like Victor Jones.

'Look, you can hang around until I finish the game. I do

good, then maybe you get paid.' Vic snaps a finger at Brandi, who takes his glass, making sure to squeak her boobs around the boss's arm while she's doing it. 'Or you can keep dropping in for a few weeks until you catch me with a couple of bucks in my pocket.'

'More than a couple. A couple of thousand more like.'

Vic shrugs like this makes zero difference. 'Whatever. Less than fifty grand, I could give a shit.'

Fifty grand. You could buy the lease on this entire club for half that.

He picks a fresh pack of cards from the table and rips off the plastic. 'Now, if you would kindly get out of my face, I got a game to play.'

Like I said, I'm not much for flashbacks, but for a second the sound of that plastic tearing has me back in a camo tent on the southern Lebanese border with Israel. There's death at our door and blast tremors rattling the tent poles, and I'm saying, *One more hand. Come on, guys, one more hand.*

Victor does a few wedge shuffles and my eyes follow the snap of the cards. One of the girls starts to cry, her bony shoulders hitching, her fake boobs bobbing like buoys in the tide.

I like that one. Buoys in the tide. Sounds like an Eagles number.

Vic's little con is as simple as it is low-down. Any time new girls come in looking to make a little money hostessing, Vic softens them up with tequila and then charms them into a few hands of poker. With Brandi looking over their shoulders and dropping her boss the wink, the girls quickly lose their first month's wages, and before they know what's happening they're toting trays for tips. Modern-day slavery is what it is.

202

'You rolling these little girls, Vic? Is this how your mother raised you?'

Vic does not bite on that hook. 'My mother was wasted by two thirty every afternoon. I raised myself. I built everything I have.'

'Let the girls go, Vic. Wipe their slate. Tell you what. You let those two out of here all square and you can keep my salary.'

I find it hard to believe that I'm saying this. Simon Moriarty would be writing *I told you so* in that little notebook of his. All capitals.

'Hey, you hear that, AJ? Big noble McEvoy, giving it up for the ladies. They only owe me a couple of weeks wages; maybe they'll win it back.'

'And maybe hell will freeze over. What do you say, Vic? It would save me having to get angry.'

Vic has an answer to that. 'Don't worry, McEvoy. You get angry and I will fucking shoot you, make no mistake. Obviously I hope it doesn't come to that.'

He's not lying. Vic shot a drunk about eighteen months ago. He didn't enjoy the intense police scrutiny and swears often and loudly that the next person he shoots is going to absolutely deserve it.

'Come on, Vic. Keep my money, let them go. They're too skinny to work here.'

'Hey!' says one of the girls.

The other pinches her friend's bare arm. 'Shut up, Valerie. The old bald guy is trying to help.'

This gets a big laugh from Vic and AJ. Even Brandi has a titter.

'Make you a deal, doorman,' grins Vic, in a good mood now. 'You wanna save these two? You wanna free them from my evil clutches? I'll give you chips for your wages and you try to win the ladies' money back.'

I should have seen this coming. This is Vic's answer to everything. He once suggested it to an IRS guy.

'Not happening. I haven't played cards since the army.'

Vic flaps his lips. 'Everything is *since the army* with you. I haven't played cards since the army, I haven't defused a mine since the army, I haven't killed anyone since the army.' He winks at Brandi, going for the big laugh. 'I hope you don't mind me saying, but you've been one boring motherfucker since you quit that army.'

AJ cracks up. Brandi actually gives Vic a round of applause.

'I'm not playing, Victor.'

'Then stop breathing my air, doorman, and let me get on with my game.'

The smarter of the girls shoots me a look of skeletal desperation. She has caught a glimpse of her future and is beyond terrified.

I grind my teeth. Another *situation* I do not want.

'Shit, Christ, bollocks. Okay, Vic. A couple of hands to get the girls clear. How far down are they?'

Vic's grin is like a smear of butter. 'Twelve hundred. Plus the vig.'

I pull out a chair violently. 'Fuck your interest. They've been here half an hour.'

'Touchy.'

'Screw you, Jones,' I say, settling into the chair. 'You're not my boss any more, so you don't get the respect you never deserved. And put out that cigar. Smoke gets in my eyes and I can't tell diamonds from hearts.'

Vic screws the fat stogie into an ashtray. 'What's the matter? You quit smoking when you left the army?'

AJ almost hacks up a lung.

'You tell your cousin to stop laughing. He might crap a statue.'

A single squeak of laughter shoots from between Brandi's ruby lips and flies around the room like a canary.

'Are we playing or talking?' says Vic, putting on his game face.

I snap my fingers at AJ. 'Gimme some chips. Two grand mixed.'

Vic clears the order with a slow blink, and soon four towers of chips list before me. I straighten them with forefinger and thumb while Vic takes a slug out of his refreshed cocktail.

'What's the game?' he asks.

'Straight poker,' I shoot back. 'Nothing wild, no wrinkles. All face down. Five and three, that's it.'

Vic nods. He's giving me some latitude because he's a player and I'm an amateur.

'Straight poker it is. Brandi, honey, get McEvoy something from the bar. What do you need? Shit, all this time and I don't even know what you drink.'

I shake my head. 'You stay right where you are, Brandi honey. I don't need you behind me feeding the boss my figures. In fact, I want to see you in front of me at all times.'

Brandi pouts, cocking her hip, boosting her breasts high with crossed forearms.

'Shit, Dan. That hurts.'

'Sure. Whatever. Also, keep that compact in your bag. You know, the one with the mirror.'

Vic chuckles, not in the least offended that I have more or less accused him of being a lifelong cheat. 'I guess you better stay where you are, honey. AJ, you in?'

'No, he is not in,' I say before AJ can answer. 'Poker is not supposed to be a team sport. One on one.'

Vic is getting a little pissed now. 'Okay, doorman. Is that it? Any more rules? Just tell me, because I don't want you bitching when I clean you out.'

'We play for the girls first,' I say. 'The smart one deals.'

'Which is the smart one?'

I nod at the terrified girl, a skinny brunette whose blotted mascara makes her look like a skull. She doesn't have the hope in her to smile.

'The one who knows how much trouble she's in. After I dig the girls out, we play for my salary.'

Vic shrugs, the magnanimous monarch. 'Green is green, doorman. The order it comes in doesn't matter to me.'

The girl deals. She's so nervous that she flips a couple of cards and has to start again. Finally Vic and I have five apiece. Too late to back out now.

I check my cards, fanning them inside the clam shells of my hands.

Two kings, not a bad start.

I suppose, Ghost Zeb grudgingly agrees. *Maybe you know what you're doing.*

Half an hour later I'm down to my last hundred bucks in chips.

Moron, says Ghost Zeb.

'Moron,' says Vic, and I cut him a suspicious look.

'What?'

'Moron,' he repeats. Obviously I have been emasculated by my unlucky streak. 'You come into my club and try to take me on. Me! Victor Jones. You know how many guys have taken a beating here?'

'It's two grand, Vic. Get a grip.'

'Two grand more that these lovely ladies owe.'

'No,' I protest. 'I lost my wages, that's all.'

Vic chews an unlit cigar. 'No, no, fuck that. You said we were playing for the girls first.'

'Those chips were my wages. Anything I won was to get these two out of the shit-pile they're in.'

AJ is snuffling and snorting, beads of sweat standing out on his red forehead. Begging to be turned loose. But Vic holds him back with a frown, magnanimous in his good fortune.

'Any way you look at it, McEvoy, these pretty things are still in the hole. You ain't saved nobody. Not since the army.'

That joke is getting old.

'I've got a hundred bucks left on the table. You never know, my luck might be about to change.'

Vic lights his cigar, twisting it slowly for an even burn. He's past pretending to give a shit what I think.

'One more hand. Why not? After today, doorman, you're

gonna have to borrow a pot to piss in. I'll give you a good rate on one of those.'

'Very funny, Vic. Let's play cards.'

It's the macho thing to say, but I don't feel very tough. Vic is crucifying me. Maybe Simon Moriarty was right and I am totally trans-parent.

A good dealer can land five cards right on top of each other so the corners match up. This girl is so rattled, one of my cards floats right off the table.

'You wanna change that, McEvoy?'

I snag the card with two fingers. 'No, Vic. I'm good.'

It's not a bad hand. Two pair. Queens and eights.

We're both in for fifty, then I tap the table and the girl slides a single card over. Vic passes his hand across his cards, like a magician. He's sticking with what he's got, which should mean that he has everything he needs, unless he's bluffing. A couple of hands back I folded on a pair of aces, lost over seven hundred dollars. I never paid to see Vic's cards, but I've seen him bluff with nothing. The problem is that when Vic has his game face on, nothing changes. His voice is steady, his features are calm, his body language says *fuck you*, no matter how good his hand. I thought I could find a chink in his armour, but I can't. My only hope is Lady Luck.

'Fifty,' I say, even though my fifth card is useless to me. Why not go for broke.

'This is going to be easy,' says Vic, pushing in a stack. 'Five hundred. You can't pay, you're gone. No IOUs here. House rules.'

'I know the house rules, Vic. You made us memorise them, remember?'

Vic relaxes a little now that the battle is won. 'AJ here can't memorise dick. That's why we call him by his initials, so he can remember his own name.'

'Maybe that torch scratched his brain.'

AJ smacks the flat of his hand on the table, but he won't move without a go from Vic.

'Okay,' says Vic. 'So you're done, doorman. Get the hell out of my club. You're barred.'

'Unless I got dollars to spend, right?'

'I don't turn down cash money. You never know, if you drop by, maybe Marcie here will give you a hand-job in one of the booths. Work off some of her debt.'

Marcie cries a river, and I reach for my wallet.

'I'll see your five hundred.'

Vic hides his surprise well. 'You sure about that?'

'What? You thought I was walking around broke? I got funds, Vic, so I see your five. You never turn down cash money, right?' I toss the bills in with a flourish.

'Never.' Vic cups his stash with two hands and pushes it all in. 'There's your five hundred, and two thousand more. You got that much walking-around money?'

I'm watching him closely. Same old Vic. I was hoping the surprise funds might throw him.

'Yeah, I got it.'

Your getaway money? Come on, Dan. Are you going to blow all that for these two airheads? They dug this hole for themselves.

I have no intention of blowing it all; just enough to clear the girls and maybe get my wages back. This pot and that's it.

'How much you got in that safe you don't have?'

Vic somehow keeps the face straight. I bet his toes are curled in his shoes.

'I got the night's float. That's twenty grand, Daniel.'

And there it is. He was all *McEvoy-doorman-moron* and suddenly it's *Daniel*. Vic never called me Daniel in his life. It's just like Dr Moriarty said: Vic's subconscious is trying to gain my trust because he's lying. Bluffing.

I realise with a rush of certainty that Vic doesn't have shit in his hand. I can win big here.

My resolve to play it safe dissolves, and in its place floats a shining Christmas bauble vision of a moment in the near future when I leave Victor Jones weeping at his own table. If I let him keep the table. This is the guy whose first thought on seeing Connie dead in the parking lot was for his own sleazy business, and I feel an irresistible urge to take that business away from him.

My poker face is nowhere near as good as Vic's, so I hide it in my hands, feigning distress.

'Twenty grand. Christ. But you're not going to risk all that. No way.'

'Maybe I will, maybe I won't.'

'Okay. Okay. I'll take five. I've got five. So that's three grand to you.'

The stash is spread all over my body. Some in each breast pocket and the rest in my socks. I empty one pocket and place the wedge gingerly on the pile, making sure Vic sees the pocket is empty.

'Sheee-it, you must be related to these dumb bitches.' Vic clicks a finger at AJ, who springs to his feet as though the gravity holding him down has been siphoned off.

'What, Vic? What? Shoot him?'

'Nope. Just open the safe and bring me the cash.'

AJ is crestfallen and actually pouts, which might make him cute if he was thirty years younger and a person was ignorant of his tryst with Lady Liberty. He trudges to the bar and successfully opens a safe hidden behind a brewery mirror.

I chuckle. 'Christ, he remembered the combination.'

Vic breaks out of his poker face for a fleeting smirk. 'It's 10–28–18–86. The date the Statue was dedicated.'

In spite of everything, I can't hold in a guffaw, and maybe for a millisecond I admire Victor Jones.

'You are an evil arsehole, Vic. But that was a good one. You'll have to change the combination now.'

Vic accepts the compliment with a royal wave, then plucks a brick of cash from AJ's fingers, plonking ten grand on the pot. 'Your three, and seven more. Now you are screwed again, Daniel. No pay, no play.'

I have him. A sense of savage victory glows like a light bulb inside my skull, and I close my mouth to stop it shining out.

Ooooh, says Ghost Zeb. *You think there's actual light shining outta your Irish mouth? I think you better phone that guy Simon.*

It's a fair point.

'Don't worry, Vic. I'm playing. I got one more pocket.'

I pull out two more wedges, each one wrapped in cling film. Any more and I have to go into my socks.

'I see the seven and raise it another three.'

Vic struggles with his expression. It's a challenge to keep the poker mask in place, and a winding vein swells between his ear and eyebrow. If he folds, he's down ten grand plus. I hear rumours that Vic owes money to some real criminals; losing ten grand could cost him a lot more than ten grand. His only hope is to bankrupt me.

'Fuck you, doorman,' he says, and is that a tremor in his voice? 'All in.' He throws in his final wedge like a grenade. 'Now go the fuck home.'

It's one of those moments that sucks the air out of a room. Whatever happens next is going to shape lives. All I need to do is up the ante by eight grand or so and I squash him. Even if I lose, I still got something. Brandi is leaning low across the table, doing her best to boob-blind me, and AJ is throwing back shots of Stoli at the bar one after the other, psyching himself up for the confrontation that is almost surely coming. I put together a quick fight plan. Soon as this is over, I deck that arsehole with my chair.

Eight grand. That's all I need. But then I flash on Vic leaving Connie out there in the rain while he cleans house. I see his fat fingers squeezing the flesh of yet another girl as he's leading her into the back room.

'Thirty-five grand,' I say, pulling the rolls out of my socks. 'And fuck you, Vic.'

Vic's breath comes hard, like he's having an attack, and to be honest I don't feel so hot myself. Both of the girls are crying now. A person would have to be deaf, blind and stupid not to realise that this can only end in violence now.

Vic's mask collapses and suddenly his face is lined like a dried fruit. 'Thirty-five grand. No way. No goddamn way.'

And I know then that Vic is screwed and that all he can do is pray that I am bluffing too.

'You done, Vic? That it?'

Vic's lip hangs fat and low like a slug. He's getting a glimpse of his own future. Come collection day, things are going to be a little tight. He can't afford to let that money leave the table.

'That cash is not mine to lose. I owe Irish Mike twenty grand.'

Irish Mike again. The man is like a cancer.

'All you have to do is buy a look at my cards.'

'I'm out. Tapped.'

I reach in for the pot, hoarding it with my arms. 'Sorry, Vic. No pay, no play.' This is fine; this will do.

Vic watches the pot move across the table like it's his life's blood draining away.

'There must be some way to work this out. I can owe you.'

'Not an option. Your rules.'

'I can kill you.'

'You can try. Bigger men than you have tried. Go for your nine, see what happens.'

Vic bought a nine millimetre because that's what the gangsters rapped about. I suspect that's because of the easy rhyme.

'It's thirty grand just to see your cards. This is Cloisters, for Christ's sake. Where am I going to get that kind of money?'

It's laughable really. Has this man never heard the word irony?

'Vic, you've been rolling girls back here for years. Every one of them begged you for a little leniency. You screwed them all. Cheated them, then screwed them.' I pile up the cash and chips. 'You still owe me for the chips. That's four grand give or take. And I'll take, if you don't mind.'

Vic's poker face has collapsed in on itself, and in its place is raw desperation.

'Fuck you, doorman. I'll see you. Let me see those cards.'

'Show me your money.'

Vic wrings his hands, and the chains around his neck jangle. 'I got the club.'

Bingo.

'You don't even own this fire hazard, shithole.'

Vic does not dispute my description. 'I got a twenty-year lease. That's gotta be worth fifty grand.'

'Yeah? And I got a shoe that's worth half a mil.'

'Come on, Daniel. I'll throw in the lease for a look-see.'

I mull this over. 'If you win, you cut these girls loose anyway. And if you lose, then this club and every stick of furniture and bottle of booze in it belongs to me. I don't want any haggling; this isn't a divorce.'

Vic nods, not able to speak the words.

I push the pot back in. 'Show me the lease.'

Brandi hurries to the open safe and fishes about. She can see where this is going. In two minutes there could be a regime change around here. She returns with a manila envelope tied with string.

'This it?'

Vic looks like he's going to puke. 'Yeah.' And then adds, 'Bitch.'

Brandi is aching to respond; it's in the square of her chin, the flash of her tawny eyes. But this deal is not sealed just yet. No one outside the game speaks, because this is one of those situations that will be talked about for years whatever happens, and details are important. Also the whole thing has an unreal quality about it, like something out of a TV show, and not the good ones with budget behind them; the afternoon reruns from the seventies with stereotype villains and a cheap set that wobbles every time a door is closed.

I check the document. Most of it is legalese; could be a guarantee for a deep-fat fryer for all I know. Even if it is legal, the entire situation is probably bullshit that any halfway-decent attorney would tear apart without spilling his latte.

In spite of all that, I say: 'Okay. Looks good. I accept the wager.'

A little formal, but it's that kind of night.

Vic's jowls are shuddering. 'Show me, goddamn you, doorman.'

Calm drapes me like a shroud and I know the club is mine.

'Two pair,' I say, flipping the cards. 'No bluffing on this side of the table.'

Vic doesn't bother with his cards. He's screwed, and killing a few people is the only way out.

His nerve-clumsy fingers crab down his body towards the nine in his belt. He's way too slow. I reach across and crush his hand in mine. Brandi puts him away with a vicious elbow to the side of his face. That girl changes allegiances in a heartbeat. No, that's wrong. Our girl Brandi only has one allegiance. Vic slides off his chair, moaning, blood pouring from a cut above his nose.

AJ is moving, but I have so much adrenalin in my system that he might as well be wading through mud, coming around the side of the table at my ten o'clock with a look on his face that's more animal than human.

I draw my little Glock 26 and put a shot in the bar mirror over his head. Fragments rain down spectacularly, glittering icicles, slicing AJ's neck and hands.

I don't have to say anything. Even AJ is not dumb enough to go up against a gun. He lies on the floor and starts crying.

I turn to Marcie and her friend. 'Go now. Don't ever come back in here. Stay off the strip.'

They kiss and hug me for a minute, like I'm an old rock star.

'Thanks, Daddy,' blurts Marcie. Then, 'Oops. Sorry. I mean thanks, mister.'

Then they're gone, skittering across the casino, sandals slapping the floor.

'Thanks, Daddy,' says Brandi, imitating the California/MTV twang that all kids speak with these days, then she cracks up laughing. 'I don't believe this, Dan. You own the club.' She stamps the heels of her Catwoman boots with sheer joy. 'That asshole's time has come. I should crack his skull for all the shit I've had to put up with these past months.'

'Don't crack anything yet, Brandi. Vic hasn't signed the lease over.'

'Hmm,' says Brandi.

She rouses her ex-boss with a sleet of ice from a steel bucket. As soon as he signs, she cold-cocks him with the bucket.

'Finally this club is going to rock,' she sings, pouring herself a healthy shot of bourbon. 'We can get some professional girls working in back. Maybe cut a deal with Irish Mike for some product. Make us some serious money.'

I can see I'm going to have staff problems.

*　　*　　*

Jason shows Vic and AJ the door with unseemly glee. He actually sings them out using the tune from 'YMCA' and his own lyrics:

> 'Get-the-Fuck-Out,
> You pair of assholes.
> Get-the-Fuck-Out,
> And don't come back here!'

I'm impressed. I haven't seen Jason this happy since his signed Lou Ferrigno T-shirt arrived.

News spreads across the club like electricity across water, spasming everyone it touches. Pretty soon the entire staff are gathered outside the back room waiting for some kind of pep talk.

Talking to staff is not my area. *Having* staff is not my area, for Christ's sake. *Travel light* has always been the code I live by, and yet somehow here I am with a casino and a dozen people depending on me for a living.

My transplants are itchy.

Thank God the wages were paid yesterday.

What about me? Ghost Zeb pitches in. *Don't forget about me.*

And Zeb is still Irish Mike's captive. Irish Mike who collects a little tribute every month from Slotz. It seems every time I crawl out of no-man's-land, the earth tilts and rolls me back in.

I hear Brandi's steel heels clacking across the casino floor and I decide to face the music before she launches into another tirade. I rise, check my skullcap in a remaining shard of busted mirror and duck under the door frame to meet my public.

It's a weird feeling to have subordinates smiling at you; didn't happen a lot in the army. Mostly in the army people muttered *gobshite* under their breath when I was dishing out orders. But here, all I'm getting is happy faces.

Jason is still riffing on 'YMCA'.

> 'Dan-Mac-Evoy,
> Is fucking awesome,
> Dan-Mac-Evoy,
> Kicked Victor Jones' goddamn ass!'

He abandons the song's structure for the last line, but nevertheless his efforts earn him an enthusiastic round of applause.

'Okay,' I say, forcing a smile. 'Okay. I thank you, Jason. The Village People thank you.'

More laughing. Marco tickles Jason in the ribs, which opens my eyes about a couple of things.

'For tonight, we do everything as normal. Except the booths; no more hands-on in the booths. Anyone has a problem with that, talk to me later. Also, anyone working off a debt, you don't owe me a dime, so from now on we all get paid.'

A couple of smiles from those no longer in the hole, but the hands-on girls don't seem too thrilled.

'If you get the opportunity to piss off Victor Jones, do not take it.'

'Too late,' chortles Jason, accepting multiple high fives. High fives? Christ, these guys are happy.

'Don't take it, because I don't know how legal that poker game was.'

'Legal?' says Jason. 'Vic's been rolling girls for years back there. How legal was that?'

This is a good point.

'You know any good lawyers, Danny?' continues Jason.

Sure he does, says GZ. *'Cept Danny here has a tendency to get lawyers shot dead.*

Marco trots across the floor, bearing a large Jameson on a scarred martini tray.

'Here you are, Dan. You earned it.'

I accept the drink gratefully. The Irish whiskey is smooth going down, but has an aftershock like a jolt from a defibrillator.

'Back to work everybody, enjoy the new management while it lasts. I need to think for a while.'

Brandi positions herself at my side. 'That's right, people. You heard the boss: back to work. We need to negotiate the booth action.'

Looks like I have a second in command.

First thing I do in Vic's office is to kick Brandi out; the second is to rip down the porn. It's not that I find naked women offensive; it's just that I prefer the real thing. Also the pictures remind me of the previous occupant, and all the acts he claimed to have performed with the various club employees. Not images you want popping into your head in the course of a work day. Plus if Vic does manage to legal me out of here, I would like out of sheer vindictiveness to mess up his system as much as I can before he does it.

I don't know how Vic got anything done. His work surface is a jumble of magazine towers, burger cartons and wadded foil wrappers. There's a trash can in the corner that looks like it exploded some time in the nineties, and the window blinds are streaked brown and yellow from decades of cigar smoke.

I wipe the boss's chair off and sit down, and that's about as far as my plan extends.

Adjust the chair.

It's a nice touch. I lower the chair six inches so Vic will get an unexpected little shock. Little nuggets like this keep a man going.

So sit down, and then what? Payrolls, overheads, rent, booze orders, cash deposits.

My transplanted follicles are begging for a scratching, something Zeb forbade me to do.

I didn't employ five students and spend eight hours separating your follicles to have you scratch the little bastards out again. No touching for a month.

Hands flat on the table, I tell myself. Do not touch the new hair. It's hard to believe how difficult not scratching is. I've waded through plenty of hard and distasteful tasks in my careers, but right at this moment, keeping my palms glued to the desk ranks right up there with any of them. Including latrine digging in the Lebanon.

I try to focus on something else, and the first thing that pops into my head is: *Kee-rist almighty beep.*

What did Sofia mean by that? Where did the beep come

from? There was no beep mentioned the first time around. Where the hell do you even hear a beep these days? Maybe there was a car passing by.

Or maybe . . . Something almost occurs to me, but I don't let the thought materialise fully in case there's something to it. I can deal with this eventuality if it becomes a possibility.

I follow the cable across Vic's desk and unearth the phone beneath a pyramid of ledgers. There's no one at the number I'm calling. Of course not, it's my own number. I count the rings until my answer machine cuts in, then punch in my password.

One message.

Hey, guy. Doorman guy. Listen, you probably don't remember me, you get schmucks all the time, right? Kee-rist almighty, I hate machines. Okay. Anyway, listen . . . Oh, this is Jaryd Faber, by the way, the lawyer you ejected last night. Deservedly so, I might add. I got your number from Vic, and the thing is that I enjoy Slotz, the club, shithole though it may be. Passing a few hours with the cards and the babes. I don't want to give that up, so I just wanted you to know that I smoothed things over with Vic, what a prince, and I'm back in. In case you see me before you see him, no need to throw a punch. What do you say, let bygones be bygones? Live and let live. Maybe I can buy you a drink or a new suit. Okay? We straight? No hard feelings. I hate saying fucking sorry for anything, but there it is. Accept it or not, you should be fucking delighted by the way, if you knew who I was and what I could do to you. Kee-rist almighty.

Then the tape runs out and there's a beep.

Kee-rist almighty beep.

I hold the phone at arm's length, like it's lied to me.

Sofia heard my answerphone. Faber was never at the apartment. I set the cops on the wrong man.

He was the right man for the cops, says Ghost Zeb. *Just the wrong man for killing Connie and trashing your place.*

And he's dead now. It's my fault.

No arguing with that.

So who did kill Connie? Who wrecked my apartment?

A shadow falls across my face and I look up.

'Well it's about time,' says Irish Mike Madden. 'I've been chasing your pale arse all over town.'

CHAPTER 12

Irish Mike stands framed by the doorway, like it was built for the purpose. He is a big man, huge, with whiskey veins popping in his nose and cheeks. His teeth are crooked and cracked from a hundred bar fights and he smiles broadly, displaying them like medals. He sports a soft fisherman's cap, worn rakishly to one side with a shamrock pin on the peak. And when he speaks, his accent is more Hollywood Irish than a living dialect.

Irish Mike. A Mick who has never been to Ireland. An immigrant who never emigrated. A plastic Paddy who learned all he knew about the old country from grandma's stories and *Boy's Own*.

'Daniel McEvoy,' he says gently, shuffling into the room, like a crooner about to break into a number. 'A hard man to find.'

'Not for my friends.'

Madden is all leprechaun charm. 'Are we not friends then, Daniel?' His eyes are dull green, and his skin reminds me of a plucked chicken.

I am too old for this.

'Cut the shite, Mike. What do you want?'

Mike chuckles fondly. 'Shite. I like that.' He leans against the wall and it creaks. 'I want the money you owe me.'

Groan. He isn't even here for me. I'm a bonus.

'Vic owes you money, not me. He owes me money too, but out of respect for you and your organisation, you can collect first.'

Mike is a little surprised by this backchat, but amused too. 'Thanks, McEvoy. Very Catholic of you. But I'd rather *you* pay.'

'Not the way it works, Mike. Even God can't transfer debt. I don't owe you a cent, and if you don't stop weaving it into the conversation, I'll squeeze my way through all that fat on your shoulders and break your thick neck.'

Might as well try bravado, see if it works.

If it was fear and submission I was hoping for, then my bluntness does not have the desired effect. Mike Madden looks tired and resigned, like he is so fed up of doing things the hard way and why can't it just be easy for once.

'Righto, laddie. I hear you. Now you listen to me. I've been searching for something.'

'Why don't you ask the universe? Seems to work for a lot of people. That's a secret, by the way.'

Madden grinds his teeth. 'You know what I'm talking about.'

We both know where this is going.

'I don't know, Mike. Believe me. But I know how you search for things.'

Mike spreads his hands wide. 'Couldn't be avoided. The disk could have been in your apartment.'

I am surprised. 'A disk? A bloody disk. What do I look like to you? Jason goddamn Bourne?'

Mike Madden hooks the flap of his tweed sports coat over the revolver at his belt.

'Any road, laddie. You're going to have to quit work early tonight.'

He's right. I can't see any way out of leaving here with him.

'I have a gun too, you know.'

'Maybe, laddie. But I have several. One hostile move from you and the floors run with blood. Wooden floors, though, so at least the blood will wipe off, if you get to it quick.'

I place my gun on the desk. 'No one has said laddie for a hundred bloody years, you phoney.'

'My heart is Irish,' objects Mike, worried more by the insult than the weapon.

'Your heart is clogged with bacon and beer and will drop you in your tracks any day now.'

Which is an unusual thing to say to a person you just met.

Two freckle-faced potato-head types squash themselves into the doorway, fumbling guns from their pockets. I know them both from Faber's kitchen.

'You put that gun back in the drawer, laddie. Or my boys will execute everyone in this club.'

That's what I thought. I glare at Madden, so the murder in my eyes is all he can see.

'If I were like you, Mike, if I didn't care about those people out there, then you would be dead right now. I just wanted you to know that and show a bit of respect.'

Irish Mike actually winks. 'Point taken, laddie. Now come over here and let's pretend we're friends.'

*   *   *

225

Mike takes my phone, then we stroll out of the office and across the casino floor like a couple of swells, and consequently none of his four escorts are forced to shoot anyone. Jason is ready to fight, chest out, arms dangling, but I calm him with a lateral two-fingered slice, which sounds a bit complicated but is one of our door signals. Doesn't matter how big your pecs are, bullets cut right through.

'It's okay, Jason. Hold the fort, I'll be back in a few hours.'

'You sure, boss?'

'Yeah. Me and Mike have a little business to discuss.'

Mike has an R-Class Mercedes Benz waiting at the kerb, and we wait an embarrassing few minutes while two of his laddies squash themselves into the rear seats.

I wink at Mike, since he's a winky guy. 'You're one hell of a mob boss. Two of your boys in the baby seats.'

Mike is prepared to argue that one. 'You think I should have brought two vehicles? What about the environment? What about my carbon footprint, laddie?'

'Laddie? You really should drop that. It is too hilarious.'

'In the car,' says Mike straight-faced. I can see I'm wearing him down.

We drive across town and I can't get to grips with the fact that it's all over for me. Once we get wherever we're going and Mike Madden ascertains that I do not in fact have this mysterious secret-agent-type disk, then he will most likely shoot me in the heart.

A disk? This is beyond weird. What the hell is Zeb doing with a disk? All he knows about computers could be written on one of those horse pills he sells to irritable-bowel patients, or the stop-go crowd, as he sensitively refers to them.

Nearly dead, I think, trying to nail the idea home. Nearly dead now.

But no sickening feeling of dread seeps through. Even the thought of torture to come doesn't penetrate my calm.

That's because I don't believe any of this. This week has been too bizarre to be real. My brain is waiting for me to wake up in a tangle of sweat-sheened sheets. You can't go from doorman to superman in a week, not if you want to survive. I do want to survive, but I can't see how I'm going to manage it.

We pass Chequer's Diner and the park. I see Carmél, the waitress, joshing it up with a customer, a guy in a hunter's cap. He swats her behind and she pours him a refill, smile bigger than a slice of melon.

I didn't know there was a backside-swatting option.

Maybe there wasn't for me.

Barely ten p.m. and already the streets are drying up. Cloisters is a daytime town. Leafy suburbs and four-wheel drives. Wooden houses filling their lots right to the fences, and expansive parks with soft-fall areas for the little kids. Our sordid world fires a shot across the bows of decency once in a while, but according to the *Cloisters Chronicle*, this small town has the third lowest crime rate in the country, and the second highest literacy rate. It's nice to live in a place where people still prefer books to TV.

Ghost Zeb doesn't let me get too deep into the maudlin. *It's a bit late for community spirit, partner. Don't tell me, if you survive the night, then Slotz gets turned into a soup kitchen and*

227

St Daniel spends his days in a soutane dispensing homely wisdom with every bowl of chowder.

'Chowder?' splutters Irish Mike. 'Jesus, laddie. Don't crack up yet; the night is young.'

Thinking aloud again. Bad sign.

I really wish that man would stop with the *laddie* bit. It's offensive. Maybe a sharp elbow in the ribs would knock the leprechaun out of him, but then I might not reach journey's end alive and find out what happened to Zeb.

Very good point. Excellent in fact. Hold on to that.

'Where are we headed?' I ask Mike pleasantly. You never know, he might tell me.

'Shut the hell up, McEvoy.'

Then again . . .

We don't drive for that long. Nowhere is too far away in Cloisters. On our short trip we pass eight churches and three patrol cars. God and guns, that's what we put our faith in here. Red bulbs buzz overhead, stretching down through the blocks like landing lights.

Pretty soon we're pulling around back of a familiar strip mall. Zeb's place. Last time I was here, I was loading a corpse into a trunk. It makes sense to finish things at the clinic. A couple of bodies in a burnt-out fire trap would have accidental death written all over them.

'End of the line, laddie,' says Mike, and I feel each stone crunch under the Benz's tyres as the vehicle slows.

Maybe, I think, suddenly gripped by the absolute certainty that if I go into that building on Mike's terms I am dead. *But not the way you expect it, laddie.*

PLUGGED

What I'm about to do doesn't seem part of the real world. It's one of those ideas that generally would never make it past the good-sense filter in my head, but for the past few days that filter has been switched off. And when a notion like this occurs to me, I fear the switch may be jammed.

So. Two men in front, two behind and Irish Mike to my left. All armed, all dangerous. But all also pretty confined in their movements and probably not expecting me to buck such superior numbers.

If I am going to act, it needs to be right now, before the seat belts come off. I snort a few breaths to psych myself up, then make my move.

Okay. Five targets. Here we go.

First I give Irish Mike the heel of my hand in his windpipe; that should keep him gasping for five minutes. His eyes bug out like he's been shot in the arse with a harpoon, a vision I will hopefully have a chance to play back for Jason. He loves that kind of thing.

The guys in the back are first to react, so I reach under the middle row seats, yank the adjustment bars and, using my legs as pistons, drive them into the men behind. The seats slide back smoothly on their rails; God bless German engineering. Shins splinter, and maybe an ankle. One guy's head cracks the rear window. No weapons drawn as yet.

Part of me feels like I'm watching this happen. It's as though someone else is taking decisive action and I'm somehow observing from a distance and not altogether approving of what's going on.

Still two guys in front.

I reach past Irish Mike's spasming torso and flick the seat levers on the front seats. Shifting my weight forward, I slam the seats till their hinges pop, pinning Irish Mike's men to the dash. One still has an arm free to reach for his gun, so I dislocate the shoulder's ball-and-socket joint with a punch in the armpit.

This is working out pretty well, all things considered. My giddy side wants to giggle, but I choke it down. Later for the girlishness.

The Benz fills up with groans like we're under water, and there's a sea anemone of blood on the windscreen. We roll ten feet and one wheel mounts the kerb, swatting a trashcan.

I give Irish Mike one more whack because he's such a dick, then I'm out of the vehicle, sprinting for Zeb's back entrance. My boots crunch on the loose stones and there's a cold mist on my face that tastes like life. I relish the movement and wetness for a moment until I reach the delivery door and I need to concentrate once more.

All the guns I own, and not one of them in my possession.

The door opens inwards and there's yet another of Mike's potato heads, coming wide-eyed to investigate the trashcan ruckus. This guy I almost feel sorry for. His gun is dangling by his side and I'm bearing down on him, snarling like an angry bear.

He manages an *oh* before I tuck my head under his arm and tackle him into the shop. The *oh* shoots up a couple of octaves, then we're halfway across the room. The guy's toes are dragging the floor and his elbows beat a tattoo on my back, for all the good it does him. Maybe if he had the wits or time to use his gun . . .

No wits and definitely no time.

'Mother,' he says. 'Mudda . . .'

Swearing or calling for his mom. Who knows.

A wall rears and I put him into it. Through two layers of Sheetrock, a timber frame and neatly on to the dentist's chair. Can't be good for a person's insides. Still, better to be safe than sorry, so I scramble through the jagged hole and clang Mike's moaning man on the temple with a handy rinsing pan.

No more moaning. No alarm either; an alarm would have been nice.

Wait. There is moaning. Behind me in Zeb's homeopathic store.

It's me, idiot. I am alive.

Zeb. No way.

Mike's man surrenders his weapon without a struggle. A nice shiny Colt .45. Seven in the mag, one in the pipe, presuming this guy, let's call him Steve, presuming Steve keeps his weapon loaded.

'McEvoy, you bastard!'

A roar from outside. Irish Mike has recovered quickly and is done with *laddie*.

'Come out, McEvoy.'

Good. That's good. They don't want to come in. There's still a slim chance. Of course I should have killed them all, and then the chance might have some weight to it.

I tumble through a haze of chalk and sawdust back into Zeb's unit. There is blood on the floor, glistening in the tube light, tracked in long arcs across the carpet and concrete. The shiniest track leads to a shivering shape in the corner. It's my friend

Zeb, taped to his own office chair. They've been playing human pinball with him.

Zeb's eyes are half closed, there's a bruise covering most of his face and blood drips from his fingertips. His crafty eyes are shrouded by bruised lids, and of his sharp hustler features there is no sign. He looks bad and probably feels worse, if he's feeling anything at all.

I spin the chair to face me.

'Zeb? Tell me, quick. What did you do?'

''Bout time,' Zeb spits through blood bubbles. 'Paramol, ibuprofen. Under the safe.'

I shake him and a cut under his eye weeps blood. 'No. Tell me. What the hell is the disk?'

Zeb coughs and something whines in his chest. 'No disk. All bullshit. Come on, Dan. Pills.'

This is how it gets. After such a beating, pain is the only thing in Zeb's life. He doesn't care about living or dying. Just pain.

'Okay. Okay.'

I pick through the bottles under the safe. Most of them have handwritten labels. Cheap generic pills. Zeb making a buck any way he can.

'Five minutes, Mike,' I shout at the ceiling. 'Five minutes to find this goddamn disk.'

No answer for a moment, just dragging footsteps and the clink of metal.

Then, 'Five minutes, McEvoy. I hear any sirens and I burn this place to the ground.'

Great. I have three hundred seconds and nothing to bargain with.

232

Paramol. I find a bottle and run a finger along the instructions.

'Fuck the dosage!' howls Zeb. 'Give them all to me.'

Not happening. In Zeb's state he would chew those things
until his heart went asleep.

I pop the bottle, shake out a double dose and Zeb eats them
out of my hand like a pony chewing sugar lumps. By the time
I've torn the tape from his wrists, my restored friend is enjoying
a little chemical calm.

'Where were you, man?' he sobs, then finishes with a jagged
giggle. 'I've been broadcasting. Sending out signals. Holding
complete conversations with you. Couldn't you hear me call?'

I didn't hear shit, says Ghost Zeb.

'I heard you, brother,' I say. 'I'm here. Now you've got to tell
me what you did.'

'I stayed alive. That's what I did. Not proud, but I did it.'

I shake him gently. 'What did you do? Come on, Zeb, tell
me.'

Zeb blinks like he's about to nod off. 'I did Mike Madden's
hair. Like I did you, Dan. Sweet set of transplants.'

Hair transplants! No way. Not all this.

'Asshole's paranoid, let me tell you. Brought in students from
China to assist, so they wouldn't know who he was. Little hands
they had, did lovely work. In six months you'll never know.
Mike will have a head of hair that would make Pierce Brosnan
crap himself.'

Time is a-wasting. 'Lovely work. Great. So what's the problem?'

Even with a mashed face Zeb manages a guilty expression.
'It was an opportunity. I couldn't pass it up.'

From outside, 'Two minutes, McEvoy. You better pull the rabbit out of the hat, laddie.'

Zeb chuckles. 'Laddie. Always with the laddie. You Irish, all retards.'

'What opportunity? Zeb, these people are going to kill us.'

'Not you, Dan. Not you, my big pet Schwarzenegger. I bet you've fucked up a few of them already.'

He has a point. 'Maybe. But why are they after me, Zeb?'

Zeb studies the blood on his fingers; no clue where it came from. 'I told Mike I filmed the procedure. Said I'd put it on YouTube. The Irish in New York would piss themselves. You should have seen him during the operation: big baby cried like a . . . baby. Wouldn't let me smoke or anything.'

'That is unbelievable.'

'I know,' said Zeb thickly. 'I'm always careful with the ash.'

'Not the cigarette. You tried to blackmail a crime lord?'

'Hardly a lord. What has he got, like a dozen men? Only twenty grand, that's all I asked for. Twenty grand to destroy the disk. 'S a bargain.'

'But there was no disk.'

Zeb hiccups and blood rims his gums. 'Course fucking not. Do you see any cameras? It only occurred to me later.'

I grit my teeth. 'And when did you tell Mike that I had the disk?'

Zeb wheels himself backwards. 'Two days, Dan. For two days I swore that it was all a lie. Two fucking days with the teeth-punching and the head-banging against the wall. Some fucking warehouse in Ackroyd. There's pieces of me all over that shit-hole.'

'Then you told Mike that I had it.'

'Yeah, I said that.' Zeb's chin drops to his sternum. 'What else could I do? You're a tough Irish motherfucker, Dan. I knew these whiskey gangsters couldn't drop you. No way. You'd kill them all and save me. It was my only hope.'

This is a lot of talking for a man with broken bones and missing teeth, and Zeb collapses into a spasm of wet coughs.

'Idiot,' I shout at his shuddering frame. 'For eight hundred years all we Irish have had is our pride, and you try to strip it away from a dangerous man.'

Zeb spits blood and a tooth. It sits like an iceberg in the sunset sea.

'A mistake, Dan, I see that now. But don't let me die here. Work something out. Play the Celtic card.' Zeb is crying, wringing his hands.

The Celtic card. I do have one up my sleeve. Maybe.

The front door booms as a forearm is repeatedly bashed against it. Lights flicker with the force. I'm guessing that the five minutes are up.

'To hell with both of you,' calls Irish Mike Madden. 'To hell in flames.'

Orange flickers beyond the blinds. Could be a cop car; more likely a makeshift torch. Mike is going to burn us out.

I rack my brain for the thread of an idea. Something to reel sanity back in. Nothing. Just more lunacy.

Concentrate really hard and teleport. Dig an underground tunnel. Call the cops.

'Brite-Smile,' says Zeb.

Bright smile? Or Brite-Smile. Of course. Go through the

dentist's where I deposited Steve. I'm a little embarrassed that a punch-drunk surgeon came up with that before me.

I take two steps towards the jagged hole before the breeze chills the sweat on my forehead. There's someone in there.

Then a voice. 'Steve's out cold. McEvoy took his gun.'

Steve? No way.

Irish Mike calls from outside: 'We got the exits covered, McEvoy. You try to run and you're dead.'

Maybe on my own I could make it, but not hefting Zeb.

I tap a finger on my temple, trying to focus. 'Okay, Mike. You win. Let's talk.'

Close quarters is my speciality. But I need to get them close before I can be special.

Irish Mike mulls this offer over for a minute. 'Very well, laddie. Throw Steve's gun next door, and your shoes too, then go stand in the corner.'

Shoes? What's that all about? What does he think, I'm a sole ninja?

I toss the Colt through the hole, and my boots, then traipse into the corner behind Zeb, feeling like a naughty schoolboy. I bet Mike would be an arsehole to work for.

'Pussy,' says Zeb, his voice barely more than a whisper. 'I held out for two days.'

If his ear was not crusted with blood and mucus, I would smack it.

'You shut up or pass out and let me handle this.'

'Yeah, maybe you can take off your pants. That'll teach 'em.'

Zeb never lets up. At least when he was in my head I didn't have to look at him.

And that is my best friend. Christ.

Irish Mike comes in the back door, flanked by two of his lieutenants. One is hobbling and the other is sporting a nose that wouldn't look out of place in a boxing ring. Mike himself wears a sunburn of anger. A little less cocky, though, I think. They shuffle slowly forward through the blood tracks and the supplement boxes, never taking their eyes off me. A third heavy appears at the hole in the wall, squinting down the barrel of a machine pistol.

Mike swallows and gags. 'You prick,' he says, gingerly massaging his throat. 'Who hits people in the neck? What kind of person are you?'

I don't answer. What's the point?

After a minute's scowling, Mike is done feeling sorry for himself.

'I'll live, I guess.' He lights a cigarette with a long wooden match, sucking hard, bending the flame. 'So, McEvoy, where's the disk?'

Zeb is whimpering softly; maybe he has the right idea. There are three criminals pointing weapons at us and I don't have any good news for them. We are flanked in a small room with no hope of escape except if these people are sufficiently dim to relax their guard again.

'Here's the thing, Mike. There is no disk. Never was.' I can't resist rapping Zeb's crown. 'This gobshite tried to bluff you, then dragged me in when negotiations turned painful.'

Mike conducts with his cigarette. 'Yeah, see that's what the doc told me shortly after he told me there *was* a disk. So what's true and what ain't? I can't tell.'

'Trust me, Mike. I'm Irish. *We're* Irish. I swear on the tricolour there's no disk. This dick wouldn't know how to use a camera.'

Mike reaches under his soft cap, scratching his head. 'That's touching, laddie, the Irish connection, but you know as well as I do that the Gaels have been cutting each other's throats for centuries. It's gonna take more than that. So what else have we got in common?'

'We got that itch,' I say, pointing a finger.

Mike whips his hand down like he's been slapped by a nun. 'What itch? What the hell are you talking about?'

'Is that what this is all about? Irish Mike Madden got some new hair and he's feeling a little sensitive about it.'

'Fuck you,' shouts Mike, then dissolves into a racking cough. Those neck jabs really take it out of a person.

'Come on, Mike. This is the twenty-first century. Surgery is a positive thing. It shows you care about your appearance. A hair transplant today is like a barber-shop shave fifty years ago. If you can afford it, do it.'

''Zactly,' mutters Zeb. 'That's what I've been saying.'

It is exactly what he's been saying. I'm just regurgitating the spiel that Zeb sold me.

'No one cares, Mike. You know how many Americans had surgery last year? Have a guess; go on, *hazard* a guess.' I don't wait for a guess, in case Zeb gave Mike the speech too. 'Twelve million. Can you believe that? Twelve mill-i-on. Chances are at least one of your boys had liposuction in the past month.'

The beefcake on Mike's left blushes a little, then points his gun at my forehead.

Mike pulls himself together. 'Yeah? What would you know about it?'

'I know about it,' I shoot back. 'Because I have that itch too.' It's time for the cap to come off. I try to do it nonchalant, like I show people all the time. I peel off the hat and stand there in all my transplanted glory.

Mike squints a little, then beckons me forward under the light. I oblige, tilting my head so the shorter guys can get a look.

'I gotta say,' the boss says finally, 'that's not half bad.'

'You should have seen him six weeks ago,' grunts Zeb. 'Fucking cue ball. Now those hairs will fall out before they grow back, but it gives you an idea.'

'Still itches a little.'

Zeb is obviously getting his second wind. 'It's all in your head. The itch doesn't last for more than a week. Mike is legitimately itchy; he has the scabs from two thousand lateral cuts. You're just a fruitcake.'

Mike pokes his scalp gingerly. 'It's driving me crazy. I wanna shoot people all the time. Last Wednesday, I almost smacked my little girl.'

I try to appear shocked, as though knowing Mike as well as I do, little-girl-smacking would be totally out of character.

'Your own little girl? Jesus.'

I must have oversold it. 'Yeah. Don't take the piss, McEvoy.'

'Well, you know, hitting daughters in general, it's not good, is it?'

Mike reaches to scratch his head, then stops himself. 'Screw this. Your hair looks good, I'll give you that. It gives me hope for the future, but this asshole tried to blackmail me.'

239

'Over what? A hair transplant? Just how sensitive are you, Mike? All of this for a hair transplant?'

Mike rears forward suddenly, kicking Zeb in the chest, forcing his chair backwards. 'This is not about the transplant. That is not the fucking point. *He* tried to blackmail *me*. I gotta make an example.'

This is priceless. 'An *example*? Who do you think is watching, Mike? Where exactly do you think you are?'

I shout the next line to the ceiling. 'This is Cloisters, Mike. Cloisters! The local PD will tolerate you until the moment you kill someone, then your arse is going to the slammer. My guess, *Mike*, is they're already up on your cell phones and have your club under surveillance.' I don't mention the multiple homicide in The Brass Ring.

Madden scowls. 'You don't know me well enough to call me Mike, laddie. Mister Madden will do just fine.'

My mouth is running away with me now. 'And another thing. Now that I think of it, no one ever said *laddie* in Ireland. That's Scotland you're thinking about.'

'Same country,' offers one of Mike's dimmer boys.

Madden is horrified. 'Same country? Same fucking country? Jesus Christ, Henry. I knew I shouldn't have hired you. In fact, you're fired!'

This gets a few laughs as the firing is performed jabbed-finger *Apprentice* style. With all the attention on poor Henry, I decide to go close quarters.

It doesn't take more than a second, and the atmosphere in this cramped reception area is so surreal, with the strip lights and dust clouds, that nobody can quite believe what's happening.

They keep right on laughing as I launch myself off the back of Zeb's chair, snag Macey Barrett's stiletto from the ceiling tile and land among them. Mike's men are knocked aside like skittles. They tumble away from me as though I am at the centre of a blast zone. Cupboards collapse and Zeb's fake marble worktop splinters and splits.

'You move quick for a six-footer,' says Mike as the steel tickles the underside of his chin. 'I'm never going to learn. That's twice.'

It's a tense situation. I can smell gun oil and nerves. My perspective is skewed by the prolonged tension and I'm seeing everything through a fish eye. Wannabe gangsters bob in and out of my vision, huge pistols bearing down on me like train tunnels.

'Stay calm, Dan. Focus.'

'Ghost Zeb? Is that you?'

'No. This would be real Zeb.'

Shite.

Mike is real angry now. 'What next, McEvoy? My boys are jumpy enough as it is. You think this kind of stunt is calming them down any?'

Time to pull myself together.

'I want to see the transplants, Mike. See how they're healing up.'

Mike's face collapses in on itself like his mouth is a black hole. 'What the . . . Are you kidding me? *See* the transplants? My shrink tells me I'm not ready.'

'Shrink? Do all you guys have shrinks now? Tony Soprano made it okay?'

241

'Soprano never had a hair transplant, laddie.'

I push the blade a quarter of a centimetre into his neck. 'One more *laddie*. One more . . .'

I hear a couple of schnicks, and wide-eyed hulks shift in my peripheral vision. Mike's boys are considering independent action.

Mike raises a palm. 'Hold it. Wait, you morons. You shoot him, that blade goes into my neck.' Something occurs to him. 'Is that Macey's stiletto?'

There's no point denying it, so I don't. 'He was doing that shuffle thing. I had no choice.'

'So the whole Brass Ring thing was a set-up?'

'Two birds, one stone. It seemed like a plan.'

Irish Mike actually sniffs. 'I gave Macey that blade.'

'Yeah? Well he should have kept it in his pants.'

'He was my best and brightest.'

'If that's true, you really are screwed.' I grab the peak of Irish Mike's hat and twist it from his head.

'Aaargh,' he screams, as though I have inflicted actual pain, and I feel a moment's regret. It's hard taking off the hat out in the world.

There are hundreds of tiny scabs ranged across Mike's freckled scalp like rows of troops.

'Dense. A lot denser than mine.'

'I had a whole team working on Mike,' mutters Zeb. 'You get what you pay for.'

'Prick,' says Mike, and I can't help agreeing with him.

One of Mike's scabs is floating a little high, so I poke it with my thumb.

'There's your problem,' I say, like I'm concerned. 'Infection. You haven't been taking your antibiotics.'

Mike's eyes flick to his lieutenants. Guilty. 'I wanted a few beers. You can't drink on those things.'

'Looks pretty painful, Zeb, this infection. Could it get nasty?'

Zeb catches on quick. 'Sure. Balls nasty. Your whole scalp is gonna feel like a septic pimple. Transplants fall out and you got a head full of scar tissue. Looks like a third-degree burn.'

Zeb is full of shit, but Mike buys it. 'Scar tissue, huh?'

'You'll be like an extra from a Romero movie.'

Mike is incensed. 'This is typical of you service guys. You never hear the downside beforehand. It's all roses until you hit an underground pipe, or you find a lump you weren't expecting, or your fucking head explodes with pus.'

Time to wrap up my argument. 'The point is, Mike, you *need* Zeb to keep an eye on you for a year. Make sure the wounds heal. Maybe put in a fresh crop. You kill him now, and it's the public clinic for you. Try keeping that quiet.'

It's a strong argument. Well put.

'So that's the case for him. What about you?'

'Me? You could try to kill me, but your organisation is going to be a whole lot weaker afterwards. Face it, Mike, you have limited resources, and Macey Barrett was your number-one guy.'

I turn the stiletto a little to focus Mike's attention on the subject. Guys like him have a hard time accepting their own mortality, unless it's tickling their jugular.

'Hey, okay. Jesus, laddie, you drive a hard bargain.'

I let him have that *laddie*.

'So, we walk?'

Mike shrugs. 'Sure. But I ain't paying for check-ups.'

Zeb chews his lip, but manages a single grudging positive grunt.

'And you cover Victor Jones's debt.'

'One-time payment. And I send one of my staff around with the monthly.'

Mike nods; any more and he'll impale himself.

'Fuck that. I collect myself, keep an eye on your operation.'

That's good enough. 'Good enough,' I say.

I withdraw the stiletto, and a rivulet of blood flows down Mike's neck, pooling in the cup of his sternum. He sponges it with a shirtsleeve.

'This is not good for me. Making deals. If word gets out that this asshole tried to blackmail Irish Mike Madden and got off with a beating . . .'

He doesn't need to say any more. That kind of rumour could be disastrous. A wave of welshers and con artists would rise up in the morning.

'Don't worry about that,' I say soothingly. 'One word from Zeb and I will deliver him to you myself.'

One of Mike's men is not taking this negotiation well. His face is drawn tight with outrage. I know the type, a bully with a gun. This guy is going to be whispering in Mike's ear how I have to die. Soon as I'm out the door, his jaw starts flapping.

I look him in the eye and wince.

'You got something wrong with your face, McEvoy? You in pain?'

'Not me,' I say, and shatter his kneecap with my heel. It's a funny thing to see a leg bend the wrong way. Not funny ha-ha. The guy goes down sideways, like a black-and-white movie drunk, snapping off shots as he goes. One hits his partner, the Scotland/Ireland guy, in the gluteus maximus. He drops to his knees, gasping.

'Go, Dan,' coughs Zeb. 'Just kill them all. We'd be better off in the long run.'

I put Irish Mike between me and the shooter in the other room, who can't do much except holler. But then another muscle man, the driver, comes barrelling in the back door. This throws me off altogether. Presumably this guy *was* out for the count, but now he's obviously awake and pissed. How pissed?

Without saying a word, the guy shoots Zeb in the shoulder. Suppressor on the pistol too. Classy.

'Scheherazade,' blurts Zeb as he falls backwards in the chair. As far as I know, Scheherazade is a character from *Arabian Nights*, and I have no idea why Zeb would say this. Maybe I misheard.

While I'm thinking about this, Irish Mike spins and demonstrates why he's the boss, unleashing a massive uppercut that takes me squarely under the chin. My feet actually leave the ground, then I'm on the floor, my head between Zeb's knees and the stiletto six feet away.

Stars are blinking before my eyes and it's all over. Two seconds, maybe three.

'Neck punch,' shouts Mike, eyes bright with triumph. 'How'd you like that, laddie? You had it coming. Fuck you and fuck you again.'

What was I thinking? This was never going to end well; too

many unknowns. My unbelievable winning streak had to peter out sometime. A pity it had to be with my head between Zeb's legs.

My ears are wet with the sticky flow of Zeb's blood and something clicked when I took the blow. My jaw? A couple of teeth? The pain is too big to pinpoint its origin.

Be nice to have a flashback now, hear some inspirational music, turn into a super soldier.

'Your head is on my balls, man,' complains Zeb, who isn't dead yet. 'That's embarrassing. I don't want to be found like this.'

Me neither. I don't want to be found at all.

The clinic is whirling and I feel sick to the pit of my stomach. I smell blood, sweat, maybe urine . . .

'Zeb. You piss yourself?'

'Screw you. I've been in this chair for ever.'

How can we be bantering like this in the face of oblivion? Is this the most important thing after all? Communication?

We lie in a tangle of limbs, like discarded mannequins ready for the bonfire, and I feel certain that this is what Mike has in mind. One little inferno and all the evidence goes away.

I crane my neck, relieving the pressure on Zeb's testicles, and looking into my friend's eyes. I have to know, before I die.

'What the hell is Scheherazade, man?'

'That just came out. It's a safe word,' says Zeb shamefacedly. 'Sometimes the S and M hookers ask for a safe word in case things get a bit out of hand. I wouldn't even be telling you this if we weren't about to die and I wasn't riding the painkiller wave.'

Christ. A safe word. They don't work outside of cathouses or Dungeons and Dragons.

My breathing seems loud and there are screams bouncing off the walls. The butt-shot guy and the busted-knee guy are yelling up a storm. I can't even hope for a quick death now.

Mike is shouting something, but it's like he's in a Perspex booth. His voice seems muffled and far away.

'. . . let you live. Why would I do that?'

Okay. I'm tuning in now. Why would he let me live? There is a reason. I almost have it when Mike stamps on my knee. No break, but painful as hell.

'You like that, McEvoy? Huh? Isn't this what they call poetic justice? I do to you like you did to my man. I am going to kill you slow, laddie. Not your friend, though. He gets patched up to keep an eye on my new hair.'

Zeb finds himself a set of brass ones. 'Screw you, Madden. You kill Dan, you better kill me too.'

'Let's see if the horrific torture you're about to witness can change your mind.'

'Yeah,' mutters Zeb. 'Torture might do it.'

Mike embraces the shooter. 'Calvin. That was outstanding work. One shot on the move, takes out the doctor and creates a diversion. You pricks see that?'

The pricks in question are writhing on the floor, but still they make time for a *yes, Mister Madden*.

'That was quite a punch you threw, Mister Madden,' says Calvin, who is no idiot.

'Yes, laddie. We make a good team. You are my new number two. Barrett is dead, long live Calvin.'

247

All this lovey-dovey gangster talk is giving my brain time to stop vibrating. I had a Plan B, in case everything turned to crap. Plan B.

And then I remember. Tommy Fletcher, my ace in the green hole.

'Ballyvaloo,' I blurt before my mind loses it.

'Not much of a safe word,' notes Zeb.

But it means something to Irish Mike. He quits hugging his new number two and walks towards me with a face like thunder.

'What did you say?'

'Ballyvaloo,' I repeat, spitting blood on my shirt.

'What the fuck is a ballyvaloo?' wonders Calvin.

I rub my tender jaw. 'Not what, where.'

Mike raises his foot to stomp on me, then thinks better of it.

'Tell me what you've done. Tell me!'

'Nothing. Not yet.'

Mike is a reasonably smart guy. It doesn't take him long to make the leap.

'Let me guess: if I kill you, then my mother is murdered, blah blah blah. You're bluffing, McEvoy. You haven't set anything up. You looked me up on the internet and found that I bought my dear mother a retirement cottage in Ireland. Period. Shoot the fucker, Calvin.'

I stare Calvin down. 'Pull that trigger and Mummy is dead.'

Calvin is conflicted. Do what the boss says, or possibly be indirectly responsible for killing the boss's mother.

'One phone call, Mike. Then do what you like. Look in my eyes and tell me I'm lying.'

It's a stupid line, but at this moment I am as serious as a shattered kneecap or a bullet in the arse. Mike glares into my eyes, snuffling like a hungry dog, and apparently finds some truth in there.

'One call, McEvoy. If you have harmed my mother ... if you have so much as disturbed her supper ...'

If I have to endure one more diatribe.

'Yeah yeah, give me my phone.'

Irish Mike tosses me my phone, which is actually Barrett's phone. It takes me three attempts to get the number in. Tiny buttons, big blood-slicked fingers, not a good combination.

'It's international,' I say, trying to sound conversational. 'So I don't want to stay on too long.'

Mike's stare could strip paint. 'Put it on speaker, shithead. For all I know, you could be calling up your bookie.'

Fair point. I find the speaker button and twist my little finger into it. A shrill double brrrrp blasts from the phone.

'Weird ring,' says Zeb, now totally in the Paramol's clutches. 'It's like brrrrp and then another one exactly the same.'

It's true. International ring tones can be surprising.

Shattered Kneecap is whining, so Mike has Butt Shot drag him out back. The tension levels in the room drop instantly. They go right back up again when the phone is answered by a gruff Irish voice.

'Aye. Who is it?'

Real Irish. From the heart of Belfast. An accent to make the hardest hard man long for a mother's bosom to nuzzle.

'Yeah. Corporal. It's me, Dan.'

'Sergeant McEvoy. Okay to drop the hammer?'

'No. Negative, Corporal. Just confirm your position.'

'Christ, Sarge. I already popped the old dear, and a few of the cousins too.'

'Bastard,' howls Irish Mike. 'Bastaard.'

There follows a satisfied chuckle that reminds me of Corporal Fletcher shooting close to desert mutts, just to see them jump.

'Irish Mike Madden, I presume. Just kidding, pal. But now you know how it's going to feel. A little taste.'

Mike is winded as though gut-punched. His eyes are suddenly bloodshot and his hands shake.

'Where are you? Where?'

'I am in the dunes above Ballyvaloo, looking down on a lovely little cottage. Smoke coming out of the chimney, a light in the window. Sure it's like a fucking postcard. It'd be an awful shame to lob a mortar on to that thatch.'

Mike gets his wind back. 'You are dead! You hear me? Deceased. You know who I am? I will fucking . . .'

Corporal Tommy Fletcher chuckles once more, this time rolling into a fully fledged laugh that overloads the phone's tiny speaker, breaking into crackling static. He keeps laughing until Mike shuts the hell up.

'You finished, Mike? Hey, I understand. You're a good son, a tough guy. But listen to me, Mike. You're in over your head now. Before Sergeant McEvoy *carried* me out of a war zone, I did some time in the Rangers. That's special operations to Joe Public. I've buried more bodies in the desert than you've had blow jobs from your hookers. I leave one coded message on a website and a hundred guys are on a plane to New Jersey. We will bury you so deep that you'll be sleeping with the dinosaurs.

I can do things to your mother that will make her curse your name. You want that, Mike?'

'I could track you down,' Mike says weakly.

Fletcher laughs. 'This is the army, Mikey. We're right here. You don't need to track us down. Listen, Sarge, I don't think he's getting it. What say I take a thumb from the old lady, maybe an eye?'

I tick-tock my head, thinking about it. 'No. I think Mike gets it. He's top man in a big operation here. You don't get to be top man by being stupid. Am I right, Mike?'

Irish Mike is having a hard time dealing with the situation. It's affecting his entire being. The power of speech seems to have deserted him and his head is bulging in places where bulges should not be. He's snorting like a bull in the ring and his hands are raised, strangling an invisible person.

'Am I right, Mike?' I prompt. 'Or do I tell my corporal to proceed?'

'You're right,' says Mike dully. 'This doesn't have to go any further. I think we can call it a day.' He lifts a hand, finger crooked to scratch his scalp.

'Nu-uh, Mister Madden,' admonishes Zeb. 'No scratching. You *want* scars, is that it?'

'You're right, of course. No scratching.'

I speak clearly into the phone. 'Did you get that, Tommy? Stand down.'

'Say again? Was it stand down or go to town? Because I can go to town on this old lady right now.'

'Stand down, you crazy bastard. Do not hurt Mrs Madden.'

'Okay, Sarge. Copy. Keep tabs, though, right?'

251

'That's a roger,' I say. Military speak always unsettles civilians.

'I'm off for a pint then, if there's no shooting to be done.
Talk to you tomorrow?'

'Tomorrow and every day.'

Tommy hangs up and I fold the phone into my pocket.

'You see how it is, Mike.'

Mike is dazed now, arms dangling by his sides, eyes heavy-
lidded.

'Yeah, I see. What do you want?'

I roll slowly to my knees, and from there make the mammoth
transition to standing upright.

'This is not a shakedown, Mike. All you have to do is go
home. It's as simple as that. Everything else stays the same.
Zeb does your check-ups, I pay protection and I'll even throw
in Vic's debt. Everyone's as happy as they can be without true
love.'

'I'm not happy,' moans Zeb. 'I got fucking shot.'

I hoist him up by the elbow. 'You needed to get shot. This
is all your fault.'

'Who you talking to? Real Zeb or Ghost Zeb?'

I really hope Zeb develops post-traumatic amnesia. Maybe
I should give him a few more of his own pills.

Mike is working his fists, like he has walnuts in there. 'Okay.
We're out of here. This never happened. One word of this
around town and I got no choice but to take action.'

My jaw is hurting now and I feel like taking a pop at Mike
to speed him on his way, but I hold back.

'Fair enough.'

'I want my Lexus back.'

'I'll drive it over tomorrow.'

'With Vic's debt, plus interest.'

These guys and their interest.

'Screw your interest, Mike. The rates are too fluid with you people.'

Mike nods slowly, trying to find some closure. This is a long-term arrangement, but a man like him needs the final word. Otherwise he may just say *screw it*, kill the both of us, get a black armband and wear a hat for the rest of his life.

The gang boss takes two steps towards the back door, then hesitates. He turns back, settling the soft cap over his head of scabs. From the look on his face I'd say he's thought of a few final words.

'My mother is an old woman,' he says. 'She could go at any time. After that there are a few cousins but I could give a fuck about them. So the clock is ticking, laddies. When Ma dies, I'm coming after you.'

Those are pretty good words.

CHAPTER 13

I call Deacon from outside the store. She's at the hospital with a guy on the door.

'So how you doing?' I ask, wasting a few seconds on politeness.

'I'm fucking freezing,' she replies. 'I got enough morphine in me to cheer up the Rolling Stones and I'm still cold. I'm gonna lose a finger to frostbite, McEvoy. How about that for a happy ending?'

'Sucks,' I say, nodding in sympathy like she can see me. 'You okay to dial the office?' And I lay out some thrown-together story about masked raiders.

'Let me get this straight, McEvoy,' she says, and I can almost hear her teeth chatter as she tries to grin. 'You just happen by your friend's store late at night and find him tied to a chair with a bullet in his shoulder. This is worse than your last effort about me busting out of the freezer.'

'Yeah, Detective. Shocking, ain't it? An Irishman who can't tell a story.'

'Dan, we've been through some shit, and you did me a solid with that tension screw.'

'And saved your life those times.'

'And the lifesaving, sure. But I'm a cop first and foremost and I am watching you, man. I don't know how a fascinating and talented individual like yourself stayed off my radar for so long.'

'I'm a quiet guy, Detective. From now on, I'm back under the radar.'

Deacon laughs. 'People like you and me, Dan, trouble sniffs us out. Maybe you can hide out for a while, maybe even a few years, but eventually someone needs to be saved or someone needs to be killed.'

'I'm out of those businesses.'

'That's right. I hear Daniel McEvoy is a club owner these days.'

'News travels fast. It's temporary.'

Deacon sighs, and I guess she's thinking about her ex-partner.

'Everything's temporary, Dan. I'll use my good fingers to expedite the 911. An ambulance should be with you in ten. See you real soon.'

'Thanks, Ronnie. I'll call you.'

Zeb has somehow managed to give himself an injection of something while I was outside negotiating with the cavalry. He sits pale under a flickering strip light, eyes rolled back in his head and blood-slick shirt sticking to his chest.

'Zeb?'

Nothing. Whatever he dosed himself with is doing the trick.

'Man, you look like a poster for a horror movie.'

'Screw you, Dan.'

Still a few marbles in the jar, then.

'What was in that shot?'

Zeb's irises roll down like slot-machine bars. 'One of my own concoctions. I am feeling no pain, Dan. You see the ponies?'

'The ambulance is coming. Sirens and lights, the whole nine yards. The medics will want to know what you took.'

Zeb smiles and bubbles burst in the corner of his mouth. 'I took as much as I could, Dan. Being shot is no joke. This blackmail thing was my worst idea ever.'

I beg to differ. 'No. That she-male last summer was the worst idea ever.'

'Don't knock it,' says Zeb, then his eyes roll back in his head.

I wheel Zeb and his chair outside just as the ambulance pulls into the lot. A paramedic jumps out of the moving vehicle like he's auditioning for Quentin Tarantino.

He grabs me by the forearm. 'Did he take any drugs?'

'Take your pick,' I say, nodding towards the store's sign.

The paramedic pokes around Zeb's wound. 'Is he allergic to anything?'

Zeb? Allergic to drugs? Funny.

'Not so far.'

'He'll live,' pronounces the paramedic after a cursory examination. 'But it's going to be a rough night.'

'Good,' I say, then go inside to get my boots.

Slotz is doing good business by the time I get back. Jason is parading the street, chatting with the university beer crowd.

'Where you gonna go?' he asks a group of guys sporting shorts and calf tattoos. 'Every other street in this town is dead. You gotta curfew or something?'

He spots me shuffling down the sidewalk. 'Hey, hey. Bossman. You all straight with Irish Mike? I was worried.'

I try to smile, but my jaw feels like there's a steam iron inside it. 'All sorted. He's a sweetheart when you get to know him. What are you doing out here? Hustling?'

'It's a new day, Dan baby. New management is good for all of us.'

Management? I don't like the sound of that.

'I don't know, Jase. Payrolls and overheads. Figures give me a headache.'

Jason flashes me his diamond grin. 'You are such a pussy, dude. I can install some small-business software on your computer. That shit will take care of everything, even pay your taxes, you feel me?'

'I feel you,' I say gratefully, resisting an urge to add *dawg*. 'What do you know about business software?'

'I took a couple of semesters in Dover. Picked up a few things. We create a file for everyone and the computer can even print their paycheques if you want. We can use it for inventory too.'

I feel a weight lifting. 'You are promoted to business manager, Jason. Get yourself a blue suit and take that diamond out of your tooth.'

'I don't do blue,' says Jason. 'And the diamond is me, man.'

'You're still hired. How soon can you get that software?'

'Soon as now, Dan. All I need is the internet and ten minutes. Shit, I could probably download it on my phone.'

Some good news. I feel like crying.

*   *   *

Inside the club, nothing much has changed. I realise I was expecting something. Not bluebirds and fruit punch, but maybe a less oppressive atmosphere. No Vic cruising the floor throwing a jaundiced eye over everyone's shoulder. No lights off over the back booth. But it's same-old same-old. The atmosphere is fake-cheery and the girls are nothing but tired.

Marco is the only ray of hope, polishing glasses like they were diamonds.

'Working hard, Marco?' I say to the little barman, pointing at the Jameson bottle over his head.

He pours me a large one. 'You ever see Jason so happy? He's out on the street selling this joint. That boy is on fire.'

I decide to make Marco's night. 'I promoted him to business manager.'

Marco flaps at me with his rag. 'Get the fuck out. You did not.'

'Yup. True as God.'

'You won't regret it,' beams Marco. 'Jason will work himself to death.'

I take a sip of whiskey, feeling it slide down my throat smooth as mercury.

'Have a word with him about the diamond. I have a feeling he listens to you.'

And I leave him open-mouthed, wondering if their secret is out.

I was hoping that the booth would be empty by the time I finished my drink. No such luck. One of Brandi's Catwoman boots is protruding from the gloom, and something is squeaking, hopefully the upholstery. This Brandi issue has to be sorted out sometime; it may as well be now. Get all my confrontations over in one night.

The booth has its own light switch under the table's rim, and I flick it without warning. First thing I see is a pale bloated stomach; second is Brandi down in the shadows, writhing like a snake.

The guy with the stomach jerks so hard he bashes Brandi's head on the table rim.

'What the . . .' His eyes focus and he sees me there, looming over him, best *grim* look in place. 'Cop? Tell me you're not a cop?'

'This is a respectable club, sir. No contact allowed.'

Brandi surfaces, rubbing her crown. 'Jesus Christ, Dan. What the fuck? I mean, what the fuck?'

I try to shame her with a look, but Brandi is impervious. 'The booth action is done. Finished. We talked about this.'

She tries the old kiss-ass routine. 'Come on, baby. A girl's gotta eat.'

Now it's my turn to be impervious. 'Maybe, but she doesn't have to eat that.'

Belly-guy has lost the urge. 'Hey, listen, you two have got some kind of employment dispute, why don't I give you some space to work it out? Communication is so important.'

I cock my head, waiting for a trademark Ghost Zeb comment. Nothing. The ghost is gone. Reunited with his wounded self in St John's hospital. Alleluia.

'Yes, sir. Why don't you tuck yourself in and try your luck at the tables.'

'I believe I shall,' says Belly-guy, formal with relief.

Brandi watches her john skip around stools in his hurry to get away from me.

She is furious; anyone with ten minutes' elementary body-language studies could see that. Her bottom lip is pushed out like a segment of blood orange and her cocked hip is sharp as a guillotine.

'Problem?' I enquire mildly.

Her eyes flash and she wants to claw my eyes out, but Brandi is the consummate survivor.

'No problem, Dan. We got a few bumps, that's all. Not even bumps . . . implants.' And suddenly her breasts are wrapped around my arm. Took all of four seconds for her mood to swing.

'No bumps,' I say, flexing my bicep so her boobs pop off. 'The booth is closed. Now, you go do your job.'

I wasn't sure I could flex enough to dislodge Brandi, but I did and it was cool. I leave her wobbling and stride towards the office.

The phone is buzzing when I reach the desk in Vic's office, but I let it ring out. I need a minute to put my pieces back together. My jaw throbs and my knuckles ache and I realise that I should have raided Zeb's painkiller stash.

I crank Vic's chair down a few more notches and settle back until my head touches the wall behind me.

My office, my desk.

That's it. Crises over.

Now I need to take stock of what's happened. A lot of new things have come into my life and I don't know which ones I want to keep. One thing is for certain, as soon as Zeb is back on his feet I am going to knock him on his arse. After that, I need to get my head straight, then take a few days' rest with nothing on my mind but food and drink.

My eyes begin to close and I don't fight it. The familiar sounds of chips clicking, glasses clinking and gamblers moaning in the casino beyond are almost like a lullaby.

Relax, I tell myself. Irish Mike is off my back for the moment. Okay, the Sofia Delano situation needs a little work, but it's not life-threatening.

Breathe in through the nose, out through the mouth. *Breathe in balls, breathe out pussy*, as the marines say, though I always thought that came off a little ambiguous.

Getting there, nearly calm now.

The phone rings again and I nearly fall out of the seat. I slap the receiver out of its cradle.

'What? What now?'

Ronelle Deacon's laugh is like whiskey and cigarettes. 'Management too stressful for you, Dan? You cracking up already?'

I blink myself alert. 'It's been a long night, Detective. A long week.'

'I sent a couple of uniforms over to your friend's store. Quite a mess. Or to quote Patrolman Lewis, *Big motherfucking hole in the motherfucking wall*. A couple quarts of blood too. You wouldn't know anything about that?'

'Not a thing. I arrived after the fact. Zeb was the only one bleeding.'

Brandi slinks in the door, making full use of her stripper

training; every movement is choreographed. I see where this is going. I'm in for a full-on booth negotiation.

'Dan,' she purrs. 'We need to talk, baby.'

I raise one rigid finger. *In a minute*. I am not good at multi-tasking, especially when there are people involved.

'Yeah, that's what I thought,' continues Deacon. 'And you didn't see anything, right?'

'Not a thing but my friend bleeding.' I decide to use a little distraction technique. 'Come on, Ronnie. It's too late for work. Why don't you check out of that hospital and come on over here for a few drinks? I'm in good with the management. You still got nine fingers, right? More than enough to pick up a beer.'

'Maybe when I solve this murder I'm working on from my sickbed. Woman killed outside Slotz; maybe you knew her?'

My stomach lurches. Connie. How could she have slipped my mind even for a moment?

'Anything I can do?'

Brandi is tapping her forearm. She doesn't like to be kept waiting. I grit my teeth and focus on the handset.

'I got some more news on the murder weapon,' says Ronnie quietly; maybe there are nurses hovering. 'I thought I could run it past you since we have such a special relationship; unofficially of course, as I am technically off duty for the foreseeable . . .'

'It was some kind of a blade?'

'No. We got some metal fragments from the wound. Too soft for a blade. Maybe a tube, like the tip of an umbrella. With some kind of glittery substance on the shaft. That ringing any bells, McEvoy?'

'Nothing pops out at me.'

'Me neither. This makes it a spur-of-the-moment thing. Our murderer could be anyone now. Could be staring us right in the face.'

Brandi sits opposite me and swings her legs on to the desk, crossing them at the ankles. Her boots shine like gloss paint.

'You'll be thinking on it?'

I don't say anything, because suddenly there is no air in the room. More than that, the room has become a vacuum, popping my ears and expanding my brain.

A *metal tube. Glittery substance.*

Detective Deacon is still talking. 'Right, Dan? Yo, Danny boy. You're gonna work with me on this?'

My fingers paw the desktop like a blind man's, until I find the phone and cut Ronnie off.

I hate people calling me Danny boy. My father used to do that, and sing that goddamn dirge in pubs, though no one asked him.

'I know you want to make changes, Dan,' Brandi is saying, doing her best trailer-trash talk-show spiel. 'I know that and I respect you for it. But I think, if you look inside yourself, you'll find that you're still in shock over Connie. She never went in the booth, so now you're gonna shut the booth down. See what I'm saying?'

Brandi's six-inch heels are in my face. Her trademark Catwoman boots. I've seen her kick sparks from the pavement with those boots.

She picks at a tiny square of body glitter on her forearm.

'I hate to speak ill of the dead, Dan. But that girl's morals were costing us all money. Hell, we lost a dozen high-rollers last month because little virgin Connie didn't want any hands on her ass. My tips were way down. And I need my tips. Cat's gotta have her cream.'

The phone is still at my ear, beeping. I can't seem to remember where it should go.

'I ain't missing her. None of the girls are.'

I can see how it happened. They met in the parking lot, words were exchanged. Connie and Brandi differed on how the job should be done. Things got heated. Maybe a slap turned into a tussle. Connie went down and Brandi put her heel through Connie's forehead. She's capable of it; God knows she's capable.

It's true. My gut knows it.

I stare at Brandi's heels, mesmerised. They are shining and wicked. After the deed was done, Brandi stood at the door beside me building her alibi. Hell, she probably had blood on her if anyone bothered to look.

'So come on, Dan. What do you say to a little action in the booth? I'll give you a free taste.'

The heel glints, and I see in the centre a tiny perfect circle of dried blood. Could be mud, coffee, anything.

It's blood, I swear I can smell it.

Jason puts his head around the door. He's half apologetic, half smiling.

'Boss, we got a lady outside, looks like Material Girl Madonna. Got a casserole for you, says she's your wife. You want me to show her the door?'

I can't talk. Can't say a word. I shake my head to defer the decision.

PLUGGED

Brandi doesn't want her meeting hijacked. 'So, Dan? Is the booth back in business? You want me to slide under that desk?'

I keep shaking.

Brandi killed Connie.

'Should I bring her through? She's pretty hot, boss. And that casserole smells amazing.'

I manage one word.

'Just . . .'

'What, Dan?'

'Just throw her out, boss?'

I try again. 'Just . . .'

Brandi is doing a few slinky dance moves. 'Just do it, Dan. Give me five minutes.'

'Bring her in? Throw her out? Keep the food though, right?'

'Just wait!' I shout. 'Just wait a goddamn second.'

The handset is still beside my ear, and suddenly the beeping is replaced by a familiar voice.

That bitch murdered me, says Ghost Connie. *She made orphans out of my Alfredo and Eva.*

No. Not another one. I slam the phone into its cradle. Not another ghost, no way.

I want to go back in time. I want to steal apples from an orchard in Blackrock and eat them with my little brother on the beach. I want to count the new stars as they switch on and stay out until we're sure Daddy is passed out drunk.

Connie. Beautiful Connie. Brandi deserves to be dropped in the river.

The look on Brandi's face tells me I've said this out loud. She wants to laugh, but is afraid to.

'Who's going in the river, Dan? Not me, right? All I want to do is sell a few hand-jobs. That's not a crime, is it?'

I try to speak calmly. 'Jason, please bring Mrs Delano to the back room, tell her I'll be with her in a minute. Brandi, stay where you are. You take one step towards the door and I swear to Christ you'll regret it.'

'But Dan . . .'

I am not in the mood for argument, so I simply take my gun from the drawer and place it on the desk. It's a clear message, hard to misinterpret, but Jason does anyway.

'Hey, come on, boss. Guns all of a sudden? Did Mike initiate you into the gang? What, you got a shamrock tattoo now?'

It's a tense situation, so I say something to Jason that I regret before the echo fades. 'Get out, Jason. Go give Marco a cuddle.'

Brandi shrieks with joy. 'Finally. Zing. Fuck you, Jason. Tough guy.'

Jason gives me a look like I shot his puppy and I feel like I've turned into my own father. He closes the door softly and I start figuring how I'm going to make it up to him. A weekend in Atlantic City at least.

'The elephant has left the room,' Brandi crows, her legs doing a little scissors kick on my desk. 'You need to get rid of that faggot, Danny. He's bad for business.'

This switches my attention back to her and gives me a nice segue.

'Like Connie was bad for business?' I say this ominously, but Brandi's self-preservation cat sense is switched off.

'No, not really. I'd say Jason would have no problem with

some guy licking his ass. I'd say that's exactly the kind of thing he'd have zero problem with.'

'So, you'd get rid of him?'

Brandi winks, her eyelid heavy with crusted glittering eyeshadow. 'Toss that boy on the street. Marco too. We gotta make some business decisions.'

'Like you got rid of Connie?'

I don't expect Brandi to fall into that trap, and she doesn't, but her eyes give her away. It's not much, just a quick flicker, but I notice.

'Got rid of Connie?' she says, haltingly, drawing her boots off the desk.

This to me seems like a crucial moment in the development of this whole confrontation. For some reason I absolutely believe that if Brandi gets her boots off the surface of Vic's desk (my desk) then I have lost whatever upper hand I had, which was pretty crappy in the first place.

So Brandi is pulling her boots away from me, knees up around her pirate earrings, but she doesn't move fast enough. I reach out and grab her right ankle and squeeze it till the patent leather squeaks, which kinda sucks the gravity from the moment.

'This smells clean,' I say, gritting my teeth with the effort of holding on to the boot and carrying on a conversation. 'Real clean. I bet you used a whole pack of antiseptic wipes on this boot.'

'Gotta keep germ-free, Daniel,' says Brandi. Her voice is super-innocent, like a girl scout, but her eyes are darting around the office like something or someone is going to pop up with another surprise.

'You should have burned this pair, Brandi. I know they're your favourites, but you've got others.'

I'm rambling a bit, but that's because half of me knows that the accusation I'm about to make is at best based on a hunch and at worst based on supernatural intervention.

'Why the fuck are we talking about my boots? First no booth, now you have something against my boots? Let go of my goddamn leg, Dan.'

'You should have burned them,' I say again, using my old trick of repeating myself to buy a second. 'Because all the blues need is one strand of DNA, caught in a stitch. All they need to do is match your heel to the hole in Connie's head.'

Brandi is a little pale under her make-up. 'Let go of my leg, Daniel. You're hurting me.'

Is this what she should say? Is this what an innocent person would say?

'Aren't you going to tell me that you're innocent? Protest and so forth?'

'And so forth? Who the fuck are you?'

I admit it. That was a little Dr Moriarty.

'I'm taking this boot to the cops. If they find nothing, then no harm done and you can jerk whoever's pecker you like for a month. But if they find some trace, then there won't be any peckers where you're going.'

Brandi sees in my face that this isn't one she can talk her way out of.

'Get your hands off me, asshole.'

'What's the problem? Just give me the boot and you get to

268

rule the roost around here, so long as you had nothing to do with Connie.'

Brandi sneers at the sheer volume of dumbness in my plan. 'I don't care if that boot has Connie's eyeball stuck on the heel, you're still the one handing it over. The jilted boyfriend.'

That takes a moment to sink in, but she's right. Even if Brandi owns the murder weapon, it doesn't mean she did the murdering.

'I'll take my chances. The police will look closely at both of us, something I have no problem with.'

Halfway through this last sentence, I try to take Brandi by surprise, standing suddenly and yanking the boot with me, hoping it will come clean off, but Brandi is ready and curls her toes going up with the boot. Now I am in the cartoon situation of holding a grown woman upside-down by the ankle.

'Shite,' I say. Seems appropriate.

'What next, Dan?' asks Brandi, her hair brushing the floor. 'I worked the pole for years. I can do this all night.'

I don't know what next. I really don't. I cannot believe the situation in which I find myself: standing in my ex-boss's office, holding the stripper who possibly murdered my potential sweetheart aloft by her ankle. It pains me to say it, but this girl is heavy and my bicep is aching already.

'Hey!' says Brandi, having a light-bulb moment. 'Are you wired?'

This thought freaks her out so much that she does a pretty impressive stripper move and folds herself upwards, swinging her other leg around, and suddenly there is an angry woman on my shoulders. I hear something scrape along the desktop and a quick glance is enough to confirm that she has snagged my gun on the way up. Brandi's legs are strongly muscled and she's doing her damnedest to squeeze my brain out of my ears. I feel a metallic ring digging into my scalp through my cap and I realise that I probably have two seconds to live before Brandi composes herself and flicks the safety. Amazingly, I am almost as worried about Brandi damaging the hair grafts as I am about sudden death.

I take two rapid steps forward, around the side of the desk. It's instinct really; I'm just trying to get away. As I clear the desk, I hear a dull bong, like a bell in a sack, and Brandi goes over backwards. Her legs are still locked but her upper half is dazed. She's cracked her head on something metal. *The ceiling beam*, I remember. *Barely six-and-a-half-foot clearance.*

The immediate danger is past and so I take a second to assess, to look at myself from afar. I see a middle-aged, craggy-looking ex-soldier standing in the middle of his office, panting like a donkey, with a stripper wrapped around his neck, and it's not even the strangest situation he's been in today.

Jason comes through the door and his face is red with choked-down rage. I don't blame him.

'Hey, screw you, Daniel,' he says, barging all the way in, still pissed about the *give Marco a cuddle* comment, eyes burning holes in the floor. 'It's bad enough that I gotta go around every second of my life . . . But then I actually try to help you and . . . you throw that shit at me.'

I gulp down a couple of breaths like there's a shortage, and try to get my middle-aged heart to slow down a little, while Jason folds his arms, apparently oblivious to the person around my neck.

The least I can do is apologise. 'Okay, Jason. That comment about Marco was crude. I was going for light-hearted: *I know about the gay thing and I don't care*, but it came out all spiteful. So, you know, sorry. I misjudged.'

Jason softens a little, but he's gonna hold it over me for a while.

'Okay, Daniel. You get one chance. Next time we find out how tough you really are.'

I hang my head in shame, which is not easy with Brandi's thigh in the way. 'I hear you, man. Do you want to hug or something?'

Jason frowns. 'What am I? A Walton?'

I am a crap modern man. I just assumed . . .

'Okay,' I say. 'You call the cops. I gotta take the boots off this unconscious ex-stripper.'

Jason seems to suddenly notice Brandi, but it doesn't faze him. In our line of work we see stranger shit than this at least once a week.

EPILOGUE

Zeb is back in business after a week bolstering his system in Cloisters General. He was finally kicked out having been caught on video loitering around the pharmacy with obvious intent. The blues questioned him for six hours straight over the incident at his store, but he stuck to his story: got hit on the head from behind, woke up in an ambulance. Don't remember anything. They questioned me too, but Deacon took the lead and she was prepared to swallow my monumental crock of shit in light of all my lifesaving efforts. I tried to mention the word *freezer* as much as possible while giving my final statement. The file is pretty much closed and I'm hoping it will be gathering dust soon.

The Brandi file on the other hand is wide open. Deacon ran the boot through the lab. They found blood, bone, brain matter, DNA. The works, Brandi's boot was the murder weapon, no doubt about it. Unfortunately Brandi fled custody from the hospital before the tests came back and fled the state shortly after that, pausing only to raise funds at a Slotz regular's house in the suburbs. She was last sighted in Florida.

So here I am, back to the quiet life in Cloisters again. All the craziness seems totally unreal. Could it have actually happened just last week? All that crap in a couple of days when things had been pretty quiet for over a decade, not a single person killed, less than a dozen in the hospital, and a couple of them were faking trauma for legal reasons, then Faber comes along and things go red all over again.

Did any of it happen? I know it did because Connie's kids are in a foster home instead of watching TV with their mom. It's not an institution and the McGuffins are good people, and I'm gonna visit every week like I promised, but it's still a foster home.

What I should have done, looking at it now in retrospect, was to walk into the casino and kick good old Mister Faber so hard in the balls that any mischief-making he was cooking up in his ginger head would have disintegrated along with his favourite executive toys.

But I didn't do that, since I can't see into the future and apply it to the past.

So it all went ahead and happened. I sat down and watched Barrett bleed out. I've still got blood on my cuff. Or I used to until I burned that shirt and flushed the ashes. It took three flushes. Crappy plumbing.

Ronnie Deacon's words echo in my mind: *People like you and me, Dan, trouble sniffs us out. Maybe you can hide out for a while, maybe even a few years, but eventually someone needs to be saved or someone needs to be killed.*

No. It won't be like that for me. I was Superman for a week, but now I'm just a bald guy with a humdrum job. No more quick thinking, crazy coincidences or lunatic plans.

*   *   *

I feel a little antsy walking into work this afternoon, because today's the day Mike's coming to personally collect his payment. Also he says the brakes on the Lexus are whistling a little and I gotta take care of it, which is a crock, cos that Lexus was braking fine when I sent it over.

I look around and the car park is empty but for the aforementioned Lexus and my ghosts. I can hear cars passing on the street and they seem a long way away.

I yank my hat off my head, defiantly revealing my head in public for the first time post-op in some kind of gesture, symbolising I don't know what. Maybe I've turned a corner; maybe there are things more important than a head of hair. Zeb says the bald patch will be gone, and that's enough for me. No more needles in the scalp.

So that's no more:

Killing.

Lunatic plans.

Needles in the head.

The club is quiet except for Jason in the foyer pulling on a giant rubber band that he swears does wonders for his abs.

'Gotta keep myself looking good for Marco,' he grunts. 'I swear that guy bats his eyes at every queer on the strip.'

This statement is more important than it sounds. Jason is being casual like this to show me I'm forgiven. I stop for a minute, trying to think of something to say that won't open the wound again.

'Hug?'

'In your dreams, Danny. You better go in. Mike's waiting.'

*   *   *

PLUGGED

Mike is waiting in my chair, which is a bit of a cheek, but after the month I've had, I'm finding myself very tolerant of things that don't threaten to immediately kill me.

'Mister Madden,' I say, squeezing into the old wooden chair on the visitor's side of the desk, hoping it doesn't collapse, which might startle Mike into shooting me. 'How's tricks? I mean business tricks, not prostitution obviously.'

Mike does not glare at me. He is calm, a man biding his time.

'Business is good, Danny boy. Booming. People always want shite, you know, so I give them the shite they want, and to be honest I can't get hold of the shite fast enough.'

Seems as though Mike is afraid of wires and likes the word *shite*.

'And how's tricks with you, Daniel? Business, I mean.'

I give the standard Irish tell-'em-nothin' response. 'Ah sure, you know, not too bad.'

Mike winces. 'Not what I hear. I hear Vic Jones is causing a few problems.'

It's true. Victor has a lawyer claiming that the poker game never happened and he signed his lease away under duress. With AJ and Brandi in the wind, the only other witnesses to the game are the two girls whose future we played for. Jason has a team out looking for them. But even if we do find them, a poker lease transfer may not hold up, as it wasn't agreed to by the owner.

But I say, 'Don't worry about Vic. You get your *shite* no matter who's behind the desk.'

Mike smiles and touches the peak of his soft cap. 'Oh, I'm not worried, Danny boy. I always get what's due to me.'

I decide to change the subject. 'How's your mother doing?'

Mike's smile grows so I can see his ivory-yellow fangs. 'She's old, Dan, and she has a bit of a flu. Let's hope it doesn't develop into something.'

I should have picked another subject to change to.

The door to my office opens and Zeb's head appears, weirdly disembodied in the gap. I wasn't expecting to see him today, but he's probably drunk or bored or both.

On seeing us he calls: 'Hey, it's the hairy boys. What's up, gangstas?'

Mike tries to rip off the armrest, but it's one of those tested-in-space toughened materials and resists his efforts. He shoots me a look and mutters, 'You know, Danny. I love my ma, but there's going to come a point with this guy.'

'I hear you,' I say, forgetting for a moment that if Zeb goes in the river, the next splash I hear will be my own.

Zeb is unconcerned by this death threat. 'Come on, guys. I'm bustin' your chops, that's all. Shoving firecrackers up your asses is what makes life worth living.'

'You're a funny one, Dr Zeb,' says Mike. 'Firecrackers indeed. You want to pull yourself together before you say the wrong thing to the wrong person.'

I add the force of my glares to Mike's.

'You should take a photo, Zeb,' I say. 'Because this is me agreeing with Mike.'

Zeb takes what looks like a clay urn from a pocket and pulls a cork out with his teeth.

'Oh, come on, motherfuckers, let's do shots. This stuff will put hair on your chests.'

Mike grabs the urn and takes a sniff. 'How about my head? Will it put hair on my head?'

'Sure,' says Zeb, dipping his fingers into a cluster of glasses on the shelf. 'Plus it's got a kick like a mule on steroids. Monks make it from yak spit. Totally illegal.'

'Totally illegal, eh?' Mike is intrigued. 'How much you paying for that bottle?'

Zeb smells a profit. 'Ten bucks. I could sell it to you for twelve.'

Mike and Zeb put their heads together and start horse trading as though the former had never kidnapped the latter who had just tried to blackmail the former.

For a second I can't remember which one of them is my friend, and when I do remember, I can't figure out why. Maybe it's time I tried forgetting instead of remembering just for an hour or two.

'Hey, Zeb,' I say. 'Pour me a glass of that yak spit.'

We can talk about the brakes later.